The Lady

&

The Marine

Book 2: Semper Fi in Love

Danette Fogarty

Dear Readers:

I want to extend my great thanks to you for choosing to read The Lady & The Marine. This is the second book in a series I hold very dear to my heart. Being a part of the Marine Corps as a spouse of an active duty Marine is something I am very proud to have done. I was fortunate to be around Crash Crew for many years and deeply respect the men and women who serve in the field. I am especially thankful to all of our service members, wherever they are serving, for keeping us safe.

I wanted to begin my writing career with a love story about something I knew.....Crash Crew and the Marine Corps. The Marine Corps motto, Semper Fi, means Always Faithful. What better description for finding the person you are meant to be with. So, after asking my husband and a lot of different people (retired and currently serving) about a million questions, I felt like the story was ready to tell. After writing the first book, I knew there were more stories and was fascinated by interweaving the lives of characters I hold dear to my heart.

The Lady & The Marine is a story about two people who, under different circumstances, may never have met. Being brought together because they each knew someone who fell in love attracted my attention. Not to mention, I am always up for the adventure of meeting new people and have had quite a few interesting conversations during a flight.

This is the follow up book to A Marine to Remember in which Chase Johnson and Eryn Fredricks-Smith carry out their own crazy love story. Be sure to read their story to find out why it took so long for them to figure out they were meant to be together.

Also be sure to look for the next book in the Semper Fi in Love Series, Moonlight & A Marine; slated for release in December, 2013. This is the story of Abi Rochelle, a Gunnery Sergeant/Crash Chief who gets the unwelcomed news that she is supposed to marry someone she's never met.

These characters are my friends and, hopefully after you read the books, will be yours too. Thank you again for helping to make my dreams as a writer come true.

Best Wishes to All of You,

Semper Fi

Danette Fogarty

Prologue

November, 2012

"Master Sgt. Frinnel," Mitch Frinnel answered at his house in Virginia.

Chase grimaced, "Mitch," he said through clenched teeth, "I need to talk to you, man."

Mitch was sitting in his study with his second cup of coffee of the day and debating on whether to start a project in the garage or do some yard work when the phone rang. He was used to interruptions on the weekends from work but he hadn't spoken to Chase since before the Ball.

Sitting back down, he smiled, "Hey, how's it going there?"

Chase was relieved that he caught Mitch at home but now he seemed unsure of how to talk to his friend.

"Mitch," he ran his fingers through his short hair, "it was great."

Okay, Mitch thought that was good but why did Chase sound like it was anything but good. "Spill."

Chase took a deep breath. It was difficult to say everything he was feeling. The insecurities of where he and Eryn were at was overwhelming.

"It was phenomenal, Mitch, indescribable." Chase let out a breath.

Wow, Mitch thought, he couldn't remember the last time he ever labelled a night with a woman as 'indescribable.'

Chase cleared his throat, "I'm going to marry her," he said quickly.

Surprised, Mitch snapped his head up, "Really?"

"Yes," Chase answered more sure than ever that it was right. "I need her."

It was amazing to Mitch that two people could find such a strong connection. His parents shared it and his sister seemed very happy in her marriage but he was yet to find someone who could make him feel what Chase described. He was torn between being happy for his friend and feeling envy for something he himself hadn't experienced.

Happiness for his friend won out, "I'm happy for you both." Now it was reality, "Of course, she's still your OIC so you want to explain how you're going to get over that little hurdle?"

Chase smiled, he spent the last day and a half going over all the possible scenarios their relationship could take. There was only one logical conclusion but he was pretty sure Eryn would fight him on it. Best to go on with his plan and not give her a choice in the decisions at this point. He loved her and they were going to be together.

"Well, I have a plan…" Chase started.

Mitch listened intently to what Chase wanted to do. He asked questions periodically but tried to listen to everything before he commented. The plan was a good one, but he agreed with Chase; Eryn wasn't going to go along with it willingly.

Mitch smiled into the phone, "Looks like you're going to be a pretty busy guy now."

Chase snorted, "I will be if I can convince a certain woman that she's the one for me."

Nodding, Mitch could relate to a complicated situation; he dealt with them at work all the time. "Just take it slow and don't run ramshod over her."

"Me?" Chase questioned. "Oh, I don't think I could do that even if I wanted to."

Mitch chuckled, "Yeah, right." He got up with his coffee cup and walked to the kitchen to rinse it out. "Just call me if you need any help with the paperwork."

"I will," Chase said.

The conversation was basically over and both men knew it. So why did Mitch feel like he needed to say something?

"Chase," he said quietly.

Chase cleared his throat, "Yeah?"

Mitch was not quite comfortable talking about feelings but he'd try for his friend's sake, "Congratulations, I'm very happy for you and Eryn."

The sentiment meant a lot to Chase, "Thanks."

They hung up and Mitch stood in his kitchen for a long time staring out the window and wondering if he would ever meet anyone that would make him want to give up everything familiar.

Chapter 1

March, 2013

Katherine hated being late! She was always criticizing others when they weren't punctual. Her family and friends said she was OCD about it but she didn't care. Being late meant you didn't think that where you had to be was important enough. And that was most definitely not Katherine. Everywhere she needed to be was important and flying to Hawaii for her cousin Eryn's wedding was definitely in that category.

Unfortunately the fates were working against her this morning. She, somehow, set her alarm for almost an hour later than she needed to be up. She'd been up late working and must have zoned out when she set it. Then, the car service that she called was late and traffic was atrocious.

Taking a deep breath, Katherine decided it was just a test of her resolve and she didn't fail tests, no matter what.

Grabbing her carry-on bag, she stepped out of the car and tipped the driver. A skycap grabbed her other bags from the trunk and wheeled them over to the curbside check in area. She tipped him generously and walked through the doors to Newark Liberty International Airport.

Her four inch heels clicking on the tiled floor were keeping in time with her thoughts. She had a phone call to make to her assistant this morning before she boarded and a couple of emails to send. The trip was planned for months but she never quite got a hold of time when she was working.

The line for security wasn't that long, a relief, so she stood patiently and sent emails while waiting. There was no use in wasting time if one could help it. Her father taught her that at a young age.

She made it through security and walked to her gate to check the status. There was still time before boarding so she dialed her assistant's number and went to a store to purchase some reading material and snacks for the flight.

Mitch Frinnel was reading a book in the gate area when he heard his name called over the loud speaker. Frowning, he got up and went over to the gate desk.

"Mr. Frinnel?" the gate agent asked.

Mitch nodded, he checked in yesterday so he wasn't sure what the problem was.

The young woman smiled warmly, "There's been some seating changes so I just need to see your ticket."

He handed her his ticket and noticed her nametag said Peggy on it. She was very polite so he didn't mind a seat change. It didn't really matter as long as he got there.

"Here you go," Peggy said and handed him his ticket. Boy the man was delicious looking. She knew he was a Marine; his haircut and demeanor gave him away. She took a chance, "Are you stationed here?"

Mitch was surprised by the question, "No, unfortunately," he smiled at her. "I was visiting my family in Delaware and drove up yesterday so I could catch the flight today."

A shame, Peggy thought, "Oh, well," she cleared her throat, "you have a great flight, Mr. Frinnel."

That was weird, Mitch thought. "Thank you, I will." He gave a short wave and walked back toward the windows.

There were dozens of planes lined up at gates and airport employees moving here and there trying to complete their jobs. Working in Crash, Fire, Rescue for so long gave Mitch a firm understanding of what was needed to run a successful airport. He looked out the windows absently trying to relax for the flight. He was happy to be seeing Chase and Eryn but found himself feeling on edge.

Ever since the call from Chase four months earlier, he felt like something was genuinely missing in his life. That was a new concept to him as he was always very content to do his job and serve in the Marine Corps. He spent the last twenty-two years devoting his time to the Corps and never once regretted it. But now he was starting to feel unsettled.

Katherine sighed loudly; this was a warning to her assistant that her patience was waning quickly.

"Ms. Fredricks, just a few more items," Suzanna, Katherine's assistant, rushed. She knew her boss was about to get on the plane but there were loose ends and Ms. Fredricks never liked loose ends.

Looking around, Katherine could see other passengers getting ready to board. She just wanted to get the call done so she could enjoy her vacation. If there was one thing she did not want to think about while on the plane, it was work.

"Okay, shoot," she said curtly into the phone.

The PA crackled, "Okay folks, we're about to start boarding flight 325 with service to Honolulu." The agent smiled.

Katherine checked her watch. "I have to go, Suzanna, I'll call you tomorrow." She hit the end button on her phone without waiting for her assistant to answer. It was time to change. She got up and walked briskly to the restroom.

Mitch waited in line for his turn to get on the plane. He smiled at the other passengers, amazed by the jockeying for position people did. What did it matter as long as you were on the plane when it took off? As he stepped onto the aircraft he looked at his ticket. This didn't seem right.

"Excuse me," he leaned over to speak to the flight attendant waiting near the door of the aircraft, "I'm not sure my ticket is right."

The flight attendant looked at the ticket and smiled, "Oh yes, sir, it's right. You've been moved to first class."

What? Mitch frowned, he certainly didn't pay for first class. What was going on? He moved slowly in the line and found his seat quickly since it was only five rows in.

Wow! He thought as he sat in the seat. It was leather and roomy. Well, well, maybe a ten hour plus flight wouldn't be too bad then. He smiled to the passengers walking by. 'Don't be smug,' he chastised himself, 'that could've been you.'

Katherine stepped onto the plane, refreshed and ready. This was, after all, the first vacation she decided to take since starting her business. After hanging up with her assistant, she went into the restroom and proceeded to remove all vestiges of her business owner attire.

Her long, blonde hair was now loose and curled around her shoulders. The dark blue, tailored suit with high heels she wore to the airport were gone and replaced with a frilly sun dress, light sweater, and sandals. It was like she just became another person when she left the bathroom.

Mitch was reading through a magazine when he noticed movement beside him. He looked up in time to see a mane of hair hanging down like a curtain. It looked soft and he had to resist the urge to reach up and touch it. Once the hair was swept back by a slim and graceful hand, he was treated to a picture of the face that belonged to it. And, oh what a face it was!

A kick to the gut wouldn't have been strong enough to compare to what his body experienced when his eyes met deep green ones looking intensely at him. And when she smiled, those eyes lit up brightly.

"Hello," Mitch squeaked out. He wanted to rap his head against the window, he sounded idiotic.

Katherine smiled at her neighbor. Oh, he was handsome. She smiled brightly as she pushed her hair back so she could sit and get her things settled before they took off.

Once seated, she looked over, "Hello."

What was wrong with him? She was just a fellow passenger; why was he acting like a teenager who had no experience with girls?

Katherine dutifully put her magazines and book in the pocket in front of her. Her bag was stowed under the seat and her headphones were at the ready in case she needed to drown out noise from others. It was good to be prepared.

Mitch didn't know what else to say so he turned his eyes back to the magazine he was reading. Of course, now he had absolutely no interest in the story since he wanted to look at the woman next to him.

The flight attendant started making the take-off announcements and everyone settled. The plane backed up and started taxiing toward the runway.

Mitch watched the plane's progress as it moved. He never minded flying; it just was a necessary thing for him to do to get from point A to point B. He snuck a glance over at the woman next to him and could see her tense up. Her hands were clenching the arm rests. Well, well, she wasn't as free spirited as she appeared to be.

Crap, Katherine thought, she hated flying. She thought that if she changed her clothes and her attitude that she would handle it better. No such luck. Deep breathing helped so she inhaled through her nose and exhaled out through her lips. The plane would be up soon and then she could relax.

"Are you okay?" Mitch asked.

She looked over at him, noting his blue eyes. They searched hers and made her feel exposed. It was like they were holding her to the spot. She could only sit there and watch them as the plane picked up speed. She didn't notice the noises or other passengers, just his eyes. They were like a beacon of blue that mesmerized her. She said nothing, only stared into them.

Mitch noticed that she didn't answer his question but she stared at him during takeoff. Words were not necessary, he knew what she needed at that moment; something to distract her from the worry. Her eyes were so green; they reminded him of a field of wild spring grass after a rain. There was solace to be found in them. The feeling was a balm to his restlessness so he just sat there and looked back, soaking up the tenuous connection they shared.

The plane leveled out and Katherine took a deep breath. "Thank you," she said softly to the man next to her.

Now she could see more than just those piercing blue eyes. She could see his strong face; good features, the dark hair that was cut very short. Oh, he was a Marine. The realization jolted her.

She'd been around Marines her whole childhood so it wasn't difficult to discern them from other service members. There was an "attitude," for lack of a better word, that Marines had. He was probably on his way to his new duty station in Hawaii.

Boy she had him on the rocks! Her eyes searched his face like she was memorizing it and the scrutiny aroused him. Embarrassed by his reaction to a woman looking at him, he cleared his throat and nodded. He finally turned his face back to the magazine in the hopes that she would look away and give him time to catch his breath.

The flight attendant came over to them and offered them a choice of beverages. Katherine gladly took a glass of wine. It didn't matter that it was barely after two in the afternoon; she was on vacation right?

The drinks were served and Katherine thanked the flight attendant with a smile. She took a drink of her wine and reveled in the cool liquid soothing her parched throat. 'The only reason your throat is dry is because the hot guy next to you is making it that way.'

Mitch looked to his side, trying not to be obvious. He watched her while she sipped her glass of wine. Her fingers were long and looked soft. Since when did he think about a woman's fingers? The thought was disturbing him even more than their stare down earlier which made him want to kiss her. If this was how it was going to be, this was going to be a very long flight.

Katherine could see that he was peeking at her and trying not to be obvious about it. How sweet! The wine was almost gone and it loosened her up. She took her right hand and rubbed it across the back of her neck, enjoying the relaxed feeling moving through her.

She was rubbing her neck and her hair moved enough to brush across his arm. The lightness of the caress was enough to leave a trail of goosebumps across his flesh. The result was a shot of desire to his groin and a blush in his cheeks.

As she moved, she noticed her hair was on his arm, "I'm sorry, I forget how long it is." Oh, that was slick!

"No problem," Mitch smiled and looked over into those eyes again, "it's very pretty."

What a nice thing to say! He was a charmer. "Why thank you."

"Oh," Mitch turned toward her and offered his hand, "I'm Mitch."

Mitch? She said his name in her head. It was a good, strong name, reflective of the man she thought. "I'm Katie."

Katie? She thought to herself. She hadn't used that name since she was about ten. NO ONE called her Katie. Except her cousin Eryn, it was either Katherine or Ms. Fredricks these days. Thinking how silly she was being, she giggled and offered her hand to him.

"Hi, Katie," he said as he took her hand in his.

If he thought the act of looking at her was intense, it didn't even compare to the impact of touching her skin. Now he knew what an atomic bomb explosion felt like because one was going off in his body.

Katherine looked down at their joined hands and reveled in the feel of her skin against his. Whoa! His hands were strong and firm without squeezing her fingers like they were twigs. She was well versed in men and their power struggles where women were concerned. She doubted that Mitch was one of those men; her instinct told her he knew where he stood and was confident with himself. A desirable trait.

The "handshake" went on way too long, neither of them really willing to release the other's hand. Finally Mitch released his hold only to feel the tips of her fingers slide across his palms and down to the tips of his fingers before putting them neatly in her lap.

An announcement from the Captain brought them both out of the moment. "Well, folks, we'd like to welcome you aboard today. We'll be flying at thirty-eight thousand feet and will land in Honolulu around six thirty local time. Please let our flight attendants know if you need anything and I'll be sure to update you on our progress periodically. Again, welcome aboard."

Embarrassed by her behavior, Katherine stared down at her folded hands. What on earth was wrong with her? The flight attendant was passing and offered to take her glass. Katherine nodded but asked for another.

Mitch looked out the window, not really looking at anything. The clouds rolled by them like large cotton balls. He wanted to be distracted from looking at the woman next to him. If he didn't find something to focus on, he was afraid he'd maul her inappropriately. She looked so demure and that was making her even more desirable. Willing himself to relax, he laid his head back against the seat and closed his eyes.

He was asleep, Katherine noted a while later. She took the opportunity to openly watch him. His features were really rather striking. A sharp jaw line that looked powerful. She thought his lips were very beautiful for a man's. Not that she studied men's lips but his fascinated her. The second glass of wine must be making her loopy. She looked away from him, trying to regain her sense of balance.

Mitch was dreaming about a woman was walking next to him and he was trying to reach out to her. She was looking at him, smiling.

When Katherine looked back at the man he had a hint of a smile on his face and she was floored at the transformation it gave him. All of his features softened and he looked happy.

Without thinking, she raised her hand and touched his cheek. She jumped when a hand shot out and grabbed hers.

He was dreaming and then he felt warmth on his cheek. He responded reflexively and put his hand up quickly only to feel fingers under his. His eyes opened and were looking into the green pools he was dreaming about. Only they looked frightened.

"I apologize," Mitch said quickly, dropping his hand from hers and sitting up.

Mortified didn't even begin to cover Katherine's feelings, "Not at all, I must apologize. I'm sitting here staring at you and touching you while you sleep. You must think I'm some sort of nut job!"

Something in her tone struck him as funny and he chuckled. "Nut job, huh?"

Katherine shook her head and looked down at her hands again.

Mitch cleared his throat, "I wasn't against you touching me, Katie. I was just dreaming and woke up." So she was staring at him while he slept? Cool!

"Mitch," she looked at him directly, "I do not touch strangers." She cleared her throat, "I am a decent person with no criminal history and no family history of emotional instability."

The explanation was more than was necessary and he found her adorable. "It's okay. The thought of touching you crossed my mind once or twice." Where the hell did that come from?

Really? Katherine was intrigued so her head shot up quickly to look at his eyes; she was good at spotting a player. He didn't seem like he said anything that he didn't mean.

"Well," Katherine smiled, "since we're both so into touching, maybe we should get to know one another a little better."

There was no mistaking the innuendo in her words. Mitch's pants were tight now. "Um," he said, not able to think of anything intelligent to say.

"I'm afraid, Mitch," she said his name slowly, "that I may be under the influence of wine and therefore I'm a little more open than usual." The smile she had while tipping her chin down just a smidgen made her feel rambunctious.

Mitch moved in his seat, trying to get comfortable, "I'm certainly all for openness," he said, returning her inflection. "I support a woman speaking her mind and touching me as she sees fit."

Oh now he was teasing her, well, she was no slouch in that department. After all, she owned her own business so she was used to playing it up with the boys.

"Well that's good," she moved her hand and placed it over his; making slow circles on the back of his hand with her fingertips. "Is this okay?"

The air was being systematically sucked out of his lungs, "Yes," he said quietly.

With no regard for acting like a fool, Katherine moved her fingers over his hand, gently lifting it and placing it between her hands. She used the fingers underneath to caress his palm while the ones on the top continued their exploration of his knuckles. His fingers were strong and she noticed there was no ring on them. A good sign since she was touching him in such a sensual way.

His mouth was dry and his eyes were glued to their hands. It was entrancing watching her fingers as they discovered the feel of his hand. There was no word that could adequately describe his reaction to this.

Katherine was in a fog of desire and they were only "holding hands." She had to do something so she looked up into his eyes and asked, "How long have you been in the Marine Corps?"

Mitch wasn't thinking straight and answered out of role, "Twenty-two years."

Then the question permeated the haze of want in his head and he jolted, pulling his hand out from between hers. "How did you know?"

The spell was certainly broken, 'good job, Katherine,' she admonished herself. "I've spent a lot of time around Marines."

Clarity was making its way through his senses; he was uncomfortable since he was allowing her to touch him and he didn't know anything about her. "Is your dad a Marine?"

Katherine shook her head, "No, he does work for the government though." She was most certainly not opening up that can of worms so she deflected the conversation. "I recognize the haircut."

Absently, Mitch ran his fingers through his hair. He was going to have it cut in Hawaii since it was grown out from a couple of weeks on leave. He was surprised that she was still able to recognize it as most people just lumped all military services together.

"Twenty-two years," Katherine whispered aloud. "Wow, that's a lot of time."

Mitch suddenly felt old. "I went in at seventeen."

As if saying that made him sound young. He looked at her, guessing that she was no more than twenty-five and definitely too young for the likes of him.

Katherine never would have guessed him to be thirty-nine. She thought he was older than her thirty-two years but didn't really care since they were only going to know one another for the duration of the flight.

"Are you glad you did?" She asked the question without thinking how awful it sounded.

"Yes," he answered without hesitation, "I am very thankful for the opportunity I've had."

Another trait, humility. The man was like something out of a book. But those guys were too good to be true so she couldn't place too much stock in that. "What do you do?"

A valid question, "I work with planes." It was a cop out, he knew it, but every time he mentioned Crash, Fire, Rescue while on a plane, the other person he was talking to usually became fidgety.

"Interesting," Katherine said.

Time to turn the tables, Mitch looked at her fully, "What do you do, Katie?" he asked pointedly.

The way he said her name was like feeling silk slide over her skin; it warmed her and made her feel pampered. "I draw." She said without thinking about the lie to much. Just once she'd like to be simple.

"Where?" Mitch asked.

Katherine smiled, "New York." She didn't really want to reveal too much about herself; he was far more interesting.

Mitch was impressed, "Rough crowd." He visited New York enough to know that it wasn't easy to have a business there. "Why did you fly out of Newark?"

Good question, he didn't miss much. "I don't really care for flying so I wanted a non-stop to get it over with." She cocked her head, "Why were you flying out of Newark? I don't remember there being any bases in that area."

Mitch was right, she was smart, "I was visiting family and this was the most convenient airport to fly out of. Plus I'd rather have the non-stop flight too."

They were two peas in a pod, Katherine thought.

The flight attendant came by and offered them options for their afternoon meal and said she'd be back in a few minutes to see what they chose. After she moved on, they each sat with their own thoughts, the intimacy of their earlier conversation gone.

After they placed their selections for lunch, Katherine asked for a water. She smiled shyly at Mitch, "I don't think I need any more alcohol."

"I'm not so sure," he responded, smiling, "I like a woman who's a little less inhibited, even if it's with the help of wine."

She tried to look stern but failed when a smile broke her lips, "I can be downright wild if given the chance, Mitch."

Her statement surprised them both.

Their meals arrived and they both focused on eating.

Katherine appreciated the break. She kept saying things she would never say to anyone she knew, much less a stranger. But there was something so intriguing about this man. He made her feel emboldened. She could blame it on the wine but it was really just her reaction to him. Something to think about, that's for sure. If anyone who knew her saw her acting like this, they would have a heart attack. She was the poster girl for control.

Mitch could feel her thinking. He couldn't blame her, he was wondering why he was acting this way with someone he just met. But it was fun so why shouldn't they have fun? Their meal trays were removed and he wanted to know more about her.

"Why are you going to Hawaii?" he asked, sincerely hoping they could maybe see one another there.

Smiling, Katherine looked over and her eyes met his. She was lost in their depths, "A vacation."

Not exactly revealing but he'd take what he could get, "Me too."

After that they both fell silent. It was like neither knew what to say now.

Katherine leaned her seat back, "Mitch, I'm tired, do you mind if I close my eyes for a bit?"

"Oh no, go right ahead." He felt like an ass since he was basically telling her to leave him alone. He picked up the magazine he was reading earlier and tried to focus on it.

Chapter 2

Somewhere Over Iowa

Katherine opened her eyes and tried to focus. Her head was against Mitch's shoulder and her hand was on his arm between them. If she didn't know better, she'd call it snuggling since she was so close to him. She could hear his deep breathing and felt his head resting against the top of hers. The intimacy of it caught her right under the chin.

She didn't know if this man was a serial killer or what and here she was, splayed over him. If her parents saw her right now, there would be hell to pay. Oh well. She closed her eyes and nestled closer to him. His other hand came up and covered hers causing her eyes to pop open in surprise. Ah, better, she thought and closed her eyes again.

Mitch woke up to movement. There was a tingling in his hand. When the cobwebs cleared, he realized it was Katie touching his hand softly with her fingertips again. A man could get used to that, he thought.

Katherine knew when she woke him. His breathing changed and his heart beat sped up like hers. When he moved, she changed her position and took a moment to watch him. He stretched, lifting his muscled arms above his head. His shirt wasn't tight, but moved across his skin enough to allow her to see the silhouette of muscles underneath. Heat bloomed in her belly and she looked away, trying to hide her lascivious thoughts.

"How long were we asleep?" Mitch asked, his voice raspy with sleep.

Katherine looked at her watch, "About an hour I think," she pulled a magazine out of the seat pocket and tried to act like she was going to read it.

Mitch softly touched her arm, "Do you mind if I get up to stretch my legs?"

"Oh certainly," she said and stood so he could get up and into the aisle.

Once he was standing next to her, she was surprised by how tall he was. He towered over her five foot two frame, making her feel small and delicate. She tilted her head to look up into his eyes and stopped moving. There was something in them that drew her in.

Why couldn't he move? Mitch asked himself. Because those eyes kept him glued to his spot and he wanted nothing more than to kiss her, that's why.

Another passenger made a noise and they broke eye contact. Katherine sat down and watched him make his way up the aisle toward the bathroom. Watching him walk was a treat too. She could see he was in excellent physical condition and wondered what was under the clothes that she couldn't see.

"Stop it!" She hissed, and cowered when she realized she said it aloud. Now she was talking to herself......great!

Luckily, the other passengers seemed oblivious to her behavior. She needed to get a hold of herself; this behavior was crazy. She was most definitely not crazy, at least not before now. Oh, he was coming back to his seat. She got up and smiled shyly as he sat back down.

The captain came on again, "Greetings from your Captain, folks, we're looking at the weather and it looks like we may be experiencing some turbulence in a little bit so we're going to turn on the fasten seat belt sign. We're going to ask that you stay seated in the meantime and we'll try to give you a smooth ride."

The fasten seatbelt sign came on and Mitch dutifully clicked his in place. He looked over and noticed Katherine looking upset. Her bottom lip was between her teeth and her brow was furrowed.

"Are you okay?" Mitch asked her, he placed his hand on her arm.

She forced a smile, "I'm fine, I'm just going to powder my nose and then I'll be back." She got up quickly.

He watched her go toward the front of the plane and wondered how bad her fear of flying was. They stared at each other during takeoff and maybe the distraction of that is what helped her. It was no problem if she wanted him to stare at her, he would be glad to do so. She was a beautiful woman. He was literally jolted out of his thoughts by a drop in the plane's altitude. Crap, turbulence!

Katherine just got into the bathroom when she was knocked against the sink by the plane's movement. Oh, she hated this! It was tricky but she did manage to use the facilities and was starting to make her way back when another jolt threw her off balance. She ended up tripping over the strap of someone's bag and unceremoniously ended up on the floor with her head banging against an armrest.

Mitch saw her go down and was up in a flash. He reached her and hauled her up into his arm. His face turned hard and told the flight attendant to "back off" with his eyes when she made a move toward them. He carried Katie back to their seats and got her into hers quickly. Once he was buckled into his, he turned to assess any injuries she might have.

Oh her head hurt. Katie was embarrassed. She looked down, feeling foolish. Another jolt in the plane made her grab for Mitch.

Yes, she was scared, Mitch thought, "It's okay, Katie," he said into her hair while holding her close.

Katherine thought it wasn't so bad now that he was holding her. He put the armrests between them up and pulled her over so she was almost in his lap. Not very comfortable with the seatbelt but she felt safe.

"Thank you, Mitch," she murmured into his shirt. She couldn't look at him.

Mitch smiled, "My pleasure."

He meant it too. Holding her was like being swept up into a cloud of pleasure. It took all of his restraint to not kiss her but now was not the time.

After a while, the plane became less bumpy and everyone started to relax. Katherine looked out the window past Mitch and saw the lightening in the distance. Were they headed for that? Her pulse sped up and she was starting to panic.

Mitch felt her tense. "What is it, Katie?" he asked softly.

She leaned away so she could look into his eyes, "I'm embarrassed that I'm clinging to you but this freaks me out." She closed her eyes for a second trying to shore up her nerves.

"Not everyone is comfortable with a plane bumping along," he tried to sound light; "it's not a problem for me to hold a beautiful woman in my arms."

The words he spoke skimmed across her skin, making her feel warm.

She tipped her head to the side, "You think I'm beautiful?" Not an appropriate question at all but, what the heck.

He snorted, "Are you kidding me!" He tried not to speak loudly as he didn't want the other passengers hearing them. "You're gorgeous, but you know that."

Katherine shook her head, "No, but thank you." She leaned over to kiss him on the cheek and he unexpectedly turned his head so their lips met instead.

The shock of the kiss hit him full force. He was not expecting it whatsoever but it was awesome. Her lips were soft and clung to his for only a second before she pulled away.

Oh no, Katherine thought. She offended him with her boldness. His look of surprise was followed up with a grin that made her eyes narrow.

"Well, well," Mitch said slowly, "if I'd known I'd get a kiss out of it, I would've ordered that turbulence a little sooner."

He was teasing her, she knew it, but she couldn't help it. "Well, if I'd have known your lips were going to feel so good against mine, I would've kissed you sooner."

A shot of desire pummeled his chest. This woman was keeping him on his toes that was for sure. "Anytime."

That was a nice offer, "I may have to take you up on that."

What was going on here? She was supposedly scared and here she was flirting and Lord knows what else with this man. It was so much fun though that she didn't want to stop. No one had to know; she didn't know anyone else on the plane, she could, just this once, let go and do something impulsive.

Mitch was trying to think of a comeback but his mind was blank. All the blood was leaving his brain and redirected to other parts of his body. Damn it, he needed to be an adult and not maul this poor woman on a plane.

She could see his indecision. He was a decent guy and her flirting made him question what he should do. Well, maybe she needed to take the decision out of his hands. Without thinking, she put her hands on either side of his face, her fingers lightly caressing his cheeks and pulled him toward her.

Mitch knew she was going to kiss him and he wasn't going to stop her. As soon as their lips met, he was sucked into an abyss of need.

He tasted so good, Katherine thought. His hands were holding her arms. She could feel his restraint and wanted to test his resolve. Her tongue darted from between her lips to touch his.

A spike of desire punched through him. With a low growl, he opened his mouth and took her in fully.

This was what a kiss should be, Katherine thought. The contact between them was so intense; she was engulfed in sensation. He tasted sweet. His tongue darted in and out expertly, asking her with his movements to join him in an exotic dance. Her hands went up to feel his hair. Although it was short, there was enough for her fingers to grab on and hold tight.

An "Uhum," from the aisle made them come up from their kiss.

One of the flight attendants was standing just past Katherine and looking at them expectantly. She hated to interrupt them, they were a cute couple, but she didn't want them to get too carried away. It was a public place after all.

Katherine looked at the flight attendant and was mortified. She nervously pushed her fingers through her hair. Lord, the woman must think they were animals. She smiled sheepishly at the flight attendant, hoping nothing would be said.

Mitch looked at both women and wanted to laugh. They got caught kissing like they were horny teenagers or something. He wasn't sorry, just amused.

The flight attendant looked from the woman to the man, "Drink, sir?"

She was professional, he'd give her that. "Water would be great," he answered with a smile.

Katherine was stunned. How could they both be so calm? She was very uncomfortable. Neither of them seemed to be bothered so maybe she should just go with it.

"I'll take another wine please," Katherine said with a small smile.

A few minutes later they were each sipping their drinks and not saying anything. Awkward was an understatement as far as Katherine was concerned. What did you say to a guy you were making out with on a plane? A guy who you knew for approximately two and a half hours. A gorgeous, sensual man who knew how to kiss like nobody's business. If her line of thought didn't stop, she was going to end up kissing him again.

Mitch could see she was unsure of what to say or do. He wasn't so blind that he didn't see she was not like this normally. His little Katie was not normally a demonstrative person. He was sure of that. Whoa, since when was she his? He thought about it... since she kissed him like no one else ever had; that's when.

He stared out the window and sipped his water, thinking of all the things he'd like to do with "his little Katie."

She wondered what he was thinking. He was looking out the window and he seemed lost in his thoughts. Well, she was lost in thinking about him. They still had over seven hours on this flight together so either she better figure it out or change seats.

"Mitch," Katherine said softly as she laid her hand on his arm.

His arm heated where she touched him. It tingled and felt so good. He turned his head and smiled at her, "Yes, Katie."

He was so calm, she noted. How did he do it? She was mixed up.

"I didn't mean to embarrass you by kissing you." She didn't want it to be weird between them.

Mitch's brow furrowed, "You did not embarrass me, Katie," he took her hand into his. "I was just thinking that I'd like to do more than kiss you."

The directness of his comment made her senses go on high alert. "Really?"

Why did she question it? "The kiss was," he took a breath, "very arousing."

She couldn't remember anyone ever saying that to her. Most guys just wanted her on their arm for decoration or status, they certainly never commented on her kissing ability. It was a heady thing, having someone tell you that you are arousing.

"Thank you," Katherine whispered, "I enjoyed it very much."

Mitch was relieved. He wanted her to be as affected by their attraction as he was.

She didn't know what to say, "Well you're not a criminal or anything, are you?" The question came out and she felt so stupid.

He laughed, "No, I don't think the Marine Corps would put up with that, so, no, I'm not a criminal." He thought she was adorable, "I am single, no kids, a solid upbringing, good personal hygiene." She was smiling and that made him glad, "I like books, movies, I'll put up with ballet but not my personal favorite, I like to grill out, ummm."

Katherine just watched him, he was graceful for a man. His movements were meant to put her at ease so she knew he was a gentleman. His "personal" resume wasn't solicited but it certainly was appreciated.

"Thank you for making me feel less awkward," she said when he stopped.

"Anytime," Mitch answered. It was so easy to please her; an unusual thing in his experience with women.

He was about to ask her about her life when the plane jolted. Katherine's eyes flew to his, looking wild and she grabbed onto him.

The pilot's voice came on, "Sorry, folks, some residual turbulence."

Mitch smiled, trying to reassure Katherine it was ok. He didn't mind the turbulence if it kept her in his arms. He could feel the heat of her skin and loved how she fit into his side perfectly. It was like she was meant to be there. His thoughts were very erratic and he didn't necessarily care for them right now.

Katherine closed her eyes and prayed the plane would settle down. Her nerves were frayed and she didn't know how much more of this she could take and still remain calm. Why did it have to be on this flight? She found a man who was interesting and she was like a scared five year-old. She wasn't showing her best side.

Mitch held her to him securely; he breathed in the scent of her hair and reveled in the feel of her next to him.

She couldn't move; it felt too good to be in his arms. She absently rubbed her fingers across his forearm. It didn't seem right to talk and break the spell.

The plane bumped along a few more times and every time Mitch thanked the weather. He kept thinking how he was very disturbed to be appreciating this.

The flight attendants came around to make sure everyone was okay and went back to strap into their assigned seats. That was never a good thing, since it usually meant that more weather was in the future. Mitch took note and hoped Katie was oblivious to it. They weren't speaking and her head rested on his chest, her face away from his so he couldn't see if she was awake or not. He hoped she was asleep and wouldn't be bothered by all of this.

Suddenly, the plane banked hard, Mitch heard a whining noise and knew, with all of his Crash Fire Rescue experience, that this was not good. Katie was grabbing him so hard, her nails were digging into his skin.

"It's okay, Katie," he murmured into her hair.

Katherine wanted to believe him but she was terrified.

The plane jerked a few more times and they watched as the flight attendants were talking on the inflight phone. Mitch guessed it was to the pilot and his thoughts were confirmed a few minutes later.

"Sorry about the bumpy ride, folks," the captain said, "unfortunately all this jostling around has been a little rough on the engines so we're going to go ahead and make an unscheduled landing in Cheyenne, Wyoming. Everything is okay but we just want to make sure the equipment is okay before we continue on."

The flight attendants got up and went from row to row.

"Flight attendants, prepare for landing," the captain said.

Katherine was looking at Mitch and was petrified. "Are we alright?" Katie asked Mitch. He said he worked with planes so he would know right?

Mitch was pretty sure they weren't in any real danger. He discreetly looked out the window while Katie was distracted by the flight attendant and didn't see any smoke or fire, so that was a good sign.

"Yes we are, Katie," he said confidently.

She believed him. There was no reason she should since she didn't really know him but she believed him nonetheless. "Okay." She smiled weakly.

He'd give anything he had to make her smile and not look so scared. "I would be honest with you if I was scared," he kissed her hand, "okay?"

The gesture was so sweet, it made Katherine smile. She was trying not to cry and was angry with herself for wanting to.

They settled back, feeling the plane decreasing in altitude as it prepared to land. Mitch listened carefully for anything that sounded out of the ordinary. As they were nearing the airport, he could see the crash trucks at the end of the runway and knew something was up. There was no way he was saying anything to Katie about it though.

The plane touched down on the runway and Katherine let out a breath. Thank goodness they were safe. She looked over and smiled at Mitch. He was smiling back but his eyes looked cautious. She didn't know him that well but she could tell something was up. Maybe he was more nervous than he let on. It was so sweet of him to be brave for her.

They taxied to the gate and the engines shut down. Passengers started talking, some commenting on what they were going to do, but most looked relieved that they landed safely.

A flight attendant stood and grabbed the phone, "Attention, ladies and gentlemen. We don't know what the disposition of the flight will be so we ask that all of you stay in the gate area when you deplane. We should have information for you very soon."

Katherine heard more grumbling but she was just thankful they were okay. She had a little bit of time before she needed to be in Hawaii so she was okay with the delay. Maybe Mitch's orders made it more difficult for him. She turned to see him gathering his bag.

"Are you going to get into trouble for being late?" she asked him.

Dawning came, "No, I gave myself some extra time."

That was nice; he was prepared like her. It was nice to meet someone who seemed to understand. Her assistants and buyers were always saying, "Loosen up," or something to that effect. There was something to be said for being diligent.

They deplaned and gathered as a group in the gate waiting area. The group was pretty calm and didn't gripe too much. Finally an airline rep came up and grabbed a microphone.

"Hello, ladies and gentlemen," she smiled, "our crews are checking out the plane right now and it seems that some repairs will have to be made." She waited for the reaction to die down, "We're going to put you up in a local hotel and then you'll all be able to fly out first thing tomorrow morning."

People were upset, that was apparent, but it wasn't the woman's fault as far as Mitch was concerned. He tried to take these delays in stride. He glanced at Katie and she seemed unfazed by the turn of events so that was good.

"How about dinner?" he asked.

Katherine could think of nothing better and smiled, "Yes."

Mitch walked out of the Cheyenne Regional Airport and thought that this day was turning out pretty differently than how he thought it would this morning. He was in Wyoming, of all places, and taking a beautiful woman out to dinner.

"Where should we go?" Katherine asked. She was open to whatever he wanted.

Shaking his head, Mitch chuckled, "I have no idea." He raised his hand, "Let's get a cab and ask."

Katherine laughed, "Okay."

They hailed the first cab, the driver was a little older and seemed harmless enough. Mitch asked about nearby restaurants and the man happily gave him some choices. They picked a chain place as that seemed safe enough and were off.

After entering the restaurant, Katherine excused herself to use the restroom. She pulled out her phone and called her cousin, Eryn. After getting Eryn's voicemail, she left a message.

"Eryn, it's Katherine. Listen, my flight was delayed. I'll be there tomorrow. I can't wait to see you." She looked toward the hostess station and saw Mitch waiving her over. "I'll call tomorrow with my new flight info." She hung up quickly.

They were seated at a table near the back of the restaurant. It was a nice place that served a nice variety of food. The hostess left them and said their server would be there shortly.

Katherine scanned the menu. She didn't eat out very often, opting for more healthy choices at home. Everything looked good and she decided she was famished. Maybe it was being scared witless…now she felt…almost wild.

The server came over and introduced himself. Mitch ordered steak and a salad then turned to her.

"I'll have a steak, salad, and a strawberry daiquiri," she said without thinking.

Mitch was surprised. He wouldn't have pegged her for a drinker but he counted three glasses of wine during their flight. Not that it was any of his business.

Not wanting her to feel bad, he stopped the server before he left the table, "I'll have a beer."

They chatted warmly about the other patrons, their flight adventure, without mentioning the make out session part, and the weather in Cheyenne, while they waited for their orders.

Katherine drank her daiquiri quickly, ordering a second one before their meal came. She looked sheepishly at Mitch, "You must think I'm a lush."

"No, ma'am," Mitch said good naturedly, "I'm not much of a drinker myself."

She smiled, "I'm not either but I was so nervous on the plane and then now I just feel," she was at a loss for words and waved her hands in circles.

Mitch understood, "Relieved?" he offered.

"Yes," she sighed. "I'm not myself today."

There were several ways to read that statement. He hoped none of them had anything to do with her behavior with him.

A song was playing in the restaurant that Katherine found pleasant so she was swaying in her seat to the rhythm. Those daiquiris were making her feel really good.

He was amused by her fun-loving behavior. It wasn't like he couldn't have fun; he was just a lot smarter about indulging in it these days. Responsibility, and age, could do that to you. Wow, he sounded so old! He motioned the waiter for another beer and stared at his gorgeous companion.

"Do you like this song?" he asked.

Katherine moved her head in time to the music, "Yes." She sipped the last of the daiquiri up through the straw and pouted.

Shaking his head, Mitch smiled, "Did you want another one?"

"Yes," Katherine answered, her head felt fuzzy but good.

Their food arrived and each of them dug in.

The food was wonderful and Katherine ate more than she normally would have. Not too much since she didn't want to get sick or gain five pounds.

Mitch thought she was picking at her food. He ate all of his dinner and felt sated. The beer relaxed him so he was more talkative than normal.

After their plates were removed and Katherine turned down the offer of a to-go box, they debated over who would pay for dinner. Mitch won but he was pretty sure that was only because she was buzzed from the alcohol. He stood and walked over to her seat to escort her out.

Katherine stood and the room spun a little. She waited a moment to get her bearings and tried to appear normal as she walked out of the restaurant. Oh, she hoped she didn't look as woozy as she felt. Once the crisp night air hit her face, it helped. She turned and wound her arm around Mitch's and laid her head on his shoulder as they walked. She was relieved she decided to wear sandals on the plane. Her heels would have had her wobbling for sure.

Mitch thought she was probably leaning on him for balance but he really didn't care. She felt good. He waived down a cab and asked the driver to take them to the hotel where the passengers were instructed to go.

Once they got to the hotel, they went inside and got their carry-on bags. The airline was kind enough to send the bags over for the guests so they could get something to eat.

As Katherine approached the front desk, she saw a line of passengers. They would need to wait a little bit for sure. Without thinking, she turned to face Mitch and wove her arms around his neck.

"We have time," she murmured and kissed him.

Never, in his whole life, could he remember a woman kissing him in the lobby of a hotel. Now he wondered why he hadn't done it sooner. This particular woman was an exceptional kisser so that was certainly a plus.

"Hey break it up, you two," a man behind them said roughly.

Katherine was embarrassed for the second time today. What was with her? She didn't make a spectacle of herself normally and yet, here she was kissing a man in public.

Mitch looked behind him at the man, "Sorry. Honeymoon."

The man smiled, "I remember those days." He was rewarded with a poke to the ribs by his wife.

Katherine covered her mouth to stifle her giggles.

They stood quietly and waited for their turn and walked to the desk together.

"Hello, a room for two?" The front desk clerk asked.

Mitch stopped. What did he say? Obviously the woman mistook them for a couple. Probably because they were making out in the lobby not five minutes earlier. He was getting ready to correct her when Katie spoke.

Katherine smiled. Ah, this was fun. "Yes," she said breathlessly. "Right, honey?" Her tone was sugary sweet. Although her smile faded when she saw Mitch's face. He didn't appear to be happy.

Giving the clerk his information, Mitch was confused. How did this happen? He needed to say something here; she would never willingly go up to his room with him. They didn't know each other that well.

"Have a great night," the clerk said and gave the room key to the handsome man.

Practically skipping out of the lobby, Katherine pushed the button for the elevator and smiled up at Mitch. Why did he look so upset?

"Are you okay?" she asked as the elevator doors opened.

Mitch waited until they were in the elevator, thankful that no one was with them. "Not really, Katie." He looked down at her, "Why did you say we were sharing a room?"

It was really very simple to Katherine, "Well I thought you wanted to sleep with me since our kisses were so friggin fantastic but maybe it was just me."

He was absolutely dumbfounded. His jaw dropped and he closed it quickly. "Well," he swallowed hard, "yes I did but I didn't think you wanted that."

"Oh, you're a sweet man," Katherine said with a smile. They exited the elevator and found their room.

Mitch gave her the key, "I'm not sure that would apply right now with the thoughts running through my head."

Katherine laughed. "Well, wait a bit and we'll see if I can change my opinion of your sweetness." She pulled the key out of the slot and pushed the door open.

The woman left him speechless. Without knowing how to respond, he dutifully followed her into the room.

They entered and Mitch put their bags down. The room was like any other hotel room, except that Katie was here with him. Having her here was like putting dry kindling on a fire. He wanted her but wanted to be a gentleman.

"Katie," he started to say that she could change her mind when she turned to face him. Something in her eyes made him stop mid-sentence.

Katherine slipped her shrug off her shoulders and let it fall to the floor. She put a finger up in the air and crooked it toward him, gesturing for him to come to her.

He was pretty sure that this woman was going to kill him.

Of course, there was no better way to go.

Chapter 3

Katherine was trembling. She wasn't sure if it was because of the need she felt pulsing through her body or because she was nervous about making love with a man she only just met. This was not her by any means but, then again, Mitch wasn't like any man she ever met.

She watched as he came toward her. There was hesitation in his eyes but she also saw want. For her. It aroused her, knowing he felt the same way. The kiss on the plane was so empowering for her. Once he was close enough she pressed her hands, palm out, gently against his chest. She could feel his heart beating as erratically as her own. She wanted to feel him so she slowly ran her palms down his chest.

Mitch watched her exploration of him in awe. Her eyes were bright and followed her hands as they made their way down his chest. They were both fully clothed but it sure didn't feel that way to him. Her touch drove him crazy but he wanted her to set the tone. If she decided she didn't want this, then so be it.

"I want you, Mitch." Katherine said softly. The admission surprised her.

Mitch smiled, "Good, I want you too, Katie," he replied.

Her chin was tilted down but her eyes were tilted up so she could see him and her grin was cat-like. Knowing he wanted her made it easier. Her hands reached his waist and she wrapped her hands around his belt and yanked him to her.

He wasn't expecting the motion but he welcomed it. She was like a drug, one he wanted a hell of a lot more of. He lifted his hands and cradled her head between them. He searched her eyes with his to make sure. She licked her lips in preparation for his kiss and he was done.

Kiss me! Katherine screamed on the inside. No man ever made her anticipate this. It was frustrating and crazy and wonderful at the same time.

"Kiss me," she ground out.

Mitch couldn't deny her demand. He leaned forward and kissed her greedily. Their lips met and danced. His belly was on fire with need for her. He moved his body closer so he could put his arms around her and hold her to him.

The kiss was everything she desired and yet it surprised her too. He was so gentle. She was sure he was giving her time to back out. But there was no way on earth was she going to.

Mitch groaned as Katie nestled into his arms and moved her hands up and down his back. The rhythmic sensation of her caress made him restless.

Katherine wanted to be closer; he wasn't close enough. "More," she said between kisses.

His hands went to the zipper at her back and slowly pulled it down. The straps of the summer dress fell down, exposing her shoulders. They looked as delectable as her lips and he had to taste them. He bent his head and tasted her shoulder, nipping the sun-kissed skin with his teeth gently. She was delicious!

His tongue and teeth were making love to her shoulders and it was amazing. How did the man know what would drive her crazy? She wouldn't be outdone so she pulled his shirt out of his pants and started to move it up. Her hands touched his skin and another log was placed on the fire of desire welling inside of her. His skin was hard and soft at the same time. The muscles rippled as he moved to kiss her neck.

No more clothes, Mitch wanted to yell. He wanted her naked beneath him. As he kissed his way across her neck to her other shoulder he pushed her dress down lower. As the dress lowered, he felt her breasts break free from the fabric and groaned again. His hands instinctively moved up and cupped them. Oh, they felt so good, filling his palms completely. Not wanting to leave any part of her un-kissed, he moved his mouth down to take a hardened nub of her nipple between his lips.

"Ahhh," Katherine moaned. Oh goodness, this was so hot!

She pulled his shirt up and he let go of his lovemaking just long enough to get it over his head. As she tossed the garment aside, she looked at him, his eyes were almost dark gray, the dim light of the room making them mysterious. He looked so sexy with no shirt and only his jeans on.

There was no going back now as far as Katherine was concerned. Her body wanted the release she was sure he would give her. They undressed each other the rest of the way and stood beside the still-made bed in the room, naked.

Mitch wanted her so much but he also wanted her to know that he would stop if she said so. Her skin glowed in the light, he slowly rubbed her shoulders, loving the ways she relaxed under his attention.

"Are you sure?" Mitch asked.

Katherine smiled slowly, "Oh yes." She kissed his chin, the tip of his nose, each cheek, and finally his lips. "Let's make love."

The way she said it made his chest do a flip. It was the oddest feeling that made his head swim and his body ache. He reached over and pulled the bed covers down. Once that was done, he brought her hand up to his lips and kissed the palm. Then he laid on the bed and pulled her up next to him.

Katherine thought the coolness of the sheets felt so good on her heated skin. This was going to be so good and she knew it. There was no way to know such a thing but she did. They were laying face to face on the bed, their fingers entwined, and kissing gently.

Mitch waited until he could feel Katie's frustration; she was ready. He rolled her over and positioned himself above her. She parted her legs to accept him and he wanted so badly to bury himself in her but he wanted to wait too. The indecision in him was maddening.

Katherine couldn't wait another moment so she lifted her legs and wrapped them around the back of Mitch's legs. Her heated center touched his hardness and she gasped. He wanted her so much; he guided himself into her and she almost melted into a puddle of ecstasy. It felt so much better than she even thought.

They fit together perfectly, Mitch thought, as he started to move inside her softness. His breath hissed from between his teeth; he wanted to make it last for her.

Their rhythm was slow and gentle at first but Katherine wanted more.

"Faster, Mitch," she sighed.

His body responded without his mind kicking in. He sped up his thrusts and the erotic feel of her multiplied.

Katherine threw her head back, "Yes, yes!" The orgasm took her fast and she looked into Mitch's eyes as she rode the wave.

Watching Katie orgasm just took him to the edge and he ground into her once more before finding his own release.

Katherine held him close as he emptied himself into her. Never before did it feel so magical. She was in awe of the experience.

Mitch didn't want to squish Katie so he moved to the side of her and pulled her to him. His arms went around her tightly and held her in place as he enjoyed the afterglow of their lovemaking.

This felt so delicious, Katherine thought. She closed her eyes and took in the sound of Mitch's still-ragged breathing, the feel of his dusting of chest hair against her back, the feel of his powerful legs entwined with hers, the feel of his arms as they held her close. She wanted to lay here for forever.

After a while, Mitch was almost asleep. He didn't know how long they lay there in the bed, neither speaking. It wasn't uncomfortable, it was just peaceful. But now reality set in and they had to talk to one another. Mitch loosened his hold on Katie so she could turn to face him.

"How are you doing?" he asked.

Katherine smiled slyly, "Very well, thank you. And you?"

He chuckled, she was adorable, "Pretty good."

She knew he was trying to make her feel better. "Don't worry, Mitch, I wanted this very much."

Her straightforwardness was appreciated. "I did too."

Katherine hiked herself up so she could place her head into her hand. The other one made lazy circles across Mitch's chest. He felt so strong.

"But," she leaned forward and kissed him, "you're worried about the "after effects."

Now he felt silly. Yes, he worried about them. Any decent man should as far as he was concerned. He smiled shyly and nodded.

He was so cute! "Don't, I'm a big girl and I'm very selective about who I sleep with."

What did that mean? His brow furrowed, "Okay?"

She realized she was probably saying it all wrong, "I just don't want you to think you seduced me and that I would regret it. That's all."

It still wasn't completely clear to him but he'd let it go. They slept together. Maybe it wasn't as profound for her as it was for him. Everyone had their own perception. The thought made his ego take a hit but that was okay as long as she had no regrets.

Mitch was becoming a bit clearer to her; he was thinking about it all. It was sweet but she was a consenting adult who made her own decisions.

"If you don't mind," Katherine smiled, "I'm going to go and shower."

He nodded, "That's fine."

He watched her as she got up from the bed and walked over to her bag to get her things. She never stopped to cover herself or act shy. It amazed him to watch her graceful movements. The woman was gorgeous; in and out of clothes. His body remembered the feel of her and responded. Dammit, he was not some horny teenager.

Katherine walked into the bathroom, a smile pasted on her face. She felt Mitch's eyes on her as she made her way across the room, the feel of his need driving her own. She liked feeling this way, it was awesome and made her feel like she could fly or something crazy. She turned on the water, letting it run over her hand until it was the right temperature.

Mitch was lying in the bed and heard the shower start in the bathroom. Why was he here and her in there? No reason for that, he thought and hopped off the bed.

"Can I join you?" Mitch asked when he entered the bathroom. He wasn't sure if she would like it but it never hurt to ask.

"Hmmm," Katherine answered. "It depends."

He smiled, "On what?"

Katherine poked her heard around the shower curtain, "Do you hog the water so I can't use it?"

Mitch chuckled, "No."

Okay, she thought, "Do you wash backs?"

He dutifully nodded.

That's two, Katherine thought, "Do you like to experiment to see what you can do in the shower?"

The kick to his gut was fast, "Of course." he answered, trying to sound serious.

"Then you can join me," Katherine smiled big and wiggling her eyebrows at him.

So she was playful, Mitch thought. He could deal with that.

They shared the shower, washing each other top to bottom, and experimenting to see what they could and couldn't do in it. It was small but definitely usable. They laughed and played and kissed and made love. It was fun! After they got out they dried each other off and ran for the bed naked.

Mitch pulled the covers up over them so Katie wouldn't get cold. She was squirming beneath him, the friction of their skin making him hard again. Geez, could he get enough of this woman? Apparently not according to his body.

Katherine was giggling at their antics until she looked up into Mitch's eyes. They were deep blue again. The desire evident in the way he was touching her skin with his hand. She loved that, the feel of his hands on her.

"Again?" she asked playfully.

Mitch tried to look sheepish but couldn't, "Again," he said.

Katherine could not deny him when he looked at her that way. "Well, we must keep you happy now."

He wanted to smile but he couldn't, the need inside him was too much. Instead he leaned forward and captured her lips with his. He poured his want into the kiss until she was writhing beneath him. Now they were even.

Katherine sank into his touch and reveled in the feel of them joined together. It was like being wrapped up in a warm blanket. She closed her eyes so she could concentrate on the feel of him sliding into her slickness. The feel of it took her to heights she never dreamed of reaching physically.

Mitch could feel her reaching her climax, her pulsing sheathed him and took him to the pinnacle quickly.

They collapsed on the bed, each panting, trying to catch their breath.

Katherine wanted to talk to him but she was physically exhausted. The craziness of the day caught up with her and she slid into the relief of sleep quickly.

Mitch felt her beside him, her breathing deep and even. He gently moved her so she was nestled in his arms and closed his eyes. This was heaven as far as he was concerned.

They slept that night, side by side, wrapped up in one another. Even in slumber, they needed to touch one another and be close.

It was still dark when Katherine woke up. There was a crack in the curtains that showed the gray of dawn peeking through. She looked over to see Mitch sleeping peacefully beside her. The memories of the night before were beautiful, making her feel more alive than she had in a long time.

She got up to use the restroom and clean up. As she brushed her teeth, she was hit with inspiration. Knowing that you didn't push that aside, she quietly crept through the room and grabbed her bag. Without a sound, she left the room in search of a place to create.

Waking up was slow for Mitch. Not his norm as he usually popped out of bed pretty quickly. Of course he didn't normally make love to a woman three times the evening before either. A smile formed before he sat up, the thought of Katie with him making him feel warm.

"Katie?" he said when he realized she wasn't in bed with him.

No answer. His smile faded as he went to the bathroom. All of her things were gone. As if not wanting to believe it, he went through the room, searching for any trace of her. Nothing.

Katherine sat out on the patio of the breakfast room at the hotel. The morning was cool but she needed space. She asked the hotel driver to take her to a twenty-four hour store for some supplies and proceeded to draw for several hours. Once the sun was well into the sky, she decided it was time to get her things together. She looked at her watch, her eyes going wide. Where did the time go? It was after noon already. Oh crap!

She quickly got her things cleaned up, neatly tucking her drawings into her bag and went to the front desk. The clerk was helpful and told her most of the passengers checked out already and headed over to the airport.

Mitch sat on the plane, wondering what happened. It was like she never existed. She was real dammit! He sat looking out the window trying to figure it out. He waited in the room for over an hour and then the airline called to say they were ready to take the passengers back to the airport. He thought he'd see Katie there for sure but was floored when she was nowhere to be found.

Did he say or do something? He must have or else she wouldn't have left him like that right? Shaking his head, he stared into the passing clouds, hoping they would bring him some answers.

Katherine made it to the airport and explained that she overslept. She hated lying but it sounded better than the truth so she let it go. The agent was able to get her on the next flight to Los Angeles and then she'd grab a flight to Hawaii. She called Eryn and left another message, cringing at how early it still was there.

The flight to Los Angeles was spent going over her drawings. She made little changes and tweaked them to suit her needs. It surprised her how she was so creative after the day before. She was pretty sure she owed it all to Mitch. The man did amazing things to her body and her mind. Their lovemaking was more than she could ever imagine it to be. Maybe that's what everyone talked about. It certainly was not like that for her up until now.

A smile played on her face as she thought of him. Of course she never got his last name or phone number so there was a good chance they would never see one another again. That was very regrettable but it was her fault for not staying in the room with him.

The flight attendant made the announcement for their descent into Honolulu and Mitch was miserable. He replayed the whole night over and over in his mind and felt keyed up and depressed at the same time. Why did she leave? He smiled at the flight attendant but it didn't reach his eyes. The only thing he could do now was paste a smile on his face and do what he promised to do for Chase. After all, that's what he was here for right? He would be the "best man" if it killed him.

The plane landed without incident and taxied to the gate. He felt some excitement for seeing his friends so that would need to be his priority from here on out.

He made his way to baggage claim and laughed when he saw Chase waiving to him. He was dressed in a blue polo and jean shorts and looked happy. Mitch walked over and gave his friend a hug.

"Well hell, man, being engaged makes you look awful." Mitch said sarcastically.

Chase punched him in the arm, "Yeah, don't let Eryn hear you say that." He smiled, "How the hell are you, man?"

"Good," Mitch said but he wasn't sure if he meant it.

Chase looked at his friend and wondered what was up. Mitch was an easy-going guy but he looked distracted. It would take a while, but Chase would get it out of him. He started toward the baggage claim to get Mitch's bags.

They got into Chase's jeep and started their trek toward Marine Corps Base Hawaii. Eryn was meeting the both of them at the Staff NCO club for a late lunch and drinks.

Mitch listened to Chase talk about the wedding plans. Eryn's mom was going all out and wanted everything to be done by the book. When a General's wife wanted something, you didn't say no. He laughed at Chase's description of the planning and how it was driving Eryn nuts. He hadn't seen Eryn in ten years but remembered her fondly from their stint at Cherry Point. Now she was a Warrant Officer but didn't appear to have changed that much from the determined woman he knew back then. They'd spoken on the phone dozens of times since the engagement was announced and Mitch really liked her. He was glad to see Chase look so happy.

The drive to MCBH was a beautiful one. They drove down the highway and went through a tunnel that burrowed through the Koolau mountains. They were lush and green and Mitch wondered if he shouldn't try to get some hiking in while he was here. He mentioned it to Chase, who nodded and said he'd see what they could arrange.

Once on base, the men drove over to the Staff NCO club and parked next to Eryn's car. They could see her on the phone talking to someone but her windows were up so they couldn't hear what was said. She saw them, smiled, and hung up quickly.

"Mitch!" Eryn yelled as she got out of her car. She came around and hugged him tightly.

Mitch smiled and returned the hug, "You're still short!" he said flatly.

Eryn stepped back and shook her head, "I could probably kick your butt."

"I don't doubt it," he laughed.

Chase got out of the jeep, "Hey, what about me?"

Eryn sauntered over and slowly wrapped her arms around Chase's neck, "I was just waiting for you to come and get me."

The intimacy of the interaction made him think of Katie. Which made him scowl. Luckily he caught himself before either Chase or Eryn saw him. The three of them went into the club for lunch.

The boys caught up on old times and regaled each other with their current job happenings. Chase was working for a government contractor out of Honolulu but had an office on the base which made it very convenient.

Mitch talked about his current duty station in Quantico, Virginia. He liked it and was fortunate to be a lot closer to his family than his previous duty station. Eryn asked questions about his hometown in Delaware and he talked about it freely. He had a good childhood with great memories. Eryn and Chase laughed at his family stories.

"How was your flight?" Eryn asked.

Whoa, he thought, before he blurted out that he met a woman. "Good," he finally said.

Eryn nodded and grimaced when her phone rang. "It's, mom," she said apologetically and got up to take the call outside.

Chase watched her leave, "She's going nuts but she'll be fine." He motioned for the bill and paid it quickly, ignoring Mitch's objections.

They left the club, said goodbye to Eryn, and went over to the golf course where the wedding would take place. Eryn's mom gave Chase a list of things he was supposed to take care of for the wedding.

"You don't mind?" Chase asked.

Mitch shook his head, "No," he clapped Chase on the back, "lead the way."

They went over and spoke to the caterer at the golf course, as instructed by Mrs. Fredricks, then they got back into the jeep and headed for Honolulu.

The wedding party and some of the guests were being put up at the Hale Koa Hotel in Honolulu. It was a military hotel on Waikiki beach that was as beautiful as any hotel in the area. The proximity meant they would all be able to meet up for wedding related functions more easily.

Mitch asked Chase to just drop him off so Chase wouldn't have to fight the traffic on his way back to the Windward side of the island. He watched as Chase drove off and turned to go in.

The Hale Koa was a gorgeous hotel/resort with great restaurants and rooms. Mitch stayed here before but it was years ago and it certainly grew since then. He walked into the lobby and to the desk. He was reminded of the night before when he walked to the lobby of a hotel in Cheyenne with a beautiful woman next to him. Stop! He yelled at himself, there was no use in this train of thought.

After checking in, he went up to his room. Even as he put the keycard in the lock, he was thinking of Katie. Their night was unlike any he could ever remember. It was more than just sex, at least to him. It was pretty clear that Katie didn't like some part of it or she wouldn't have left without a word.

Mitch walked over to the window in the sitting area and looked out to see a stretch of Waikiki Beach and the Pacific Ocean laid out before him. It was stunning to see; he stood there and stared, wondering what his Katie was doing right now.

Katherine grasped her seat, wishing the plane would land already. She just despised flying. Thoughts of Mitch and his care for her yesterday played out in her mind, making her smile in the midst of her anxiety.

She managed to get an earlier flight from Los Angeles so she wouldn't arrive in Honolulu too late. Eryn promised to meet her and drive her over to the hotel. The wedding party was scheduled to have dinner the next evening so she had tomorrow to compose herself and take care of her wedding assignment.

Excitement bubbled up in her belly, thinking of how Eryn would look. Of course, her cousin could wear a paper bag and look stunning but this was a work of art, if she did say so herself.

The plane's wheels touched down and Katherine sighed with relief. She didn't have to do this again for a week; that was a blessing.

As Katherine came down the escalator towards baggage claim, she searched the crowd for Eryn. There was a sea of people so searching was difficult but she shouldn't have worried, there was a sign sticking up in the crowd that said "KATIE."

Katherine giggled as she neared her cousin. "Oh my, you are a snot!"

Eryn laughed, "I learned everything I know from you."

The women hugged then stood back so they could look at one another.

"Love does good things for you, cousin," Katherine whispered, trying to keep the tears back.

Eryn nodded, emotion building in her chest, "Thank you." She grabbed Katherine's hand and led her toward the baggage carousel.

They waited for Katherine's bags then went over to the airline's office. Eryn looked questioningly at her cousin.

Katherine spoke to the attendant and waited impatiently. Finally, the woman came out with a large box.

"What's this?" Eryn asked.

Katherine winked, "It's a surprise," she nodded toward the door, "let's get out of here."

They drove in Chase's jeep since Eryn's car didn't have a back seat. Thank goodness Eryn thought of that since it didn't occur to Katherine. She was simply not a woman for details and that's what she hired assistants to do. Not that she was a snob, it was just how she got through life. "An artist," her mother used to say, "operated on feeling, not practicality," and that's what Katherine did.

"What are you daydreaming about over there?" Eryn asked. She was driving but looked over a few times to see her cousin looking distracted.

Katherine didn't want to give too much away but it was fun to bait Eryn, "I'm just thinking about you being practical and me not."

Eryn nodded, "That's the truth."

They were silent for the rest of the drive to the hotel. Eryn's parents arrived the day before and Katherine's were due in tomorrow. Pretty soon Hawaii would be flooded with the Fredricks clan.

Eryn parked outside and the women made their way to the lobby. As they walked in, they saw Beverly and Tom Fredricks heading toward them. Katherine smiled brightly as she was engulfed in hugs.

"How was your flight, Katherine?" Aunt Beverly asked, concern on her face.

Katherine tried to hide her blush because mentioning the flight made her think of Mitch and their night together, "It was fine." She tried to sound casual.

Uncle Tom grabbed her bags, "Well let's get you up to your room."

The foursome walked toward the elevators. Katherine had never been to the hotel before so she was looking around curiously when she thought she saw Mitch. Her heart stopped, followed by her footsteps. When she looked again, he was gone.

"Something wrong?" Eryn asked.

Katherine shrugged, "No, I thought I just saw someone I knew." She didn't want to say anything about her little adventure. It was hers and hers alone.

Once she was settled in her room, Katherine washed up and changed into another sun dress. The weather was so mild here. She planned to have dinner with Eryn and her parents. She hoped Chase would join them but he was picking up some of his family and friends at the airport. Just as well, then she could spring her surprise on Eryn.

The restaurant was lovely; the foursome ate and laughed a lot. There was a bit of reminiscing about the girls' childhood with a few stories thrown in about their dads' rambunctious adventures as children. The wine loosened them up a bit but Katherine was careful not to over-indulge. It simply was not acceptable to act impulsively in public. Not according to her father anyway.

She watched the interaction between her aunt and uncle and cousin. It was easy-going and full of love. Katherine was envious. Oh she knew her parents loved her; they were just regimented and had years of expectations shape their public image. She was excited and nervous about their reunion tomorrow.

Dinner concluded with the four going out on the veranda to walk around the grounds. The hotel was gorgeous with grounds that were no less stunning. It was such a change from New York with its harried pace. She didn't speak much, instead letting Eryn and Aunt Beverly discuss wedding plans. It was easier to let her mind wander and absorb her surroundings. Little did she know her family stopped and was looking at her expectantly. Oh darn, she zoned out again.

"I'm sorry," Katherine said sheepishly. "What did you say?"

Beverly responded first, "We were just asking about your surprise?" She winked at her niece in unspoken conspiratorial agreement.

Katherine nodded, "Oh yes," she wrapped her arm around Eryn's, "I left it up in my room. Would you like to see it?" she asked.

"Sure," Eryn said, knowing something was going on here but not sure what it was.

Tom Fredricks cleared his throat, "That's my cue to leave ladies," he kissed his wife, "I'll see you later."

The three women made their way up to Katherine's room. With great pomp and circumstance, Katherine motioned for Eryn to sit on the sofa and went into the bedroom.

She very carefully opened the shipping box, being sure not to use anything sharp. As she peeled away layers of tissue, she smiled. The dress was in perfect shape. Katherine pulled it out and hung it on the back of the bathroom door to inspect it for any imperfections.

"Hey," Eryn shouted from the sitting area, "what are you doing in there?"

Katherine shouted, "Just hold your horses."

Very carefully she picked up the garment and started toward the other room, "Close your eyes!" she yelled through the door.

Eryn closed her eyes as directed and almost opened them when she heard her mother's hitched breath beside her. What was going on here?

Katherine closed the bedroom door and hung the dress up on the back of it so it could be displayed. She tried to contain the butterflies doing back flips in her stomach, she was so excited for Eryn to see it. If her aunt's reaction was any indication, Eryn was sure to like it.

"Okay," she said softly, "open your eyes, Eryn."

Eryn opened her eyes and all thought left her brain. The tears filled her eyes immediately. Before her was the most beautiful dress in the history of dresses. Without saying anything, she stood and walked toward it. The gown was white with an overlay of very light tool. The bodices was fitted with a silk fabric. It flowed down like a cloud. Eryn didn't want to touch it because her hands were trembling.

"Oh, Katie, it's breathtaking," Beverly said as she smiled at her niece.

Eryn lifted a finger to feel the fabric. "Why?"

The question was totally Eryn. Her aunt told Katherine that Eryn bought a dress a month ago but Katherine wanted to make this for her cousin. If she chose not to wear it, then that was okay. Katherine created it after a phone call in which Eryn described her feelings for Chase. The inspiration hit her and she was helpless to stop it.

"You don't have to wear it. I was just thinking of what you and Chase have and this is what I came up with." She was a little embarrassed by the admission but it was the truth.

Tears flowed down Eryn's cheeks, "It's perfect." She hugged Katherine tightly, "Of course I'll wear it. I'll just donate the other dress to someone who needs it."

Hearing Eryn's excitement made Katherine happy. It was not often that she felt as though she actually belonged anywhere. Usually she felt like an observer watching everyone else live their life. It was moments like this that kept her connected to the rest of the world.

"Don't feel obligated," Katherine played it off as no big deal but it really was.

Eryn's eyebrows rose, she knew her cousin was very insecure and would not accept anything akin to charity. Of course she would wear the dress; it was angelic and she knew it would make her feel so beautiful.

As if being jostled out of her musings, Katherine looked up, "Oh, I haven't shown you the best part."

She turned the dress around and watched as Eryn and her mother gasped. The back of the dress was corseted with red and gold ribbon. At the base of the back was an Eagle, Globe, and Anchor pin done in gold. Since that was the Marine Corps emblem, Katherine thought this was the best way to incorporate it.

"Oh my Lord," Eryn exclaimed, "it's amazing, Katie!"

Eryn grabbed her cousin in a fierce hug. Beverly snapped a picture of them with her phone and laughed.

After she released Katie, Eryn just ran her fingers gently down the back of the dress. She wanted to memorize every detail of it. This was the dress she would wear when she and Chase became a family. There was nothing she could think of as more appropriate.

The woman gushed over the dress and made plans for a fitting the next day. Eryn insisted on wearing it at least once before the wedding.

Beverly left soon after, saying she was going to her room to meet up with Tom. Both Eryn and Katherine were too keyed up to sit so they went downstairs to one of the bars to have a drink and catch up.

After they were seated and ordered their first round of Hawaiian Sunsets, Eryn caught Katherine up on the other members of their wedding party. There was her sister, Sarah, and two friends of Eryn's from the Marine Corps; Abi Rochelle and Emma Cantrell. Sarah and Emma were flying in the following day and Abi worked with Eryn so she was already here. They discussed the dresses for a bit with Eryn apologizing to Katherine for not asking her to make them.

"I understand, Eryn," Katherine said, "it would have been awkward had you not liked them." She was trying to be pragmatic about it.

Eryn shook her head, "Oh no, I just didn't want to impose on you since you were working on your spring collection." She took a sip of her fruity concoction. "How's that going?"

Katherine shrugged, "Good I guess, I don't pay attention to that side of it that much." She sipped her drink, liking the sweetness of it.

That was Katie, Eryn thought, not worried about anything but the art of it all. "Are you aware of how famous you are?"

To Katherine, it was all relative, and she just didn't care. Certainly she worried whether or not anyone would buy her creations but she didn't care if she made one hundred dollars or one million dollars.

"I have been stopped a few times on the street," she answered her cousin who sat there staring at her.

Eryn sighed, "I don't even tell anyone that I'm related to THE Katie Fred, designer," she smiled slyly, "although maybe I should. I might get some perks."

Katherine snorted, "I doubt it," she waived to the waitress to get another round, "nobody cares about fashion designers."

How did Katie not know how spectacular she was? It boggled Eryn's mind and made her worry that her cousin wouldn't find love like she had with Chase. Women who were about to be married wanted everyone to be as happy as they were.

"Well, I do!" Eryn said loudly.

The next round of drinks arrived and the cousins discussed sightseeing and plans for the wedding. It was fun and they laughed a lot. Eventually the conversation came around to sex. They laughed at their bad dates and Eryn hinted that making love with Chase was wonderful. The alcohol was making Katherine's mind fuzzy and she didn't want to be upped by her cousin so she gulped her drink and slammed her hand on the table.

She shook her head, "Nope, I had the best lovemaking experience just last night."

Eryn stopped lifting her glass to her lips and stared at her cousin. What!! "You'd better spill right now," she said in a whisper.

Katherine laughed and leaned forward. "It was with a guy I met on the plane and it was mind-blowing." Just remembering Mitch's hands on her made her tremble.

"You met him on the plane," Eryn leaned in close and said accusingly.

Katherine rolled her eyes, "I know," she knew that anyone else would judge her actions far more severely than Eryn would, "I figured you would understand, Eryn."

Eryn sat back, her brow serious, "Me?"

Nodding, Katherine took a long drink of her cocktail, "Yes, you," she cleared her throat, "it was like how you described your connection with Chase."

Oh crap, Eryn thought, "What if he was some maniac?" She was worried about Katherine, she always was.

"Nope," Katherine shook her head quickly, "he was amazing. He held me, Eryn," she took a breath, "like I was the only thing that mattered in the world."

Eryn turned the information over in her mind. It was amazing to have that feeling and she did experience that with Chase all the time. That's why she was marrying him in three days. She could never begrudge Katherine for feeling that.

Smiling, Eryn patted her cousin's hand, "I can see why then." She took a drink, tapping her glass to Katherine's in an unspoken toast, "So, what's our wonderful man's name?"

Katherine looked down into her drink, she was embarrassed about not getting more info about her lover but what was done was done. "His first name is Mitch and I don't know his last name," she said quietly.

The bottom dropped out of Eryn's stomach. She looked at Katherine smiling, but inside she was fuming.

"Is he a Marine?" Eryn asked, trying to sound calm.

Katherine smiled, "Yes, for twenty-two years," she looked around her nervously, "at least that's what he said."

Dammit, dammit, dammit! Eryn didn't know whether to be happy or sad for Katherine or kill Mitchell Frinnel.

"Are you okay?" Katherine asked.

Eryn blew out a breath, "Yes, I am," she smiled, "just a little dizzy from the alcohol."

Katherine nodded, "Well let's get the check then."

"Yes, let's," Eryn answered.

Chapter 4

The morning light was peeking through the curtains of Katherine's room. She didn't want to get up but her mind was up and ready to work. Darn it, why did she take a vacation if her creative side just didn't want to take the time off? With a sigh, she threw the sheet off of her and got up to do some creating.

Outside there was a lovely landscaped park area next to the hotel. There were beautiful trees and flowers everywhere so you didn't even realize you were in the city. The smells of the flowers and the gentle breezes felt wonderful to her senses so Katherine meandered around to find a place she could work.

She set her paper and pencils up neatly on a table that was deserted. Not that she minded company necessarily as she could zone most people out, it was just that people wanted to ask questions and she didn't want to answer them.

Designing fashion was her career and she loved it but this was art and it was sheer pleasure. She sat down at the table and started drawing whatever came to mind. It took no time for her to be lost in the picture she was drawing, wanting the details to be as perfect as she could get them. It was only when she sat up an hour later that she saw what she drew. It was Mitch lying on the bed in the hotel room.

Shocked by the intimate portrait, Katherine looked around to make sure that no one was looking and studied it more closely. She drew him as he was waiting for her to come to bed and make love with him. His muscles were clearly defined and the grin on his face was seductive.

The picture was unlike anything she ever drew so that made her wonder what kind of effect the man had on her. Her body remembered every kiss, every touch, every sensation he made her feel. And now, he heart ached because she would probably never know that again.

Determined not to let the sadness of missing a stranger interrupt her time here with Eryn, she tucked the picture at the bottom of her pile of papers and started to draw some flowers she saw. That was much safer on her mind and in her heart.

Mitch stood at the window of his room looking out at the view. He should be happy, he was here for a happy occasion and yet here he sat, sulking. The reason was because he was still fuming over Katie and her disappearing act.

The woman tied him up inside and out and he'd known her for what.....twelve hours or so. Ridiculous! He glanced at the clock and frowned. He was due for a golf outing in two hours and he had yet to get his butt in gear.

Mitch was about to go turn on the shower when his phone rang. His caller ID said Eryn.

Smiling, Mitch hit answer, "Well if it isn't the bride. How are you today?"

"I've been better," Eryn said through clenched teeth.

She was debating with herself all night as to whether or not she should call Mitchell Frinnel and give him a piece of her mind. She stayed in her parents' room since they had a suite here at the hotel and she didn't want to drive after drinking with Katherine.

This morning she took a walk with her mom and spilled the story. Her mother nodded in all the right places and asked a few questions. In the end, it was decided that they would leave Mitch and Katherine to figure things out themselves.

But now that she had him on the phone, Eryn wanted to pull him through the phone and throttle him. Of course that was far too unladylike for her so she didn't.

Mitch could hear something in Eryn's voice; probably wedding jitters, "What can I do for you?"

Eryn sighed, her mother was right. They didn't need her interfering, "Well, I was hoping you could pick up some things for the dinner tonight."

"Sure," Mitch answered. He got a pen and paper out, "Shoot."

Oh she wanted to alright. But, in the end, he was her friend and she was pretty sure Katherine would take care of whatever was between them herself. She gave him the list and hung up as quickly as she could.

When Eryn turned around, she saw her mother standing there with her arms folded across her chest. "I know," Beverly said, "you wanted to smack him, right?"

Surprised at her mom's insight, she nodded. "Yep."

Beverly gave her daughter a hug, "Good girl for refraining."

Eryn nodded but she wasn't so sure she agreed.

"Besides," Beverly said, "Katherine will handle her own life her own way."

Nodding again, Eryn sighed, "I know but I don't want her hurt."

Beverly looked at her daughter, "You've always spoken so highly of Mitch before. Does he seem like a womanizer?"

Eryn wanted to laugh at her mother's use of words, "No, he's honorable."

"Then he will be polite and treat Katherine with respect no matter what their relationship may entail." Beverly was sure of it. If not, she knew a few Marines who could make his life tough.

The gleam in her mother's eye gave her pause but Eryn believed she was right. It was almost time for their fitting so she got her things together. There were supposed to meet Katherine and her seamstress at Katherine's room in twenty minutes.

Outside, Katherine glanced at her phone and snarled. Darn it, why did the time have to fly when she was sketching? She had a meeting with Eryn and Aunt Beverly in a few minutes so she finished her sketch and signed it quickly. She collected her things and walked over to a family sitting nearby on a blanket in the grass.

She smiled as she walked up and handed her sketch to the woman sitting and playing with her daughter. The woman smiled, surprised by the gift from the young woman. She looked down at the drawing and her breath hitched. It was a sketch of her holding her little baby girl and it captured the love between them perfectly. She looked up, tears escaping down her cheeks to find the woman gone.

The fitting went well, only very minor alterations were necessary for the dress to fit perfectly. Katherine held her breath the whole time Eryn was putting it on, worried that it wouldn't look as she imagined while creating it.

When Eryn came out of the room, she looked like she was floating on a cloud of love. The dress was her. Katherine beamed at her cousin, knowing it was right.

After the seamstress left with the dress, the women went downstairs to catch a cab for some sightseeing and last minute wedding details. Abi was still at work and wouldn't meet up with them until the dinner later and the others were landing in a couple of hours and would be met by the guys.

The shops full of neat wedding decorations and fanciful creations were amazing. They went into a few shops with Hawaiian themed gifts and picked out a few things. It was fun and pulled Katherine out of her earlier funk. Sometimes she was so lost in the feelings that she forgot to function as everyone else did.

They stopped for lunch at a bar where the motif was dedicated to Hawaiian surfers. The atmosphere was festive and relaxed which made the afternoon even more delightful.

"What are your plans for the trip?" Beverly asked her niece.

Katherine cocked her head, trying to think, "I think I might hop over to Kauai for a day or two after the wedding." She took a bite of her fish and found it delicious.

Eryn nodded, "Oh, let me know," she leaned in, "I know some great spots."

Her cousin's enthusiasm was contagious, "Okay, I will."

They finished their lunch and made their way back to the hotel, stopping off at whatever shop interested them. There weren't a lot of purchases, just time together was enough.

Back at the hotel, the arriving wedding guests were getting situated in their rooms and Chase and Mitch were down at the bar having a drink.

"That was fun," Chase said sarcastically.

Mitch chuckled, "It actually wasn't so bad," he said. "Everyone was on time at least."

Chase nodded, "Yeah, I just miss Eryn."

Understanding how Chase felt frustrated Mitch. They played nine holes of golf this morning and went to the airport to pick up family for the wedding and the whole time he thought about Katie. When was she going to get out of his head? He thought maybe he should look for her but there were dozens of hotels in Honolulu. And he didn't even know if she was going to be staying in the city, she might be staying somewhere else on the island.

Chase watch Mitch and was wondering what had his friend's face scowling like that. "Earth to Mitch," he said.

"What? I'm sorry," Mitch returned.

Clapping his friend on the shoulder, Chase smiled, "It's okay. Is there something you want to talk about?"

No! Mitch shouted in his mind. "I'm good," he answered, finding something really interesting to stare at in his beer bottle.

"Who is she?" Chase asked. In his experience, the only thing that ever made him think that much was Eryn.

Mitch laughed, "No one."

Oh so that's how they were going to play it, Chase thought. "Okay but I'm here."

Mitch sincerely appreciated the offer but he had to figure this out on his own. After all, the woman was with him for one night, big deal! Yes, keep telling yourself that, his brain said sarcastically.

"Isn't it time to start rounding people up for our dinner thing?" Mitch asked, clearly wanting to change the subject.

Nodding, Chase smiled. Mitch would open up when he wanted to. "Yes, let's get this show on the road."

They left the bar, Chase started texting Eryn to see where they were. There was an hour before their reservations but they figured it would take that long for everyone to arrive. Chase and Mitch were in charge of corralling everyone into the private room they were having dinner in. As it was the night before the rehearsal dinner so there was a large number of people. Most of Chase's and Eryn's family had never met so this was the 'get acquainted' dinner.

Mitch and Chase were standing in the lobby when they spotted Eryn and her mother. There was another woman with them, a cousin Mitch was told, but he couldn't see her with all the people moving around.

Katherine entered the lobby and took the bags from Eryn and her aunt. She was going to take them up to her room and hold them there until the rehearsal dinner and wedding. It was the least she could do to help out.

She made a mad dash for the elevator when she noticed the door was opening. The ride up took forever, probably because she was tired. All the walking and travelling caught up with her. Maybe she'd take a quick nap before dinner. As she entered her room, she heard her phone ring.

Putting down the bags, she looked at the screen. It was her mother. Here we go, she thought as she answered, "Hello, Mother."

The group was in the large, private dining room and Mitch thought it was organized chaos. Both families inter-mingled, which was nice, but the sheer enormity of it was a bit overwhelming. He was introduced to so many people that he was pretty sure he'd never remember everyone's name. He used his manners, his mom would be proud, but it was not exactly his type of function. Not that he minded, he was just distracted.

Chase asked him to get everyone seated. The wedding party was scattered around the room so he wouldn't meet everyone until the next day at the rehearsal. He had yet to meet the maid-of-honor. He assumed it would be Eryn's sister, whom he met, but it wasn't. A cousin, he was told. Well, she better be up for this, he thought as he surveyed the group around him.

"What are you thinking about?" Tom Fredricks asked. He watched Chase's Best Man standing there looking lost.

Mitch stiffened automatically, the man was an officer after all, "Sir," he put his hand out to shake Eryn's father's.

Tom shook Mitch's hand, "No formalities here, son, I'm just Tom for the next couple of days."

Relieved, Mitch relaxed, "I was just thinking that the two families mesh well, sir." Crap, he said sir.

Chuckling, Tom looked around the room, "Yes, I think so." He spotted his wife who was waving him over, "I don't envy you getting this group organized."

Mitch watched Eryn's father walk over to her mother and start up a rousing conversation. Sometimes it was better to watch than to participate.

Katherine was taking deep breaths on the elevator. She was meeting her parents at their room and then they were all going down to the dinner together. She loved her parents but they tended to be more formal than Eryn's and it always seemed awkward. Maybe it was because she was flighty by comparison, choosing art as her passion. Her father always commented that her choice in careers confounded him. He wanted her to go into public service like he did.

The elevator doors opened and Katherine put on her game face. She walked to the door of the room number her mother provided and knocked.

Victoria Montrose Fredricks opened the hotel room door and smiled warmly at her daughter, "Katherine," she said as she gathered her daughter into her arms.

"Hello, Mom," Katherine answered, hugging her mother.

A noise from the other room made the women part.

"Vicki," Marcus Fredricks came out of the bedroom, "have you seen my cufflinks?"

At the sight of her father, Katherine smiled. He was a handsome man, years of stringent self-discipline kept him young.

Wearing his suit, he looked far younger than his fifty-three years of age.

Victoria shook her head, "Dear, you won't need them until Saturday. Your daughter is here."

It always amused Katherine that her mother referred to her as her father's daughter. Some things never changed.

Marcus smiled, "Ah, Katherine," he came over and kissed his daughter on the cheek. "You look lovely."

Always a charmer, Katherine thought. "Thank you, Dad."

Her father stopped and really looked at her for a moment. His attention made her nervous, even though she tried to look like it didn't bother her. His gaze could make the strongest of men cower down but she'd developed an immunity over the years.

Victoria could see something in her husband's eyes but she wasn't sure what, "Well, let's get going or we'll be late."

Marcus looked at his wife and smiled, "Yes," he offered his arm to her, "Let's go."

The three of them walked silently to the elevator. Katherine discreetly looked at herself in a mirror as they walked by to make sure she looked okay. Her father was staring at her so she thought maybe he disapproved of her attire or something. The feeling of being on display was there whenever she was with her parents for a function. A hazard of her father's job she supposed.

The elevator doors opened and the three of them walked to the private room. Two ushers were standing at the door and gestured for them to enter. Katherine looked around for Eryn. Being maid-of-honor gave her an excuse to be away from the looks her parents were bound to garner. It was that way every time they went out.

"Excuse me," she said to her parents. "I have some details to attend to for Eryn."

Her father nodded and her mother smiled. Victoria knew how Katherine hated the scrutiny that usually accompanied her father.

Katherine wove her way through the crowd; running into a few relatives she hadn't seen in a long time. It was fun catching up. She grabbed a glass of wine from a passing waiter and settled into the revelry. Before she knew it, there was a tapping of a microphone. She was seated in the back so she couldn't see who was up front talking. As soon as the speaker started though, her stomach dropped to the floor.

"Excuse me, ladies and gentlemen," Mitch announced into the microphone. "We're going to ask that everyone be seated now."

The guests started moving, people finding their seats and shouting out hellos to those they missed during cocktail hour. He smiled as Chase and Eryn made their way up to him. His friend looked happy. Eryn, on the other hand, looked tense.

Maybe his earlier thoughts about her getting cold feet were true. He'd try to reassure her of course.

Chase and Eryn were seated so Mitch looked up to make sure everyone was seated. That's when he saw her. His Katie! What was she doing here? He looked at his friends who, thankfully, were lost in their own conversation. When he looked back up, she was gone!

It was him! He was here! Katherine thought. Her thoughts were racing and she was confused. If she didn't get some air, she was going to hyperventilate. She stood to go out and had to wait for a couple of guests to move in front of her. As she looked up, her eyes met with his. Oh Lord! He looked as unsettled as she felt.

Even though she wanted so badly to run away, it wasn't an acceptable thing to do. This was for Eryn and Chase; it wasn't about her so she did what was expected and made her way around the crowd to sit at the table with her parents.

"Um," Mitch mumbled, his thoughts were in tatters, "I guess I'll turn the microphone over to the groom now." He thrust the mike into Chase's and sat down.

Katherine found her seat and was thankful that her parents were seated in such a way that Mitch was not in her direct line of sight. She needed some time to compose herself.

"Are you alright?" Victoria asked. Her daughter looked pale.

Not wanting to have this discussion right now, Katherine nodded, "I'm fine."

She looked up at Chase and tried to smile. It was excruciating but she would do it for Eryn.

Mitch half-listened to his friend as he thanked their families and friends for making the trip to Hawaii for the wedding festivities. The joy in Chase's voice was unmistakable and Mitch was thankful for it. His friend deserved the happiness he found with Eryn. Then he heard Chase announce that he wanted to introduce the wedding party.

"This is my best man, Mitch Frinnel," Chase said, "stand up so everyone can see you."

Mitch stood up and felt like a teacher just called on him. He waived awkwardly and sat down quickly. The other groomsmen were announced and he was relieved they were put on the spot like he was. Then Chase introduced the maid-of-honor, Eryn's cousin, Katherine, and his heart stopped.

It was her! He wasn't hallucinating. She was here and she was stunning. Her hair was piled up loosely on her head and she was wearing a light blue dress with thin straps over her beautiful shoulders. Shoulders he remembered kissing all too well. The thought made him blush. When she sat down he could no longer see her.

He looked over to see Eryn staring at him intently. Oh hell, she knew! Her face was tight and he could see she was pissed.

What did Katie, or Katherine, tell her? He stared back at her, not ashamed of his role in the night in Cheyenne.

Chase sat down and wondered why Eryn looked so upset. "Are you okay, baby?" he asked her.

Looking at her fiancé, Eryn's face transformed into a bright smile, "Yes, I'm fine." Inside she was a mess of anger but it wasn't because of anything Chase did. "I love you," she whispered and kissed him.

The rest of the dinner was uneventful. Mitch was relieved he wasn't required to make any more announcements or speeches until the wedding. He kept trying to get a peek of Katie but couldn't see her. In between bites of steak and lobster, he was dodging glares from Eryn. It was an awkward test of his resolve. Chase looked oblivious so he was pretty sure his friend had no idea about what was going on.

The music started as dessert was served. There was a small dance floor off to the side of the room and the guests slowly started to get up and sway to the slow tune playing. Mitch watched as people congregated here and there to offer congratulations to the parents or Chase and Eryn. He was startled by a hand on his shoulder.

Eryn couldn't take it any longer; she wasn't able to hold her tongue. Excusing herself and whispering into Chase's ear, she went over to Mitch. When he looked up at her in surprise she smiled.

"Would you like to dance?" Eryn asked.

Oh this was like going into combat, Mitch thought. The woman was imposing when she wanted to be. But he was a gentleman and she was the bride so he agreed with a slight nod.

They walked out to the dance floor, Mitch placing his hand lightly on Eryn's back to guide her to the music.

He wasn't going to give her a chance to strike first, "What do you know?" he asked Eryn.

"She said she had and amazing night with you," Eryn answered in a dead pan voice. She was still not sure if she was mad at him or Katherine for acting so impulsively.

Her response was not what he imagined Katie would say, "We met on the plane and she was scared of the turbulence so I offered her comfort." Okay, even he thought the explanation was lame and sounded perverse.

Eryn scoffed, "Comfort?"

His temper was flaring, "Eryn, you know me, I'm not one of those guys," he moved her around the floor as if there was nothing wrong, "besides, she's an adult, you know."

She did know it, and if it was anyone else besides Katherine, she wasn't sure she'd be this upset. Katherine always seemed so fragile to her and Eryn always considered herself her protector. Looking at Mitch though, she could see he was tormented about something. In his defense, she watched him when he noticed Katherine and he looked dumbfounded. She believed neither of them knew the other would be here.

"I know," Eryn responded. She looked into his eyes, "Mitch, just don't hurt her."

He didn't know whether to be pissed or impressed with Eryn's obvious protectiveness of her cousin. He shook his head, she didn't know everything so how could she think it was him who would do the hurting. He was hurt by Katie's rejection the morning after their lovemaking. He was mad now. Why did women always assume it was the guy who would be the jerk?

He stopped at the edge of the dance floor and looked down at Eryn, "Did she tell you she left ME the morning after our supposed amazing night?" He looked around them to make sure no one was listening, "Not one word, Eryn."

That didn't sound like Katherine to Eryn. Her cousin wasn't that cold. Her insides warred; her loyalties were divided.

Mitch did not think now was the time for this particular conversation, "Listen, you should be celebrating with Chase, not worrying about what Katie and I are doing or not doing."

His tone was quiet and calmed her. He called her cousin Katie and that meant something. Katherine did not let many people use the nickname. Plus, Mitch was right. She nodded, hugged him quickly to let him know they were okay, and went back to her fiancé.

Katherine stood in the shadows at the edge of the room, watching her cousin and Mitch dance. They were dancing but their body language said everything. Eryn knew he was the man she was referring to the other night. Her stomach was in knots wondering what to do.

Mitch could feel awareness and knew Katie was looking at him. He looked around and finally located her standing alone in the corner of the room. She was observing everyone. He understood the need to just watch sometimes. His gut was flipping but he couldn't keep away from her.

Oh Lord, he was coming over. Instinctively, Katherine smoothed her hand down the side of her dress. Did she look as scared as she felt? She never was any good at the games between men and women.

As he approached Katie, he could see her nervousness. Good, he was pretty unsettled himself. She looked gorgeous, her eyes bright and searching his. His body responded to her and that made him mad; it defied his head which said, don't give an inch.

"Katie," he said quietly.

She looked up into his eyes, they were dark and looked angry. "Mitch, I didn't know you would be here."

Katherine felt silly, she wasn't saying anything right. His reaction made her think he was definitely mad.

"I'll bet," Mitch said tightly.

Mitch cupped her elbow and, without another word, guided her out of the room. He didn't stop until they were outside on the patio away from the other guests.

"Why?" Mitch demanded, it took all of his control to not scream at her.

She didn't understand, "Why what?"

He walked a few steps away, trying not to lose what was left of his temper, "Why did you just leave?"

Katherine shook her head quickly, "I didn't leave." That was what he thought?

Clenching and un-clenching his fists, he looked at her. She looked small and fragile but he was hurt. "Yes you did! You were gone when I woke up and I couldn't find you." He looked away then back to her, "That's leaving, Katie!"

Looking at him, she knew they would get nowhere right now. He was too angry and she was feeling foolish. She didn't leave but now was not the time to try and convince him of that. There certainly was no reason to make a spectacle in front of the guests so she nodded and turned to go back inside.

What the hell! She just walked away? He slammed his fist down onto the railing of the patio and was glad for the pain the movement caused. He needed something to focus on. He stared out into the black of the night for a while until he was composed enough to re-enter the party.

Chase was talking with his brother about something when he noticed Mitch crossing the room. He looked pissed. Chase excused himself and caught up with Mitch as he was reaching the door.

"Hey, Mitch," Chase called out.

Mitch stopped and turned, "Hey, what's up?"

Anyone else might be fooled by Mitch's tone but they'd known each other too long, "What's up with you?" Chase asked with a worried tone.

Mitch looked around him, "I think I'm just worn out, buddy. I'm going to get some fresh air but I'll be back."

"Okay," Chase said. He didn't believe his friend but he wasn't going to force Mitch to talk about something here.

As Chase turned to go back to his guests, he locked eyes with his bride-to-be. Something about the way Eryn looked made his neck hairs stand up. She wasn't mad exactly but something was up. He made a beeline for her knowing he was damn well going to find out.

Katherine sat at the table with her parents. They were involved in conversations with friends and other family members. She was content to sit back and watch them. She saw Mitch walking out, Chase catch up to him, and then Chase walking over to Eryn. The embarrassment she felt before was tenfold now. She was the cause of trouble during a time that should be happy. She excused herself from the guests at the table and made her way toward Eryn.

Chase walked over and took Eryn into his arms. If there was one thing he knew, it was find the tactical advantage. He kissed her deeply, his lips melding with hers and making his heart speed up. The woman could undo him in mere seconds with a kiss.

"Now," he whispered when he was done kissing her senseless, "are you going to tell me what's going on?"

Eryn was about to answer when her eyes focused on something behind him. He turned to see her cousin, Katherine, standing there and wringing her hands. He'd only met Katherine once before and found her a very delightful woman, if a little meek for his tastes.

Katherine looked down at her hands then up at her cousin and Chase, "I'd like to apologize for any discomfort my actions have caused you both. It certainly was not Mitch's fault."

Okay now he was really confused, "Does somebody want to fill me in here?" Chase asked.

It was Eryn's turn to step up, "Chase, would you mind taking your bride for a walk?"

Katherine smiled as the couple left the room. So, Mitch thought she carelessly left him in their room after their night of passion and now that was affecting her cousin's wedding. Is there any way she could mess things up more? Feeling a headache come on, she decided to say her good nights and head up to bed.

Chase and Eryn went down to the beach and walked arm and arm. It would always hold a special place for him as this was where they made the decision to finally make love for the first time. Was that only four months ago?

Eryn watched her fiancé and knew he was thinking of the night of the ball last November. She was thinking of it too and so glad they were getting married. She loved him so much!

"Okay, I don't know the whole story yet," Eryn started to explain. "But they met up on the plane and had a night together."

That last part stopped Chase, "What! Your cousin and Mitch?"

Eryn nodded.

Chase shook his head, "What was he thinking?"

Eryn could appreciate his feelings, she was torn as well, "I guess they didn't exchange last names or backgrounds so neither knew who the other was."

He sat down on a bench and waited for Eryn to join him. He put his arm around her and held her other hand in his on their laps. "Are we mad or do we let them be?"

She couldn't help it, she laughed, "I don't know."

"Listen," Chase said and moved so he could face her, "the next two days are you and me, lady." He kissed her softly. "I don't care what anyone else does; I want you with me forever, okay?"

Eryn nodded, loving him so much. "Yes, sir," she whispered.

"That's about the only time I think you're going to address me as sir, isn't it?" he joked and kissed the tip of her nose.

Eryn stood and pulled him up, "Probably."

They started walking back to the hotel, hand in hand.

Chapter 5

Friday morning was gorgeous and helped lift Katherine's spirits. She woke up early again. The need to create drew her outside once again. With her tote over her shoulder, she walked around the hotel to where she sat yesterday. She laid out her paper and pencils once again and sat there staring into space. Even though she wanted to draw, nothing came to mind.

A breeze picked up the papers and would have scattered them if not for a hand snaking out and holding them down.

Katherine saw the hand and followed it upward until her eyes met up with the blue ones she knew so well. "Good morning," she said quietly.

Mitch looked down at her; she looked ethereal, her gauzy dress moving with the breeze, her skin looking so soft, wisps of her hair caressing her cheeks. He couldn't just stand there and watch her, he had to say something.

"Good morning," Mitch said.

At least he didn't seem as mad as last night, Katherine thought.

He started to straighten the papers he held to the table when a drawing caught his eye. It was a sketch and his breath hitched when he pulled it out and looked at it. His eyes flew to hers then back to the paper. It was him in the sketch. He was laying on the bed, the sheet draped over his hips barely concealing his modesty. It wasn't the sketch that caught him but the beauty of it; the details were amazing. Especially since it was a pencil sketch.

Katherine watched him look at her drawing, she wondered what he thought. His eyes covered every inch of the paper. Did he see what she saw? He was a beautiful man physically and emotionally.

Mitch finally put the paper down with the others and sat down to face her, "Why did you draw that, Katie?" His voice barely audible.

Katherine smiled, it was very simple to her. "It's you, that's why?"

He didn't understand. "What do you mean?"

"Our night was wonderful, Mitch," She would not dramatize the situation; "I woke up and felt like drawing so I went out to the hotel's patio area." She saw him nod. "I tend to lose track when I work so when I looked up, it was after noon and you'd already gone to the airport."

She described it so simply, but to him, it wasn't. "Weren't you mad at me for going?"

"No," Katherine said matter-of-factly, "you had a plane to catch."

Mitch shook his head. Did she think their time together was nothing? She said it was amazing but what she was saying now contradicted that.

Katherine dropped her chin, "I don't take things like this personally, Mitch." She knew he didn't like her comment. "I see it as how we work as individuals."

Normal people were not this rational, Mitch thought. "So did you like our night together?"

"You have to ask?" Katherine was dumbfounded.

He sighed, "Uh, yes." He stood, frustration pounding through him. "I looked everywhere for you at the hotel."

Katherine sighed, "Obviously not, since I was there."

Was she trying to goad him? "What?"

"Mitch, I don't know what to say that will make you believe me." She sighed again when she saw the anger in his eyes.

Resignation filled him, "You don't have to say anything, Katie."

He turned and walked away from her.

Katherine watched him go and wondered what she did.

An hour later, Katherine looked up to see her mother standing nearby. She smiled and motioned for Victoria to sit.

"I didn't want to disturb you," Victoria said.

Katherine rolled her shoulders, "You weren't. I needed to take a break anyway."

Victoria nodded, she looked down at the sketches Katherine had on the table. "May I?"

Nodding, Katherine was happy that her mother showed an interest in her drawing. As a child, her mother was always supportive of her artistic interests, unlike her father. Katherine was proud of her work and wanted her family to be as well.

When Victoria got to the drawing of a man, she looked up at her daughter quickly, then back at the paper. It was a stunning depiction. He looked familiar to her somehow. The intimate pose led her to think that this was the man her daughter was currently involved with. Of course, she couldn't ask about it. They weren't close in that way.

Katherine watched her mother gently place the paper back down on the table. Her mother didn't comment which didn't surprise Katherine. It did, however, disappoint her.

Victoria smiled, "Are you going to meet us for lunch?

And we're back to reality, Katherine thought. "Of course." She silently grabbed her supplies and got up to return them to her room.

Mitch stood at the window of his room looking down on the hotel property. As soon as he got back up to his room he looked out and saw her right away. The soft set of her shoulders contradicted her total absorption in her work. He watched her as she sketched although she was too far away for him to see what was on the paper. He saw another woman approach and look at the papers she had and wondered if the woman saw the sketch of him.

When he first saw it, he was blown away. He had no idea she was such a good artist. Now he wondered what else he didn't know about her. She was confusing as hell and yet he stood up here and watched her for a good hour. Was he any better at communicating his feelings? What were his feelings exactly?

His phone rang, interrupting his thoughts. "Hello," he said absentmindedly, his eyes watching Katherine and the other woman walk toward the hotel.

"Mitch," Chase said, "we're waiting for you to come down so we can pick up the tuxes."

Dammit, how did he forget? "Yep, on my way down." He grabbed his room key and his wallet and quickly left his room to catch the elevator.

Lunch was fine, Katherine thought. They went to a restaurant a few blocks from the hotel. Eryn and her parents met up with Katherine and her parents. Eryn's sister Sarah was supposed to meet them but the travelling left her tired. She was pregnant so she decided to rest until the rehearsal in a few hours.

The conversation revolved around wedding plans for the most part. There were a few questions aimed at her father regarding her parents' current assignment so that kept the focus off of her for most of the meal. That was just fine with her; it gave her time to consider the conversation between her and Mitch this morning.

She honestly did not know what he wanted her to say. It wasn't like they were in love. The word was so foreign to her that she wasn't sure she'd know it if she saw it. However, a person did not fall in love in the space of one day. It wasn't practical at all.

Eryn watched her cousin mull over something. Probably Mitchell Frinnel. Lord knew she spent countless hours thinking about Chase over the years. What was Katherine thinking? Eryn felt bad for judging Mitch and she would apologize when she saw him later. There were always two sides to everything. If her tumultuous trip through love was any indication, there was a lot of misunderstanding. She was thankful that she and Chase found one another in the end.

Beverly Fredricks watched her daughter watch Katherine. Every once in a while she'd catch her sister-in-law, Victoria, looking at Katherine too. Why was everyone so worried? No one gave Katherine enough credit.

"Well, I'm full," Marcus said while he patted his stomach.

Tom Fredricks laughed, "Not feeding you well in France, Marc?"

Marcus frowned, "Serving sizes are small." He smiled at his wife, "Thank goodness Vicki is a great cook."

Victoria playfully tapped her husband's arm, "I have to be if we want to eat."

Katherine was curiously watching the interplay between her parents and her father and her Uncle Tom. How was it that they could joke with each other but shared none of that with her? Anger was rising up in her chest; an emotion she was not thrilled at feeling.

Eryn stood quickly, "Well, folks, we should get a move on." She noticed a change in Katherine's demeanor and wanted to avoid any awkwardness.

The group stood to leave and Eryn came around so she could walk out with Katherine. She whispered into her cousin's ear, "You're riding with me."

Katherine nodded, relieved that she didn't have to sit in the car with her parents for the long ride to the Marine Corps base.

Eryn walked over to speak to her mother and asked if she and her dad would ride with Uncle Marcus and Aunt Vicki. Her mother nodded so she returned to her car.

They got into Eryn's convertible and started the ride over to the base. The breeze was light and the sun was shining, so Katherine laid her head back against the headrest, just taking in the peace of the wind in her hair.

"Did you and Mitch talk today?" Eryn asked. Her curiosity getting the better of her.

Katherine looked at her cousin, "Yes but I don't think it went well."

That was cryptic, "Would you like to explain that comment?" Eryn asked.

"I don't know as I can," Katherine sighed, "I explained what happened in Wyoming but I don't think he believed me."

Not knowing what to say, Eryn nodded.

Katherine looked out her side of the car, they were out of the city now and headed down the H-3 toward the base. The mountains loomed gracefully in front of them.

"He seems so upset," Katherine said, "I think he wanted me to be more emotional about it."

Eryn snapped her head to the right to look at Katherine, "Really?"

Katherine nodded, "Yes and I was," she shook her head, "but not in the same way he is apparently."

Eryn laughed, she couldn't help it. "Welcome to a relationship, Katie. There will never be a time when you both see things the same way."

Oh that was sad, Katherine thought. "I don't see this as a relationship, Eryn." She threw her hands up helplessly, "It was a fantastic night of lovemaking and that's all."

Speeding down the H-3, Eryn thought that she'd been seeing her cousin in the wrong light for a long time. Katie was the man now and Mitch was the woman! It would be funny if it were anyone else. She loved these two people and they had some inexplicable connection. There had to be something said for that.

The women arrived at the golf course a few minutes before their parents. They got out and grabbed some of the bags out of Eryn's truck that contained decorations and supplies for the ceremony the next day.

As they walked over to the clubhouse, Katherine looked around. It was spectacular. She would love to draw it. Maybe she would get some time to sneak away for that later.

Chase was standing in the clubhouse talking with Mitch and his other groomsmen when the door opened. Mitch was to his right so he saw him first before he turned around. When he noticed the way his friend's face changed, he stopped turning. There was a transformation; a lightness in his eyes that made Chase just stare at him. He wondered if that was how he himself looked when he saw Eryn. Finally, his gaze followed Mitch's to where Eryn and Katherine were standing.

"Hello, my love," Chase said as he crossed to Eryn.

Eryn smiled brightly, "Hello, my love," she replied.

The intimacy of the interaction awed Katherine. Not having the openness in her own relationships, it was interesting to observe it in others. Once she turned to give the couple some space, her eyes met Mitch's across the room.

The floor shifted, he was sure of it. Once her eyes were locked with his, he couldn't move. All the blood left his brain and concentrated lower. The urge to not embarrass himself won over his need to look at her and he finally looked down at his drink.

Was that what it was like for others, Katherine wondered? Did Mitch feel the emotion bubble up like she did? Even though he looked away, she still sensed a tangible link between them. Feeling brave, she walked over to him.

"Hello, Mitch," she said softly and stood on her tip toes to kiss his cheek.

He smiled, "Hello, Katie." He covered her elbow with his hand to keep her next to him. Her kiss left a swell of heat on his cheek and he didn't want her to move.

Katherine wasn't sure what he wanted but she stayed where she was.

The group gathered closer and the Reverend conducting the ceremony spoke up and explained what the rehearsal would entail. Everyone's eyes were on him as he spoke except Katherine's. Hers were on Mitch, wondering what he was thinking.

Mitch felt Katie's eyes on him but he pretended to hear the directions form the Pastor. The woman made him tingle from head to toe when she looked at him. He didn't understand it and certainly couldn't explain it.

Katherine started moving because everyone else was. Mitch released her elbow and moved his hand to her lower back to guide her as they walked. The simple gesture made her feel warm all over. She liked it and wanted to tell him but they were surrounded with everyone and didn't really have the privacy needed for that kind of conversation.

The group was paired up for the processional at the ceremony site. Katherine was distracted by the beauty of the place. There were gorgeous cliffs only yards away that gave way to the Pacific. The white tips created by the water hitting the rocky shore was mesmerizing.

It was clear to Mitch that Katherine was lost in her artist mode. That was the only way he could describe it. He noticed her looking much the same way when she was out on the grounds of the hotel. What must it feel like to be transported like that away from reality? He noticed that they were supposed to be lining up for the rehearsal and leaned closer so only she could hear him.

"It's almost our turn," Mitch whispered into her ear.

His breath kissing her skin jolted her back to the present, "Yes, of course," she looked over her shoulder into his eyes, "I apologize."

Mitch wrapped her arm around his and started down the aisle. "We'll talk later, okay?"

Katherine nodded and walked with him. She looked ahead of them at Chase who was looking at her and Mitch.

Once everyone was in place, the Reverend went through the ceremony. Both Chase and Eryn wrote their own vows so they gave a copy to him. The whole thing only took about fifteen minutes and then the Reverend organized them for the recessional.

Once back at the Clubhouse, the group went into a room reserved for their dinner.

Katherine laughed out loud at the décor. It was Hawaiian but not traditional, the walls were covered with paper Hula Dancers and straw grass skirts. The tables were set with plastic tiki torch glasses and bamboo placemats.

Everyone joked about the decorations and sat down. The feeling was laid back and happy. Once the couple walked in, the cheers started. Mitch whistled as Chase and Eryn found their spots at the head of the table.

"I know," Chase laughed, "we wanted this to be really relaxed."

Katherine looked over at her parents, sure that they would be offended at such frivolity but they were laughing with everyone else. Was everything different than she thought? She looked over at Mitch and saw him watching her. She was forced to sit down because her head was swimming.

Chase stood and started speaking. He was thanking his friends and family and asked the guys to accept a gift from him and Eryn. Mitch and the others went over to him so he could give them each an engraved flask. Chase mentioned out loud that it was filled with a twenty-five year old scotch. That drew cheers from the men.

Eryn stood then and asked her ladies to come up and accept their gifts. As soon as Katherine went up, she was given a small, wrapped box. She waited for the others then they all opened them up together. It contained an exquisite gold chain and a small pendant engraved with their names. It was delicate and brought tears to Katherine's eyes.

Eryn hugged each of the women tightly and then they returned to their seats. Dinner was served and everyone sat down to eat.

Katherine nibbled at her plate, the food was tasteful but she wasn't particularly hungry.

"Are you okay?" Mitch whispered as he leaned closer to her. He'd been watching her and noticed she wasn't eating.

She nodded, "Yes, thank you."

He didn't believe her. "Would you like to go for a walk?" He wanted to ask her a few things.

Katherine looked over to see Eryn watching her. She asked her cousin silently what she should do. The almost imperceptible nod was all she needed.

She turned to Mitch, "Yes, thank you."

They stood up, a few people looking at them questioningly.

Eryn said loudly, "Thank you for doing that Mitch and Katherine."

She was giving them a reason to excuse themselves and Mitch thanked her with his nod.

"What are they doing?" Chase asked Eryn.

She winked at her love, "I'll tell you later."

Mitch placed his hand at Katherine's back to guide her as they walked. Anytime he touched her, his body was on high alert. It was very difficult to think clearly but he didn't want to argue with her either.

They ended up walking back up to the spot the ceremony would be held the next day. There was little light left from the sinking sun but it lit the horizon in front of them up so it looked as though the water was on fire in the distance.

"Beautiful, isn't it?" Katherine asked as she admired the scene before them.

Mitch rubbed her back gently, "Yes, you are."

She looked up and into his eyes. They were reflecting the horizon, shining brightly at her. When he looked at her like that, she felt off-balance.

"Do you want to make love with me again?" she asked.

The question threw him. She was so straightforward. "Yes," he answered. There was no point in lying.

She nodded and smiled slowly, "Good because I want to make love to you too."

The punch to his gut was fast, he had to refrain from taking her into his arms and starting right now. Instead, he held his hands at his sides as he leaned down to kiss her.

Once his lips met hers, Katherine hummed in contentment. His lips were soft and possessive at the same time. They made her want to question everything but she was too busy feeling to speak.

Mitch decided he had to pull away because if he didn't he would embarrass himself right here.

Slowly he lifted his head and looked at her. "You are amazing!"

Katherine shook her head in denial. "Not really, but I appreciate you saying so."

He looked at her, a frown forming. How did she not know how intense she was? How did she not know she made him feel things he never thought possible?

They walked back to the Clubhouse and entered the dining room to find everyone milling around. The conversations varied from Marine Corps to the weather to the stock market. Eryn was the first to greet them.

"Okay, you were getting some last minute items from my barracks room," she said through her smile.

Mitch nodded and smiled conspiratorially at Katherine. "The mission was a success."

Eryn nodded and smiled, "Well, you both better be coherent tomorrow at my wedding or I'll have your butts!" She smiled sweetly and left them so she could go join Chase.

Katherine watched her cousin and giggled. The conversation was absurd but it was Eryn showing her support of their budding relationship.

Mitch guided Katherine as they walked over to where the other wedding party members were gathered. Katherine noted a mischievous look in the men's eyes.

"What are we up to here?" Mitch asked the group.

Chase's brother, Spencer, laughed, "We're discussing the merits of short sheets compared to beer cans on the car."

Katherine was appalled; those things would most certainly upset Eryn. She looked at Mitch hoping he would be the voice of reason. He smiled at her and asked the guys to join him outside.

When the men left, Katherine was left with Eryn's friends, Emma and Abi. She smiled, not knowing what to say.

"So you're an artist?" Abi asked her.

Katherine shook her head, "No, I'm actually a fashion designer." Her eyes kept going to the door that Mitch just left through with the others.

Emma smiled, "Oh really, what's your brand? Maybe we've heard of you."

She appreciated them trying to speak with her, "Oh, I go under Katie Fred."

Abi looked at her friend and then back to Katherine. "Are you kidding me?" she asked, not truly believing it.

"Yes," Katherine looked at the women, "why would I lie about that?"

Emma was waving her hands, "Oh my goodness, I love your dresses!" she said loudly.

People were starting to look at them and Katherine worried that her parents would be upset by the scene.

"I'm a huge fan," Abi said, "how come you didn't design our dresses?"

The question drew Katherine's full attention, "I wasn't asked to," she said matter-of-factly.

She was disappointed in herself, because she was being rude to Eryn's friends. She turned herself to face Emma and Abi, a smile on her face. "I'd love to show you some sketches of my upcoming designs if you'd like."

Both women nodded anxiously so they walked over to a sofa and sat down. Katherine pulled up the sketches on her phone she took the morning after her night with Mitch.

She watched the women as they poured over the pictures, commented on some things, and asked questions. They seemed genuinely curious and were kind with their comments.

Emma handed the phone back to Katherine, "How do you come up with your designs?"

That was easy, "I just feel inspiration, get a few key designs down, and then create some pieces to accentuate them."

Abi smiled, "That is so amazing," she said breathlessly.

That's the second time someone used that particular word with her this evening. She found it odd that someone thought what she did was that impressive. But not understanding their view did not mean she should be rude.

"Thank you, Abi," she squeezed Eryn's friend's hand. "Why don't you both make sure I have your address before I leave and I'll make sure you have tickets to my next show in New York?"

Emma was almost hopping in her seat, "That would be so exciting, thank you, Katherine!"

It was the least she could do; these women were important to Eryn. They deserved to be treated with respect, plus, she liked them. "No problem at all."

The three got up and went over to speak to Eryn before they all went back to the hotel for the evening. Abi got a room at the Hale Koa for the night so they could all meet for their makeup and hair appointments the next day.

Eryn hugged her cousin tightly, "Are you ready?" she asked Katherine.

Katherine didn't know. "I wasn't sure if I would be going back with you or Mitch."

With a sly smile, Eryn handed Katie the keys to Chase's jeep. "We'll take my car so you and Mitch can go back in Chase's jeep."

Nodding, Katherine smiled, "Thank you."

Eryn hugged her again, "Have fun, okay?"

That was her plan. "I'll see what I can do," she said softly in Eryn's ear.

Katherine stood outside the Clubhouse and watched as Chase tucked Eryn into her car and went around to the driver's side. They were laughing at something and Katherine felt a pang of envy for their closeness. Look at what it took for her to just be courteous this evening? How was she supposed to find that kind of tenderness? Did she even possess it?

Mitch found her standing by Chase's jeep, lost in thought. She didn't notice him so he took the time to study her. She looked so delicate with her pale blue dress dancing softly around her with the breeze. He noticed wisps of her hair as they touched her shoulders and cheeks. When she finally noticed him, her face transformed from serious to intense with her smile. His body responded immediately, wanting her, needing her.

"Are we driving back?" Mitch asked as he started toward her.

Katherine walked to him, her arms coming up around his neck and playing with his hair. The shortness of it created a delicious friction on her fingertips. He was beautiful for a man. She thought about the sketch of him and how it sat right beside the bed in her hotel room.

She stood up on her tip toes and kissed him softly, "I would very much like it if you would escort me back to the hotel, Mitch." Another kiss, "And then I would like it if you would undress me and make love to me until I cannot think or breathe."

His heart raced, "It would be my pleasure, Katie."

With a gleam in his eye he stepped back and took her hand into his. He led her to the jeep and helped her in. He was backing up the jeep from the parking space when he saw Katherine's father standing by the doorway of the Clubhouse looking at them. He looked over and Katherine was looking down at her hands so she hadn't noticed their audience. He finished pulling out of the parking lot and wondered if Mr. Fredricks would want a word with him tomorrow.

Marcus Fredricks watched the interplay between his daughter and the Best Man and wondered why he was angry. The man seemed nice enough, well-mannered. So why did he want to punch the young man in the jaw?

"Is everything okay, Marc?" Tom Fredricks asked as he met his brother outside.

Marcus looked at his brother, "Tell me everything you know about Chase's friend, Mitch."

Tom started walking toward their car and thought that his brother looked just like he did when he found out about Eryn and Chase over a decade earlier. If there was one thing he prided himself on, it was being able to learn from his mistakes.

Tom turned to his brother, "May I ask why?"

"Well," Marcus took out a cigar he only indulged in when his wife let him, "I just saw Katherine kissing him by Chase's jeep and I was wondering if I should confront him about his public behavior with my daughter."

The proper quality in Marcus' tone had him laughing. "Geez, Marc, it's not like they draw and quarter men anymore."

Marcus didn't appreciate his brother's teasing but he realized he was being slightly irrational.

"I know that, Tom," Marcus sighed and shook his head, "I just am not used to seeing Katherine kissing a man."

Tom stopped and looked at his brother, all joking aside, "Marc, I don't know if I'll ever get used to it." He looked behind them to make sure their wives weren't coming. "I wanted to kill Chase the first time I saw him and Eryn together." Now he could smile because he knew his daughter loved Chase, "But I figured out after interfering that I would have been better off to let them figure it out."

Marcus considered what his brother said. It was logical but he didn't like it anyway.

"I see," Marcus said.

The two brothers waited for their wives, smoking cigars, and wondering how their daughters grew up so fast.

Chapter 6

Katherine didn't know what she should say during the drive back to the hotel in Honolulu. She watched the darkening landscape outside of the jeep and thought it was beautiful, even at night. The silvery light from the moon illuminated the branches of the palm trees as they swayed in the breeze. As they neared the tunnel that led through the mountains, she wondered what Mitch was thinking.

Mitch drove and was getting nervous. They were together again and he wanted her so much, but even as strangers on the plane, they didn't have this uneasiness between them. He couldn't exactly pinpoint the moment this awkwardness started but he certainly didn't like it.

"I would understand, Katie, if you wanted to go back to your own room tonight." He looked over at her, the light from the dashboard leaving shadows across her features. "Tomorrow will be a busy day."

Katherine looked at him and knew he was being a gentleman, "I appreciate the offer, Mitch, and if you prefer to not make love, I understand."

Mitch's head spun, "No," he said more vehemently than he intended. "I was just thinking that you may have some reservations."

She didn't quite understand his reasoning, "I know what I want. I want to be naked in bed with you and have you show me everything you did the other night and I want to try new things."

The bluntness of her needs made his head swim with want, "I would very much like to do that too." What else could he say?

They continued the drive and finally reached the Hale Koa Hotel. Mitch dropped Katherine off at the front and went to park the jeep in a nearby lot. As he hopped out of the vehicle, he thought he was one lucky son of a gun.

Katherine waited in the lobby for Mitch and was thinking about their night together at the hotel in Wyoming. The alcohol definitely helped her relax and be more open about her wants. Now she didn't have that and yet she still wanted him more than anything else. He walked into the lobby and her heart skipped a beat. It was not something she expected to happen. Men didn't normally create this primal reaction inside her body. She'd had her share of sexual experiences, sure, but nothing like this and nothing that involved her feelings.

Mitch walked toward Katie and saw her thinking again. After meeting her parents, he could understand a little better how she worked. Her father seemed very intellectual and driven and her mother was more laid back and supportive.

"Are you ready?" Mitch asked once he was close enough to take her hand in his. He brought her hand to his lips and kissed the back of it gently.

Tingles skipped along her skin, "Oh I think so," Katherine responded in a breathy whisper.

They walked hand in hand to the elevator and waited quietly as the floors ticked off. Passengers entered and exited and didn't seem to notice the two people in the back, waiting anxiously to be alone and in one another's arms.

The elevator stopped on Mitch's floor and he waited for Katie to exit before him. He placed his hand on her back to gently guide her to his room. He unlocked the door and opened it.

Katherine walked in and was happy they were finally alone. She turned around and pushed Mitch up against the door he just closed. She didn't want to make small talk or feel uneasy; she wanted him with her, in every way, and she wanted him NOW!

Mitch was surprised by Katie's sudden move but he sure did like it. Her lips were pressed to his and her arms were around his neck. The way she held his head in her palms made him respond quickly.

His hands were on her sides, exploring her curves, and making her feel wanted. Finally his tongue found her lips and she was helpless to think anymore. She just wanted to feel.

They made their way to the bedroom slowly. Since neither was willing to release the grip they had on one another, there was a lot of bumping into walls and furniture. But finally, Mitch had her through the doorway of the bedroom. When the bed was right behind her and he pulled his lips away just enough to put his forehead to hers.

"My Lord, woman, your kisses are intoxicating," he said while catching his breath.

Katherine giggled, "I think you can hold your own in that department, sir."

He looked down into her green eyes, the dim light provided by a lamp in the other room shown little flecks of lightening in their green pools. She appeared to him as if in a dream, her softness surrounded him physically and emotionally.

Katherine lifted her right palm up and cupped the side of his face. She could feel a hint of whiskers on her palm, making it tingle with awareness. As her fingers trailed down his neck and across his shoulder, she reveled in feeling his lean muscles. He could hold her so tightly and yet so tenderly at the same time. His eyes stared into hers as she explored his body with her hand. They didn't touch anywhere else.

Her hand traveled down his arm and flitted off the end of his fingertips. He thought she was done but then both of her hands came up and were spread across the top of his chest. She brought each of them down and to the sides of him so they tickled along his rib cage and to his hips. The clothing between her hands and his skin created a delightful friction on his sensitive nerve endings.

Mitch watched her eyes and they never left his. She was feeling him through his clothes and it was so erotic that he ached. How did a woman make him want so much and they weren't even undressed yet? The intensity of her gaze was too much and he wanted to feel her too.

Katherine grabbed Mitch's hands as they rose to touch her. She was afraid that she would succumb to her wants too quickly if he touched her and she wanted to please him first. The uncertainty in his eyes made her smile slyly. She wiggled her eyebrows.

What was she up to? He didn't know but he couldn't resist her. He dropped his hands to his sides and let her explore him. He could wait.

Katherine reached behind her and unzipped her dress. Once the zipper was low enough, she pulled the straps off her shoulders and let the fabric fall off of her onto the floor. His eyes followed her movements closely and gave her a powerful feeling. She reached the clasp between her breasts and released it, allowing her breasts to escape the lacy fabric of her bra. Her nipples were hard with wanting; his intense gaze making them swell even more.

She decided to take more control and brought her hands up to her hair. Without speaking, she took out the pins that held up the mass of curls. Her hair spilled down over her shoulders. She tilted her head back and shook it, allowing her hair to splay over the tops of her breasts and across her shoulders.

Mitch was in agony as he watched Katie's display of pure female power. She was a minx and he loved everything about her.

Reaching up, Katherine touched her neck with her hands, feeling her body as if for the first time. She moved her hands down, across her shoulders, and filled them with her breasts. When she saw Mitch lick his lips in anticipation she knew she'd fulfilled her goal. She spread her hands and slowly brought them lower over her hips until she encountered the lace of her panties. Then she slowly slid the fabric down until she could let them fall to the floor and step out of them.

Once free of all clothing, except her strappy heels, she stood in front of Mitch, her feet spread and her palms massaging her thighs and hips.

Mitch was not able to just watch anymore. He wanted to feel what she was feeling. With a low growl, her grabbed her and pulled her to him, his lips taking hers with all the energy he could contain.

His kiss was electrifying, making Katherine's already taut band of need want to snap her apart. She wanted him to take control now; she wanted to give up all thought and just feel him possess her in every way he could. And when he was done, she wanted him to start all over again.

This was not like making love. It was like being bewitched and having absolutely no bearing on whom you were as an individual. They were intertwined and there was no way to tell where one began and the other ended.

Mitch turned, bringing them down onto the bed but letting himself fall first so he would catch Katie in his arms.

Katherine giggled when they landed on the bed, limbs flailing.

Mitch loved to hear her laugh; it was as much an aphrodisiac as her body was to him. "Come here," he said slowly.

"I am here," Katherine responded, the smile playing on her lips.

He started kissing her shoulder and moving down to capture her nipple in his mouth. He felt her tense as he suckled the small nub between his lips. The pressure in his gut intensified as she squirmed on top of him.

Katherine sighed as he flipped them so she was laying on her back and he was kneeling next to her, trying to get out of his clothes. She watched him remove the fabric, feeling jealous of it for being so close to his skin. What an odd thought? As his skin was exposed, she reached up to touch it. The tickling of hair on his chest made her fingers itch to touch it. She watched her fingers as they wound their way up and down his body.

It was taking far too long for him to get his clothes off and he was getting frustrated. Of course, Katie looked amused at his difficulty, which only served to heighten his awareness.

Finally, he was naked and stretched out beside her. Even though there was no barrier between them, he wanted to take his time exploring her. She responded so openly to his touch, arching her back to bring her breasts closer for him to take into his palms. His fingers moved down her body, loving the softness of her skin and hints of shape only a woman possessed. He moved over so he was straddled between her thighs, his palms moving down each of them, kneading the lean muscles of her legs. She shifted, spreading her legs wider so he could see all of her.

Katherine sighed when she looked at Mitch's eyes. They devoured her; looking at every part of her and making her feel warm. Her breathing was becoming shallower. She wanted him to touch her.

"You are so beautiful," Mitch whispered.

She wasn't sure if she agreed with him but the words settled her heart while her body was on full alert. The contradiction amazed her.

"Touch me," Katherine said as she arched her hips up to meet him.

Touch would never be enough, Mitch thought. He grabbed her bottom and held her so he could taste her. She was like a feast to his senses. He tasted and tasted, using his tongue to seduce her moist nub of desire. She was arching which only increased the sensation his attention created. He knew she was close to climax as her muscles tightened.

Katherine was going to explode. Mitch's loving of her womanhood made her feel so exposed and so in tune with her body. She wanted him to stop because the sensation was overwhelming but she couldn't because the feeling of craziness would stop.

Katie arched one last time, "Mitch!" she yelled and crashed into her orgasm.

Mitch was more aroused by her climax; he tasted her until he felt her body relax into the cloud of afterglow. Then he kissed the inside of her thighs and worked his way up her glorious body. Each kiss was an exploration of Katie and her secrets.

Katherine was lulled into a numbing sense of contentment as she lay on the bed. She could feel Mitch's attentions but had no strength in which to reciprocate. Never before had an orgasm been so fulfilling. He brought out a reaction from her body she didn't know she could have. She closed her eyes and let the feelings envelop her as her body settled down around her.

She was gorgeous, Mitch thought. He ran his fingertips over her shoulders and down her body, delighting in her body's reaction to his touch. Her hair was spread around her like a blanket of silk. His other hand absently brushed through the strands as he drank in the sight of her.

Katherine opened her eyes and looked into dark blue ones staring at her. He was a beautiful man, his muscular physique combined with dark features made her want to draw him more. From an artist's perspective, he was fascinating. From a woman's perspective, he was a genius! A smile played on her lips remembering that she now owed him a release.

She was up to something, Mitch thought. The change in her expression was quick. Before he could say something, she sat up and moved to straddle him. He delighted in her determined expression.

"Your turn," Katherine said seductively.

Without waiting for a response, she moved down so she could take him inside her. He filled her so completely that she had to take a moment to settle in to the new sensation. Then she started moving slowly back and forth, loving the look of desire on his face. She scraped her nails over his shoulders and down his sides. His quick hiss of breath told her he enjoyed the pain as well as the pleasure. Her speed quickened until she was riding him in unyielding abandon.

She was a sexual goddess as she rode him fast. His feelings of desire engulfed him body and soul until he wanted to scream her name over and over. Words were not possible as any strength he possessed was focused on touching her and feeling their lovemaking as she rose to reach her own climax. When Mitch saw she was close to losing her control, he allowed his body to reach for its own explosion. They both burst into oblivion together which made the experience even more intense.

Katherine fell onto Mitch's chest, all physical power sapped from her. She felt their hearts as they beat quickly, as if they would both burst out of their chests. A smile formed as she remembered how his face shone with satisfaction as his climax took him over the edge of madness. Female satisfaction was something she was new to and decided it was quite exhilarating.

Mitch lay there, running his fingertips along Katie's beautiful back in mindless circles. Their lovemaking was intense and he should be exhausted but he only wanted to stay here and touch her forever.

"Are you okay?" Katherine asked when their pulses were settled.

Mitch slid to his side, tucking her in so he could face her. He laid her head on top of his arm as a pillow. The silkiness of her hair tickled his skin.

He brought her hand to his lips in his and kissed it lightly, "I am most definitely okay."

"Good," Katherine smiled, "because now I'm hungry."

Mitch sat up and pulled her to him so she was laying against him and he was against the headboard of the bed. He would give her whatever she wanted at this moment.

He cocked his head, "What are you hungry for?"

Her mind kicked into overdrive, "Is that a trick question?"

"Well, give me a few minutes for that but," he lightly tugged a tendril of her hair in teasing, "I was actually referring to food."

Katherine considered for a moment, "How about an omelet?"

Mitch smiled, "Let's see what we can do about that." He gently moved her over and hopped out of bed.

Katherine watched his body as he moved to throw on some shorts. Oh she wished he would leave his clothes off; she loved the play of muscles his limbs created with each movement. She would need to sketch that.

Mitch looked over at Katherine and couldn't decipher the look she had on her face, "Is everything okay?"

Jolted out of her musing, Katherine smiled, "Yes," she blushed at being caught looking at him, "I was just thinking that I'd like to sketch you like you are."

He remembered the sketch he saw the other day, "Didn't you already sketch me?"

Nodding, Katherine shifted to the edge of the bed and grabbed his shirt. She buttoned it up half way. "Yes, but that was from memory. I want to capture you just after we make love."

How could such a statement make him hard with need? She was a crazy dichotomy; how she was very artistic and yet so analytical.

She could tell he wasn't sure how to respond to her statement. She supposed most people didn't know how to respond to her. She encountered that hurdle a lot in her career, but over the years she realized it wasn't necessary to pretend to be any different than who she was.

He knew she was chewing on his reaction. She thought she hid her feelings well but he was starting to catch on to her tells. He sat down next to her and pulled her onto his lap.

"When you say things like that, so matter-of-factly, it makes me crazy thinking of us together and making love." He kissed her hard on the lips, trying to emphasize his need for her.

To know she evoked such a primal reaction in him made Katherine happy. He did the same for her and she was still at a loss as to how to deal with such physical and emotional responses to someone else. She appreciated that he explained things from his point of view.

Katherine touched his cheek with her palm, "I'm glad."

"Now," Mitch kissed the tip of her nose, "let's get you something to eat so I can make love to you again."

She laughed, "Okay."

They walked into the sitting area of his room and sat on the sofa. The curtains were open so they could see the hotels down the beach. They were glittering lights reflected off the ocean waves. Mitch called room service and placed an order for an omelet for Katie and an order of French toast for himself. After hanging up, he pulled her to him and they sat looking out the windows of his room until room service arrived twenty minutes later.

The food was good, Katherine thought, but the company was even better. He was as famished as she so they ate in relative silence. Once their bellies were full, he came around the table and lifted her up into his arms as if she weighed nothing. She kissed him and could taste the sweet maple syrup on his lips. That prompted thoughts of food in bed which caused a giggle to erupt.

"What?" Mitch growled as he carried her to his bed.

Katherine allowed her head to fall back as he kissed her neck, "I was just thinking of what foods I'd like to pour on your body so I could lick them off."

How did these thoughts pop up in her mind? He didn't care as they made him think of other things.

"Well, you think on that and get back to me." He started tasting her neck again.

Katherine didn't bother to think any longer. The feelings were too good to ignore. She ran her hands over his body and rejoiced in how she reacted to his touch. The flames of desire licked at her skin, making it burn. She ran her hands over his arms, his shoulders, his ribs, lower to his abdomen; the tautness of his body made her imagination run rampant with fantasies of gladiators rescuing maidens.

Their lovemaking was slower this time. It was like a slow burning fire; constant in its heat and energy but taking its time to turn into a full-fledged inferno.

Mitch loved her every way he could imagine and yet, he wasn't sated. Even after feeling her climax once more and following with his own extreme release, he still wanted her. If this kept up, they would probably be unable to move in a matter of days.

After they both quieted their breathing, they snuggled up together and fell asleep tangled in one another's arms. Each seeking peaceful slumber and never parting.

His phone was ringing and, with a grimace, Mitch reached over to pick up the receiver. Whoever was calling should be shot.

"Hello," he said gruffly.

Chase smiled. Good, he was still in bed, "Hey, Mitch, how are you today?"

Mitch growled, "What the hell, Chase!"

"Well, if you would remember I'm getting married today," Chase responded.

Shit! Mitch sat up quickly, how the hell could he forget? He looked over and saw Katie sleeping beside him, her hand on his side. Her deep breathing rhythmic. That's how.

"I'm sorry, man," Mitch said, softer.

Chase laughed, he knew what it was like. "Well, my bride-to-be is looking for her maid-of-honor and I was wondering if you knew where she might be." He wasn't going to let Mitch off easy.

Mitch took a breath as real life invaded their intimacy. "She's sleeping, I'll get her up. Where does she need to be and when?"

Chase was about to answer when the phone was taken from his hands. Beverly Fredricks gave her soon-to-be son-in-law a censured look, "Mitchell Frinnel, you get that girl up to her room now!"

Mitch knew that tone; his own mother used it often enough and he knew you didn't mess with a demanding mother. "Yes, ma'am," he answered and hung up the phone.

He bent down and kissed Katie's cheek. She smiled and stretched.

"Hmmmm," Katie purred. She liked waking to Mitch's kisses.

Mitch cleared his throat, "Katie, your Aunt Beverly just called and told me to get you up to your room now."

It was like having a bucket of cold water thrown on her. Katherine sat up straight and looked around quickly. Oh Lord, how did she forget her commitment to Eryn and her family? Today, of all days, she needed to be there for them and here she was, in bed with Mitch. She looked at him and wanted to laugh. He looked as scared as she was. It seemed that kids were still kids no matter how old they were.

"Oh gosh," Katherine said as she jumped out of the bed and looked for her clothing.

Mitch got up and helped her. If he wasn't so intimidated by Eryn's mother, maybe he'd try to convince her to stay here with him for a little longer.

Katherine looked around, "What time is it?"

Mitch looked at the clock next to the bed, "It's about eight-thirty," he replied.

Good, at least she wasn't late for anything. They planned to have brunch at nine-thirty and then meet afterward to go and get their hair and makeup done.

Once she was dressed, she looked over at Mitch. He was mussed from sleep and their lovemaking and she'd rather stay here with him and get wrapped up in their new-found intimacy.

"Excuse me for a moment," Katherine said and went into the bathroom.

Mitch watched Katie disappear and wondered if something was wrong. She had a weird look on her face for a moment and he thought maybe she regretted their night. He sure as hell didn't! If he had his way, she'd spend every night with him until they left Hawaii.

Katherine washed her face and used the bathroom. She felt...funny. Not bad, not good, just not herself. Now wasn't the time to fixate on her "morning after" thoughts; it was Eryn's day. She needed to remember that. She quickly finger brushed her teeth and tried to make her clothes look presentable before leaving the bathroom.

Mitch was in the sitting area waiting for the coffee to finish. He needed the infusion of caffeine. Plus it gave him something to do while Katie was in the bathroom. Once she came out, she looked better.

"Are you okay?" he asked and wondered why he always asked her that.

Katherine nodded, "I'm fine, just worried that if Aunt Beverly knows then so do my parents."

Mitch nodded, "Is that a bad thing?" They were adults.

She shrugged, "They have certain expectations of my behavior and I don't think this is really a part of that."

In the space of a sentence, Katie managed to make their sensational night sound so wrong. His temper flared before he could help it.

"So I'm not acceptable?" he asked sarcastically.

He was picking a fight and Katherine knew that this might be his way of dealing but she wasn't going to rise to the bait.

She walked over to him and kissed him gently, "No, that is not it." She grabbed her bag and phone from the table, "I have to get going, I'll see you later."

Mitch stood there and watched Katie walk out the door. He was mad as hell and couldn't figure out why.

Katherine reached her room without seeing her parents so she was grateful. Not two minutes after she put down her bag, she heard a knock at the door. Praying it wasn't her mother, she peered through the peep hole. It was Eryn. She opened the door and let her cousin in.

"I was just jumping in the shower, I won't be late," Katherine rushed.

Eryn shrugged, "We've got time."

Katherine expected her cousin to be more nervous but surprisingly, Eryn was very calm. Katherine stripped and stepped into the shower. She heard Eryn enter and assumed she was in the bathroom to talk. Of course, Katherine didn't know what to say but she needn't have worried since Eryn started in right away.

"So how was last night?" Eryn asked while checking her face in the mirror.

Katherine was hurriedly scrubbing her body. It still remembered Mitch's touch and was being very mutinous by making her head remember it too. She sighed, "It was fun."

Eryn's eyebrows rose and she walked over to a chair in the room's corner, "Really? We're going with fun?"

There was an understanding between them when it came to boys and, later, men. They didn't skimp on details. Katherine grimaced knowing she couldn't break the rule.

"What do you want me to say?" She scrubbed her scalp with the shampoo, "That it was the most phenomenal lovemaking I've ever experienced in my life?"

Eryn stood up quickly, "I knew it," she pointed to no one in particular, "I could feel the steam between you two."

Katherine shut off the water and opened the shower curtain. Her eyes were bland and gave her cousin the "that's enough" look she'd mastered over the years. Too bad it didn't work on Eryn.

"Oh, Katie," Eryn looked at her cousin and felt sorry for her. "I know what it's like."

Of that, Katherine was sure. She talked to Eryn not long after she and Chase started dating and knew her cousin was in love. When they spoke again and Chase left her without a word, Katherine knew he'd broken Eryn's heart completely.

"I know," Katherine sighed. "I just don't want to put too much into this, Eryn. It's just a fling while we're both on vacation."

Eryn walked over and hugged her cousin quickly, "Katie, if that's what you really think then it's more than you are willing to admit to."

Katherine was confused by what her cousin said but knew now wasn't the time for them to talk about such things. "Well," Katherine said as she clipped her hair back, "we'll see about it later. Right now it's time to get you ready for your wedding."

There was a knock at the door and Eryn left the room to answer it. Katherine went into the bedroom and grabbed a sundress out of the closet to get dressed. She looked over and saw the sketch of Mitch. The picture made her remember every minute of the previous night which made her mad. The man didn't need to invade her mind! Without thinking, she walked over and turned the paper over. There, take that, she thought and walked out to meet the other ladies in the bridal party.

Mitch rode the elevator down to the lobby an hour later and found Chase there waiting with a friend and his dad. He walked over to the group and smiled.

Chase clapped his friend on the back, "Nice of you to join us, Master Sgt."

Mitch wanted to punch his friend but that wasn't appropriate given it was the man's wedding day. "My pleasure," he said sarcastically.

A few minutes later the rest of the men arrived and they took off to play some golf before the ceremony. All the tuxes and uniforms were at the Clubhouse already so everyone would just get ready there. Everyone piled into cars and took off for a few hours of fun.

Katherine sat next to Eryn at the brunch and tried to listen as everyone talked about weddings and dresses and the honeymoon. She wanted to be attentive to Eryn but found her mind wandering more than it should. She was a focused person normally, so why the flightiness now?

Beverly Fredricks looked from her daughter, to her niece, to her sister-in-law. Victoria kept looking at Katherine like she was going to disappear or something. She herself harbored fears over her own daughter's happiness. Unlike Victoria and Katherine, she and Eryn had a more open relationship.

This morning she had no choice but to intervene with her niece. She knew Katherine spent the night with Mitch but she was unsure as to whether Marcus and Victoria knew about it. While Katherine was a consenting adult, her parents tended not to treat her like one.

Eryn stood and raised her mimosa, "I want to thank you all for being here today." She looked around the table, "Katie, Emma, Abi, Sarah, you are all gems for being bridesmaids." She shook her head quickly to push back the emotions. "Mom, Aunt Victoria, Aunt Colleen, thank you for your love and support." The tears started anyway. "And to Chase's mom, Rebecca, thank you for being my mom."

There was not a dry eye at the table. Every woman knew they were loved and that the bride was truly happy on this special day. What else could any woman ask for?

Chapter 7

Mitch stood at the front of the aisle and waited with his best friend, Chase, as the music started. All day, the mood was light, but now that the ceremony was starting, he could feel Chase's nerves. They permeated off the man in waves. In an effort to help, he clapped his hand on Chase's shoulders and leaned in.

"You are the luckiest son of a bitch on the face of the earth, you know that right?" he said softly so only he and Chase could hear.

Chase smiled and looked over his shoulder at his Best Man. Mitch sincerely deserved the title at this moment.

He whispered, "I do. Thanks."

Emma was the first to walk down the aisle. Mitch watched Eryn's friend and smiled as she winked at several of the guys. She was, according to Eryn, a spitfire. Somehow Mitch thought that description might be a little understated.

Then came Abi; he knew her through Chase and respected the Gunnery Sgt. She worked with Eryn and Chase during their "reunion" and managed to keep her cool. That feat was admirable as far as Mitch was concerned.

Next down was Eryn's sister, Sarah. She was pregnant and certainly had the "glow" his mother always mentioned that pregnant women had. She smiled at Chase as she neared the altar with a trellis lit with white lights and filled with flowers.

He turned from Chase to see Katie coming down and his heart fell straight to his feet. She was a vision in the pale pink gown and she literally floated down the aisle. She looked straight ahead and smiled shyly as she made her way toward the altar. He hoped she would look at him but she didn't. He was disappointed but his attention was averted by the guests standing for the bride.

Katherine found her place at the altar and turned to wait for her cousin to make the walk down the aisle toward Chase. She moved elegantly down the aisle on her father's arm and Katherine could not contain the swell of emotion in her chest. She watched as Eryn and Chase made eye contact; the connection between them was so strong it was palpable. She thought it akin to looking up at the sun, its brightness blinding but so warm and welcoming.

As Eryn came closer, Katherine could see the tears in her eyes. It was obvious she was very much in love with Chase and this was the culmination of a decade of love. Their story gave her hope.

Just then she looked over to find Mitch looking at her. His eyes were dark and intense and made her feel very vulnerable for some reason. The guests sat down and the Reverend started the ceremony, drawing Katherine's attention to the couple.

The service was short but sweet. Chase and Eryn decided to recite their vows to each other quietly so only the two of them could hear the words. Katherine watched with wonder as the two were united as man and wife. Once the Reverend announced them as married, Chase took Eryn into his arms and kissed her. Katherine watched them with tears in her eyes, hoping that someday a man would look at her like that.

As the music of the recessional started, the happy couple moved down the aisle to gather nearby. Katherine and Mitch were next to proceed toward the area the wedding party was to gather.

As he offered his arm to her, she looked into those blue eyes and fell into a well of sensation. They promised her excitement and pleasure and something else she couldn't quite figure out. She tried to keep her calm as her nerves skittered around in confusion.

They reached Eryn and Chase and exchanged their congratulations. The other members of the wedding party arrived and everyone lined up in the receiving line to greet guests on their way into the Clubhouse.

Katherine did her duty and greeted everyone warmly, accepting their congratulations for her cousin and her new husband. She was happy for Eryn. Every few minutes she would glance over at Mitch, who stood on the far side of the newlyweds. Sometimes he would be looking at her with that look she noticed just after the ceremony.

After all the guests made their way into the building, the photographer herded the wedding party together for pictures. The atmosphere was laid back and fun so everyone posed easily.

Once that was done, the group headed into the Clubhouse for dinner.

Katherine looked around for Mitch but didn't see him as the bridesmaids made their way inside. She accompanied Eryn to the restroom quickly to freshen her up and make sure the dress was in good shape then they found their way to the head table.

Once everyone was seated, a microphone was handed to the groom so he stood up and cleared his throat.

"Welcome to all of our family and friends," Chase announced. "I want to give a special thanks to this gorgeous woman beside me," He turned to face his new bride. "Eryn, there are no words to express how happy you have made me today. We are a family now, you and I." He choked up a bit, "I look forward to having children with you and grandchildren." He looked up trying to control his emotion, "And being with you for the rest of our days."

The speech was so unlike Chase that everyone simply sat there for a minute trying to digest his words. They were beautiful and elegant and said everything any woman would want to hear on her wedding day. If Katherine wasn't so happy for her cousin, she would certainly be jealous.

Chase sat down and Mitch scowled at his friend.

"What?" Chase asked as he handed the microphone to Mitch.

Mitch took the microphone and wanted to hit Chase with it, "How the hell am I supposed to follow up that speech?"

Chase laughed and clapped Mitch on the shoulder, "I'm sure you'll think of something."

Mitch stood and looked around the room. He wasn't a novice at giving speeches but his were usually work related so well within his comfort zone. Now he was expected to say something heartfelt. He'd try his best but he wasn't sure he would succeed.

"Chase told me it was mandatory for me to make a speech so here I am," Mitch started. "I want to say that I've known both Chase and Eryn for a very long time and I think they are both excellent Marines." A few chuckles. "But we're here today not because they are Marines but because they fell in love." A few ahhhs from the crowd. "I have to say that I do take some credit for getting them together in the first place," he looked at Chase and nodded, "but really it was these two people who decided that they would rather be with one another over any other person in the world."

Katherine stared at Mitch as he spoke and was taken in by the simplicity and honesty in which he spoke. He got right to the heart of the matter.

"They found something in one another that filled the gaps in their souls and, God willing, that connection will stay strong throughout the good times and the bad." He cleared his throat,

"Here's to the two of you," he raised his glass, "and here's to the love you've found and the life you've created."

A few "here here's" and "Amen's" from the crowd followed his speech so he was satisfied that he hadn't blown it. He looked over to see Eryn blow him a kiss through tears and Chase smile at him.

Dinner was served and everyone made small talk. Katherine attended to anything Eryn needed and chatted nicely with the groomsman seated beside her. It was very pleasant and the food was very nice but she felt something was missing and felt very guilty for thinking so.

Once the dishes were cleared, the DJ announced that the music would begin in a few minutes. Katherine looked over to see her father motion her to their table. She excused herself and went over to speak to her parents.

Mitch watched Katherine like a hawk. The woman moved like a ballet dancer. She literally floated around. Or was it just his impression of her? He'd had no time to speak to her after she left his room this morning and he missed her. The guys played golf and he thought of her. They went to the Staff NCO Club for a few beers and he thought of her. They dressed for the ceremony and he thought of her. She was stuck in his mind like a skipping record and, he realized, he didn't mind it one bit.

Katherine sat down with her parents and was tucked into their discussion of traveling and Europe with her Aunt Beverly and Uncle Tom along with their friends Colleen and Ben. It was good conversation but she certainly didn't need to be included in it for she gave no relevant take on it. She would comment when addressed directly but didn't understand why her father called her over.

A few minutes later, Eryn came over to their table and interrupted a lively discussion about security issues at the European embassies.

"Excuse me, folks," Eryn smiled and placed her hands on Katherine's shoulders, "but I need my maid-of-honor."

Everyone nodded and Katherine was relieved.

Katherine got up quickly and hugged Eryn, "Thank you."

"You looked like you needed to be rescued," Eryn returned, "besides, we're going to be announcing the wedding party with a dance."

Oh fun, Katherine thought dryly. She didn't like to be in the spotlight but knew it was her part to play for the day.

"I know," Eryn said, sensing her cousin's nervousness, "that's why it's during a dance so you won't feel like you're being inspected."

Smiling, Katherine hugged her cousin again, "You are so good to me."

Eryn snorted, "We'll see if you feel that way later."

Katherine didn't understand what Eryn meant but she let it go. There was no need to borrow trouble. She waited at the edge of the dance floor while Eryn met her new husband in the middle of it. The music started and the couple began dancing to the music. The DJ announced them as the bride and groom and everyone clapped.

"Next we have the Best Man, Mitch Frinnel and the Maid-of-Honor, Katherine Fredricks." The DJ announced.

Katherine felt a hand at her side and knew it was Mitch. She looked over and smiled. He held out his other hand for her to take and she was guided onto the floor. She felt so free as he took her into his arms and began moving her around the dance floor. She could hear the DJ announcing others but her eyes were set squarely on Mitch.

She was looking up into his eyes as they moved to the music. Her hair whispered around her face and was done up in some fancy braid thing. Her makeup was darker than he'd seen it but it made her look sophisticated. Truthfully, he was kind of intimidated by her presence now. The music was slow and sultry so he pulled her closer.

Katherine closed her eyes and tried to "feel" everything. She could feel the material of his uniform, the ribbons on the front of it a testament to his service. He was holding her close but not too tightly, showing her how he wanted her to be with him right now. The thought was erotic and a little scary as they were in a public place. But when their eyes met and she could see the tenderness and could remember the passion, the rest of the world seemed to slip away.

Tom Fredricks held his wife as they danced with the wedding party. He nodded toward his niece as Chase's friend, Mitch, held her and shook his head. He could understand how Marcus must feel knowing his little girl was falling in love right before his eyes. He scanned the crowd to find his daughter and her new husband and smiled. He was proud that his little girl found a man to be her equal in every way. It didn't make her love him any less but allowed her to love more.

Beverly Fredricks smiled wistfully as she watched Katherine and Mitch swirl gently around the dance floor. Seeing two people fall in love was a sweet thing. She looked back up at her husband and smiled. It didn't feel like that long ago that she fell in love with a Marine who swept her off her feet and made her crazy.

Marcus Fredricks stood at the bar and watched his daughter. He tried to think of what his brother said the night before but knowing it and not wanting to throttle the young man were two very different things. He tipped back the drink and relished in the way the alcohol went down smoothly.

The music stopped and everyone clapped. A fast number started and Katherine had no interest in dancing to that so she moved off the dance floor and returned to her seat at the head table. She was surprised when she noticed Mitch sitting beside her.

"You could've stayed on the dance floor," Katherine said, trying to be heard over the loud music.

Mitch shook his head, "I'm too old for this stuff."

He was being silly in her opinion, "You are most definitely not too old."

"What makes you say that?" he asked as he ran his fingers down her back.

Katherine looked directly at him, "You wouldn't be able to make love to me so completely and so earnestly if you were too old."

Here we go again, he thought, "Earnestly?"

Katherine smiled, "Yes, earnestly. Is there something wrong with that word?" She had the distinct feeling he was making fun of her.

"No," Mitch put up his hands in defense, "it's just that you don't talk like someone your age."

Now her shackles were going up. "What age do you think I am, Mitch?"

Mitch took a quick breath. One of the things his mother told him to never ask a woman was her age, "It is rude," she used to say. And now he was on the spot.

"Um," He said, "Twenty-five."

Katherine looked at him for a moment, then broke out in laughter. "Really?"

What was so funny? Mitch was wondering what he said. "Yes, really." He looked around then back to her, "I know I'm a lot older than you are."

"Well, you're right about you being older," she leaned over and kissed him out of impulse, "and I thank you for your thoughts but I'm thirty-two."

Mitch's eyebrows furrowed, "Really?"

Katherine laughed, "Would you like to see my birth certificate?" Why would she lie?

She was adorable to him, "I'm sorry, you just...you know, look younger."

If she wasn't sure he was complimenting her, she'd slap him. "Thank you, I think," she said dryly.

"Oh, Katie," he leaned in and kissed her ear, his lips lingering, "It was most definitely a compliment."

The way he said the words made her spine tingle and the hairs on her skin stand up in awareness. She noticed her father heading their way and straightened her posture and moved away from Mitch.

One minute they were flirting and then she was acting like he was the plague. Mitch was confused until he looked over to see Katie's father coming towards them. As the man got closer he started to sit up a little straighter himself.

"Katherine," Marcus nodded to his daughter, "Mitch," he nodded to her companion, "I'd like to dance with my daughter if that's okay with her." He no longer looked at Mitch.

Katherine smiled but it didn't quite reach her eyes, "Of course," she said softly and put her hand into her father's.

Mitch watched them as they went to the dance floor. He studied them with curiosity as they moved; Mr. Fredricks was an excellent dancer but seemed to be doing the movements by memory rather than by enjoyment and Katie looked like she was being forced to endure rather than dance with her father.

"Tough, isn't it?" Eryn asked as she came up behind Mitch.

Mitch turned and looked at her questioningly.

She sat down and took a drink of champagne, "My uncle is an excellent Ambassador but not very warm in the father department."

"Ambassador?" Mitch asked. He had no idea.

Eryn nodded, "Yes, and so his daughter was expected to be a perfect little lady during her childhood."

She was, as far as Mitch was concerned, pretty darn perfect.

"She isn't sure what she should do, especially in social settings. She's so studied that having fun isn't something she's used to." Eryn explained.

Mitch had the feeling this was leading up to something, "Something you want to say, Warrant Officer Johnson?"

Eryn smiled at the title. This was the first time anyone used her married name with her rank. She loved it. Of course that wasn't the point of this particular conversation.

"Well, Master Sgt." Eryn replied pointedly, "it just means that if you mess with my cousin and break her heart, I'm going to inflict an immense amount of pain on you." She looked over as her new husband came up beside her, "Or I'm going to have my husband do it for me."

Mitch looked from Eryn to Chase, who was nodding, and then back to Katie dancing with her dad. He was torn between telling his friends thanks and telling them to mind their own damn business. Instead, he nodded and took a sip of his drink.

Katherine could see Eryn and Chase with Mitch and wondered what they were discussing. No one was really smiling and that made her think they were talking about her. Her father held her snugly as if he was protecting her. She realized her family's intentions were honorable but wholly unnecessary. She and Mitch were just having some fun while on vacation.

The song ended and Katherine leaned up to kiss her father on the cheek, "Thank you for the dance."

Marcus Fredricks squeezed his daughter, "You're welcome." He released her and went back to the table where his wife was sitting.

Victoria watched her husband and daughter and noticed Mitch watching them too. One didn't need to be blind to see that the young man was very interested in their daughter. Of course, her husband noticed it too and was blatantly saying, "hands off," in his not-so-subtle way. She almost felt sorry for him but he always had a difficult time expressing his feelings to Katherine.

"Did you have a nice dance?" Victoria asked her husband.

Marcus nodded as he sat, "Yes, thank you."

She couldn't help it; she patted his arm. "She's an adult you know."

His wife was very smart, "I know."

"You know but you don't like it one bit," Victoria replied. There was some fun to be found in teasing her husband.

Marcus squeezed his wife's hand, "Yes, dear."

Katherine made her way back to her seat and watched Mitch with Eryn and Chase. Once Mitch's eyes met hers, he smiled warmly and stood.

Mitch was glad Katherine was back with him. He didn't like the ganging up approach Eryn and Chase took in warning him about his behavior with Katie. He thought about her saying she was thirty-two. She was certainly old enough to make her own decisions and he wondered if her family always protected her like this. Not that his wouldn't; his family was loud and rambunctious but they tended to take the "fend for yourself" approach.

"What are you thinking about?" Katherine asked as she sat down.

Mitch smiled, "My family."

Interesting, she thought, "Tell me about them."

Mitch took a sip of his drink, "Well, I'm one of five." He smiled at her look of shock. "Yep, I have three brothers and one sister."

It was hard for Katherine to imagine that many siblings.

"My parents live in a little town called Milford in Delaware." He smiled, "It's very green and it was a lot of fun when I was a kid."

She was intrigued, "What did you do?"

Mitch laughed, "More like, what didn't we do?" He smiled and placed his hand on hers. "We went swimming and exploring and it was a pretty normal childhood."

That was so fascinating to Katherine. Her childhood was very privileged but also very austere compared to what he was describing. She spent some summers with Eryn's family but not enough to get a taste of what some would say was the "average" child's life.

Mitch described his siblings and the escapades they got into as children. How during the summer someone usually sustained a broken bone and spent the rest of the summer in a cast or how his parents encouraged their adventurous spirit and took them rafting or swimming or boating or hiking.

Katherine listened to Mitch and envied his relationship with his family. She loved her parents but they weren't as close as he was with his. They never had a rowdy family get together. She knew her parents did the best they could given her father's choice of careers and she was very lucky to have had the exposure to different cultures as a child. While he was scraping his knees and learning to climb trees, she was learning how to entertain a Prime Minister with her piano playing or using her newly learned French.

Finally Mitch stopped and realized he'd been talking about his family for a long time. He probably sounded like a ruffian or something to her. She watched him closely and laughed at his childhood shenanigans. It wasn't something he was used to revealing but her rapt attention made it easy to open up.

"I'm sorry. I'm boring you I'm sure." He smiled and kissed her hand.

Katherine shook her head, "No, not at all." She was going to say more but the DJ piped up.

"Attention, Ladies and Gentlemen," he played a drum roll, "All the single ladies and single guys come on down to the dance floor. We're going to throw the bouquet and toss the garter belt."

Mitch stood and offered Katie his hand. She looked reluctant to go so he pulled her up and led her down to the dance floor.

"Okay girls," the DJ shouted, "Get ready!"

Katherine walked out onto the floor, embarrassed. She knew this was a customary thing at a wedding reception but she wanted no part of it. Trying to be a trooper, she pasted a smile on her face and stood behind Emma and Abi, who appeared to have some sort of plan as to how they were going to catch the bouquet.

Mitch watched Katie and noticed that she looked miserable. She obviously did not want to be on the floor for this. He felt sorry for her but, if Eryn was right in what she said, it wouldn't hurt her to let loose a little.

The DJ started some goofy music, "Okay...One...Two...Three."

Eryn tossed the bouquet and turned around quickly to see who caught it. There was some shuffling as the group moved to catch the flowers.

Katherine stood there, as still as possible, and felt foolish. Then, a bouquet was in her hands and she had no idea how it got there.

"Yay!" Eryn yelled. She was relieved that her cousin caught the bouquet.

Katherine smiled and walked off the floor, eager to be back at her seat.

"Now, gentlemen," the DJ started some rowdy music, "it's your turn."

Mitch assisted in getting a chair for Eryn to sit on. She sat and let her new husband reach up her leg to slowly take off her garter belt. They decided that they wouldn't make too much of a production out of it since her parents would not find it tasteful. Chase got off the garter and stood to toss it behind him. He jabbed his thumb in the direction behind him to let Mitch know he was expected to participate.

Katherine watched as Mitch stood in the crowd of single men. He was laughing at something Chase said and she admired his carefree attitude. She cocked her head to the side as she thought about what he said this evening. He somehow thought he was too old for her which made her smile. If anything, she thought maybe it was the other way around. She laughed as the garter was tossed and caught by a young man who was around fifteen if her calculations were correct.

"Okay, now the young lady who caught the bouquet and the young man who caught the garter will have the next dance." The DJ started a slow song.

Katherine came down to the dance floor and let the young man take her into his arms. She smiled at him and thought maybe fifteen was a bit off but he was certainly much younger than she was.

Mitch watched the young private as he danced, in his opinion, way too closely with Katie. If he would've realized he'd get another dance with her, he'd have tried harder to catch the garter.

Chase stood next to his wife and watched his best friend look totally pissed. If it was anyone else but Mitch, it would have been a lot funnier. Chase remembered all too well how he felt when he thought Eryn was married. The jealousy ran hot and fast through his body and he wore the same snarl his friend now wore as he watched Katherine dance with the poor guy who caught the garter. He smiled as Eryn looked up at him with the loveliest smile on her face. Chase would remember how she looked today for the rest of his life.

The song ended and Katherine smiled at the young man she danced with. He was sweet, not quite a man yet, but nice just the same. She looked around for Mitch and didn't see him so she excused herself to use the powder room.

The bathroom was, thankfully, empty when Katherine entered. She needed a moment to compose herself. She always needed that after some time in the spotlight. She never understood why she was so shaken but it was how she was and she would probably never change. When she heard someone enter, she quickly washed her hands and left. She would need to find somewhere else in which to find some peace.

Mitch stopped to talk with some guys from Crash Crew. They were reminiscing about times together and compared some emergencies each partook in over the years. It was fun but made him feel old when he looked at the ages of some of the guys. One of the guys came up and asked him a question about his duty station in Virginia so he hung around to talk to him for a bit.

Katherine came out of the restroom and smiled at her cousin and Chase as they twirled around the dance floor. She loved the way the gold and red ribbons that trailed down the back of the dress danced in the light. The glint of the gold Eagle, Globe, and Anchor would shine like a beacon when the spotlight hit it. She hoped they were always as happy as they were tonight.

It was now time to sneak away though to find some time for herself. She left out the front door and found her way to Eryn's car. She stashed some of her supplies in the trunk before they left the hotel this morning. Just in case, she told herself but she knew full well she'd draw. Anything that prompted an emotional response from her made her feel the need to find expression through art.

Mitch looked around the room and didn't see Katie. She was the Maid of Honor so maybe she was helping Eryn with something. The DJ announced the cake cutting so he made his way over to the area where the wedding cake was displayed. He laughed as the bride and groom nicely cut and fed one another. He clapped with the other guests but was surprised when he still didn't see Katie. After the group spread out and cake was being served, he walked over to Chase and Eryn.

"Have you guys seen Katie?" he asked the couple.

Chase shook his head, "Not since she danced with the kid who caught the garter."

Mitch looked around, a frown on his face, "Can you let her know I was looking for her if you see her?"

Eryn nodded but didn't say anything until Mitch walked away, "I think, Master Sgt," she kissed him, "that our dear friend might be falling for Katherine."

"My love," Chase held her close, "I think you are mistaken. I would revise that to *has* fallen." He kissed her back, "I love you, Warrant Officer Johnson."

Eryn hummed with love for her husband; he allowed her to be who she wanted and needed to be. How could she not love him for that? Maybe her cousin would find someone like him; she had an inkling that Katie already had and hoped she and Mitch would both make the right choices.

Katherine sat by the ceremony site where Chase and Eryn exchanged vows. The light was waning, just as it was the night before when she was here with Mitch. The building was lit up and was close enough to cast some light her way. She meant to sketch but once she sat down, her eyes were drawn to the landscape.

The scene before her was a contradiction of power and serenity. She could see the waves crashing against the rocks near the shoreline and then the water was like dancing diamonds as she looked across the expanse of it toward the quickly fading sun. She would not soon forget it, as it would now inspire some of her creations for her next line. Funny that work was not far away from her mind. She supposed that she was more like her father in that respect.

Mitch came outside to ease his frustration at not finding Katie when he spotted a figure by the trellis where the wedding ceremony was earlier. He knew it was her, not by seeing her, but by feeling her. She exuded an energy that he could not describe, only feel. He moved quietly, not wanting to disturb her and wanting some time to study her as she sat there.

Katherine felt Mitch before she saw him. He was quiet but she was aware of him and that created a splendid chaos inside her body.

"You found me," she said quietly without turning around.

Mitch smiled, "I did."

Katherine turned around slowly and looked up to his face, "And why were you looking for me?"

Such an odd question he thought, "Because I wanted to be near you."
He wasn't going to lie so he figured if she could be direct then so could he.

"Good," Katherine stood and crossed the few feet that separated them and put her hands on his chest, "I want to be near you too."

Chapter 8

The Indy Five Hundred was taking place in his chest; his heart was beating so fast. Just words from her pretty lips did that to him.

"You do?" he asked quietly.

She dropped her hands from resting on his chest in frustration, "Why do you doubt it?" She turned away in frustration, took a breath, and then turned back to him, "I remember how we made love when we spent the night together."

Her honesty humbled him, "I'm sorry."

Now Katherine was confused, "You're sorry we spent the night together?"

"No," Mitch said, leaning down to kiss her, "I am sorry that I ask silly questions." He kissed her again, slower, "I remember every second of our nights together."

A blush ran up into Katherine's cheeks but she couldn't figure out why. She wasn't ashamed of making love with Mitch but her body acted like she was. His kisses made her head swim in a fog of desire so she just held on to him and went along for the ride.

Mitch deepened the kisses, bringing her body flush with his. His mind was saying, 'slow down' but his body was saying, 'let's go.' Remembering where they were, he slowly pulled his head away and tucked her into his arms, resting his chin on the top of her head.

"Why did you stop kissing me?" Katherine asked against his jacket. The fabric was a little course against her cheek but smelled of Mitch.

Mitch sighed, "Because if I kept kissing you like that, I would not be able to control myself and we're too close to where your family is."

Pulling back enough to look into his eyes, Katherine smiled. "I see your point." She took his hand and started back toward the Clubhouse. "Let's get a drink then."

He was about to follow but saw something out of the corner of his eye, "What's this?"

How could she have forgotten her sketch paper and supplies? He made her forget, that's how. "Oh my drawing things." She walked over and picked them up.

Mitch watched Katie pick up her things and turn to go into the building. He imagined she looked like that a lot in her life, toting around drawings and just examining the things around her. He wondered if that was something he could do and decided probably not. His life was way too regimented and he liked it that way. But sometimes it was nice to wonder about how it could be different.

They entered the ballroom to find most of the wedding party and guests doing a line dance on the dance floor. Katherine almost gasped when she saw her mother and her aunt joining in the fun. Not that her mother didn't dance, she did all the time at the formal functions they attended, but she just didn't let loose the way she was now.

"It looks like your mom is having a good time," Mitch said from behind her.

She turned and looked at him with a smile then back at her mother, "Yes, she is."

Katherine walked back over to their table and waived a waiter over to take her drink order. She sat and watched the guests as they danced crazily around the floor. She supposed the alcohol helped loosen everyone up. She turned to see Mitch taking a drink of his beer and studied his form. His head was tipped up to accept the liquid so she could see his long neck and the corded muscles that wrapped his shoulders. Even the simple act of drinking a beer made him look so sexy.

Mitch noticed Katie looking at him and looked over. "What do you see?"

Katherine's eyes widened briefly, she was embarrassed at being caught looking at him. "The way your muscles move, the way you look; it is very erotic."

The punch to the gut; he blushed. "I can't be that interesting." He meant it.

"I guess," she turned her body to face him, "you just don't see what I see."

Mitch put the beer down and turned to take her hand into his, "I guess you'll have to show me."

Oh yes, Katherine thought, she would. "Would you like to go now?"

It was hard to breathe when she was so direct; she said the things he was thinking. "I want to, but it's a little early to leave the reception, don't you think?"

Katherine didn't play games, "No, I don't but you do so we'll stay." She smiled at the waiter as he placed her drink on the table.

Now it was Mitch's turn to watch her. She lifted the glass to her lips and sipped the wine. He wished he was the glass and her lips were on him. The thought gave him a jolt. She gave him a jolt. She was so unlike any woman he ever met.

A slow song started to play and he stood, silently offering his hand to Katie. He smiled wider when she looked up at him. No words were needed. She put her hand into his and he guided her down to the dance floor and pulled her close.

The music drifted around them like the waves they saw landing on the shore outside. The melody carried them together, moving them softly to their very own beat.

Eryn watched her cousin and no longer wondered if she was falling in love with Mitch. The signs were there and Katie admitted that something was between them so it was a probability. But Katie had some deep seated issues and Eryn wasn't sure Mitch was the one to be able to put those to rest.

Looking over at her new husband, she could've said the same about him only months ago. And now here they were, married and she knew, with certainty, that he was the one to ease all of her pain and help her put her past to rest. She smiled when he looked over from the conversation he was having and their eyes met. She mouthed, 'I love you' to him.

The song ended and Katherine looked up into Mitch's eyes. "When do you think we'll be able to leave?"

The question gave him a new determination, "I'll be right back," he walked over to where Chase was standing with a group of Marines.

Katherine watched Mitch speak to Chase and wondered if they were leaving now. Butterflies flew around her stomach in anticipation of their time alone. She jumped when a hand touched her shoulder.

Marcus Fredricks knew his daughter was preoccupied but wanted to speak to her, "I just wanted to say that you look beautiful and your mother and I were proud of you for standing up for Eryn and especially for creating that beautiful gown your cousin is wearing."

Katherine was dumbfounded. She could not recall the last time her father voiced a compliment to her directly. "Thank you," she said quietly.

Not wanting to end their talk just yet, Marcus took his daughter into his arms and hugged her. The open display of affection was foreign to both of them but he didn't want to leave without letting her know he was trying.

Katherine put her arms around her father but as a gesture of kindness, not because she actually hugged him back. The conversation and hug were throwing her off-balance and she didn't really know what to say or do.

Mitch was making his way back to Katie when he saw her father hugging her. She looked surprised by the action which made Mitch wonder again how Katherine felt about her parents. She seemed so surprised by certain things he would take for granted with his family. He watched as her father kissed her on the forehead then left.

Katherine was put so off kilter by her father's words and actions that she didn't know what to do. Her parents were never unkind to her, just very absorbed in the duties and commitments of her father's job. As she stood there and wondered about the change in attitude, she felt Mitch behind her.

"Are you okay?" he asked softly into her ear as his hands kneaded her shoulders gently. He always asked her that.

Katherine rested back into him, "Yes, just surprised by my father's open affection."

That was sad to hear, Mitch thought. No one should ever by "surprised" by love and kindness from your family.

Shaking off the moment, Katherine turned to him, "What were you speaking to Chase about?"

"I was asking him," he smiled and put his arms around her waist, "when they were making a break for it so we could too."

Smiling brightly, Katherine kissed him quickly, "Good, I'll check on Eryn to make sure she's ready."

She moved away, leaving Mitch to think about them being alone.

Katherine moved through the crowd and found Eryn speaking to her Aunt Beverly. They were laughing about something and a shot of envy tripped through Katherine. She shook the feeling off quickly and walked up with a smile on her face.

Eryn turned to see her cousin and smiled, "Well, we're off to a secluded resort on Kauai for a week." She looked pointedly at Katherine, "I wonder who could've arranged that."

Katherine shrugged, "I'm sure I don't know. I hope you have a great time though."

Beverly hugged her daughter quickly and then turned to her niece. Katherine was so beautiful and talented and deserved all the happiness she could find. She hugged Katherine just as tightly and whispered, "thank you," in her ear.

Katherine smiled but was exhausted from all of the display of emotions today. Not that she wasn't okay with it; she just wasn't used to it. "You're welcome," she whispered back to her aunt and gently pulled away.

The DJ announced that the couple was leaving and everyone should line up with their little container of bubbles to send them off. Katherine lined up outside with Emma and Abi and blew the bubbles as Eryn and Chase rushed past. There was a lot of good-natured teasing and laughing.

Mitch was in the Clubhouse helping Beverly and Victoria get the gifts together to be taken to Chase and Eryn's house. He waited for direction from the ladies and laughed at some of their comments about the day. Women could be really tricky at social gatherings. His mother reminded him of that every time they had a get-together. He made a mental note to call her next week when he returned to Virginia. He stopped when he noticed two sets of eyes on him intensely.

"Um," he said.

Beverly shook her head, "Typical male, tuning us out like that."

He wanted to say something but couldn't come up with a comeback that wouldn't have offended them so he smiled.

Victoria patted his arm, "It's okay, Mitch. We were just asking you what you thought about the wedding."

Oh, he thought, easy subject, "I thought it was very nice, ma'am."

"Very neutral," Victoria replied, "you'd make a great politician."

Mitch snorted, "I don't think so, ma'am. Too much bullsh-um, negotiations."

The women laughed.

Even though he thought this conversation was going nowhere, he didn't want to be rude to Eryn and Katie's mothers. "I'll just take these out to the car."

He got out of there as quickly as he could while balancing boxes with his arms. Any lengthy discussion with women could be like quicksand. He deposited the packages into the trunk of Eryn's car and closed the trunk. When he looked up, he saw Katie standing a few feet away and staring at him. It wasn't the fact that she was staring at him but how she was staring at him. Her face was almost neutral, the only give away was the look of pure want in her eyes. His whole body responded. All of his thoughts were now focused on her.

Katherine watched Mitch as he helped her mother and aunt and she was surprised at how he seemed at ease around them. It fascinated her that he was so casual around people he barely knew. He was helpful and courteous and the fact that he was so nice made her want him. She followed him outside and waited for him to finish his errand.

"Katie," Mitch said as he rounded the back of the car and made his way to her, "are you ready to go?"

Katherine smiled slowly, "Yes, I thought you'd never ask." She wound her arm around his and they walked to Chase's jeep.

Mitch pulled the jeep out of the parking lot and started to drive to the main road on the base. He had one goal and that was to get Katie alone and naked in his bed.

"Would you take me to see what you do?" Katherine asked.

The question was such a surprise that he didn't answer right away. "I'm sorry?"

Katherine looked at him, "I'd like to go to Crash Crew and see what you do."

He was flustered, trying to get his brain in gear was tough with his body on its own course of want and need. "I don't work here in Hawaii. My Crash Crew is in Virginia." He felt stupid for stating the obvious.

She nodded, "Maybe we could see Crash Crew here next week. Abi could give us a tour and you could explain what you do."

He smiled, the woman amazed him, "Sure, I don't see why not."

"Good," Katherine turned to him and laid her hand on his thigh, "now I'd like you to take me to the hotel and make love to me until we're too tired to move."

Now those were the words his body was willing to interpret quickly. "It would be my pleasure, Katie."

She rubbed her fingers along his thighs, "I love the way you say my name."

Mitch swallowed hard, "I like the way it flows off my tongue."

Katherine's hand moved up higher, "I like the way your tongue feels on me."

Whoa, Mitch was hard and didn't want to embarrass himself in the car. "Katie, you've got to stop talking like that or we'll never get to the hotel."

"Okay," Katherine whispered as she moved so she could lean over the counsel between them and taste his ear lobe, "what do you propose we do, then?"

Well they weren't going to make love in the car; he wanted her in his bed. He covered Katie's hand with his, enjoying the feel of her skin under his. "Just hold on a little longer and we'll be there."

The urgency of her needs excited her. To feel something so desperately was very powerful and she enjoyed it. The feeling wasn't exactly new; she felt it when she was creating for work but never in a sexual way before now. She pictured him as he was in her sketch, lazily lying in bed, the sheet draped low on his belly.

Mitch tried to concentrate on driving but Katie's hand massaging his thigh was wreaking havoc with his senses. He jumped when her fingers lightly moved over his swollen sex. He took a deep breath.

"Katie, honey, if you want to touch me, I'm great with it but not while I'm trying to drive to get us to a room with a bed so I don't pull this car over and make love to you on the side of the road." He was trying not to look at her for fear he'd do just that.

The power she had over him sexually was intriguing. "Really?" she asked in a husky voice. Her lips were mere millimeters from his ear.

He could feel her hot breath on his ear and neck and it was making him harder; something he didn't think was possible.

They drove silently for a while, passing through the tunnel that separated Honolulu from the Windward side of the island. Once in the city limits, Katherine started her teasing again.

"Are we almost there, Mitch?" She leaned in closer, "I want you so much."

Mitch's breathing was shallow and he was trying to think of anything he could to do to keep his body from reacting. The woman beside him was not making it very easy but that was part of the attraction, wasn't it?

"Katie, you've got to stop that or I'll turn you over my knee and spank you." The thought he gave enough credence to the threat.

Katherine slid her tongue across her lips, wondering…
"Well, I've never tried that but if you wanted to spank me, I'd let
you." She wanted to break out in laughter at the look of utter
shock on Mitch's face.

The woman was going to kill him, Mitch thought. He could
see the hotel in the distance, sitting among the row of them
along the shore. Finally, he pulled onto the street and located
the first available parking area. He pulled into the spot, shut off
the jeep, and pulled Katie to him.

Katherine wasn't expecting his kiss in the car, but she was
happy to give as good as she got. His tongue played with her lips
and created a warm glow low in her belly. The bloom of heat
spread throughout her body as he kissed her and held her to him
there in the jeep.

Mitch did not want to get too carried away since they still
needed to get up to his room. He reluctantly pulled away and
growled as he turned to get out of his side of the jeep.

Laughing, Katherine jumped out of her side of the vehicle
and waited for her Marine to come to her. He came around and
lifted her up into his arms. She felt like she weighed nothing in
his arms, his strength carrying her physically and emotionally
across the parking lot to the hotel.

It didn't matter to Mitch that people would think they were
crazy; they were. If she wanted him half as much as he wanted
her then they were probably going to hurt one another. That

didn't matter either, he just wanted her, all of her, with him in every way they could imagine together.

Katherine didn't remember getting to Mitch's room. She held her head tucked under his chin, listening to the sounds around them. There were whispers about them, some commented that they must be newlyweds. It was ridiculous but, on some level, she believed it was a lovely thought. She heard the key click in the door and lifted her head.

"I was wondering if you fell asleep. You were so still," Mitch said as he gently placed her on the sofa in the sitting area.

Katherine looked up at his face, the smile he wore was so warm, and for her, "I was listening."

Mitch sat down next to her, his knees brushing hers, and he pushed a wisp of hair off her face and behind her ear, "To what, sweetheart?"

His tone was so soft; it contradicted his strength in her opinion, "To what others were saying about us and to your heartbeat. It was fast." She smiled shyly, "Am I heavy?"

Coming from any other woman, Mitch would have thought it was a dig for a compliment but he knew Katie well enough now that she would be serious when asking. "You are light as a feather, my sweet Katie," he whispered before taking her lips with his.

The kiss was gentle and sweet and made Katherine's heart swell exponentially in her chest. His lips tasted a little of cake and he was a little sweaty from carrying her upstairs in his uniform. It was a crazy but endearing thing for him to do. She wanted to repay the favor.

"Come with me," Katherine said and stood with her hand outstretched to him.

Mitch took her hand and let her lead him. He'd go wherever she wanted as long as he could kiss her.

Katherine walked into the bathroom and stopped in front of the large mirror behind the vanity. She could see the question in Mitch's eyes but didn't say anything at first. She wound her arms around his neck and reached up to kiss him. Her teeth nipped lightly at his bottom lip, the intake of his breath was all the prodding she needed. She backed up until the vanity counter was at her back then, not taking her eyes off of him, she hopped up on the counter and wound her legs around Mitch's. She pulled him in for another kiss.

Mitch was lost in the sexual web she created. He was all for trying new things but wasn't sure the bathroom counter was what he had in mind. Of course, he would never deny Katie anything she wanted so he decided to just go along for the ride.

Deepening her kiss, Katherine absorbed all the passion he was willing to give her. His hands travelled up her back and shoulders, massaging all of the tension of the day out of her muscles. His touch settled her and excited her at the same time, pulling her feelings in all directions. When she thought she would explode from the desire he built up in her, she pulled away.

Mitch watched as Katie smiled at him and hopped off the counter. She circled him and was standing behind him, her arms wrapped around him. He tried to turn around but she stopped him.

"No," Katherine whispered when Mitch tried to face her. "I want to show you something."

Whatever she wanted, he would give. No questions asked.

Katherine was behind him, her hands moving up and down his still clothed chest. They were both looking in the mirror at the reflections of themselves, the desire in their eyes shining brightly.

Reaching up, Katherine started unbuttoning Mitch's uniform jacket. The buttons felt so solid beneath her fingers, the emblem on them creating a friction on the pads of her fingertips. She slowly watched him watch her as she undid the buttons. At his waist was his uniform belt. She unclasped it easily and gently laid it on the counter in front of him. After undoing the last buttons of the jacket, she pulled it off his shoulders and gently set it on a chair.

Mitch did not understand what she was doing but he was drawn to her eyes in the mirror. Once his uniform jacket was off, he was a lot cooler but his skin burned where her fingers touched him. He felt fire spark between them in every place they connected.

Katherine ran her hands up and down Mitch's arms, the little hairs on his skin tickling her nerve endings. She looked back at the mirror and started to pull his t-shirt out of his trousers. His shoulders were so broad compared to his tapered waist. Her fingers skirted over solid muscle, feeling empowered by the shivers she felt in him.

"Katie, let me touch you," Mitch said softly.

Katherine shook her head, "No, I want to show you something," she repeated.

He didn't understand but followed her lead. He nodded and let her explore him with her fingers. He helped her pull the t-shirt over his head.

Once he was bare from the waist up, Katherine's eyes were glued to his form. She ran her nails lightly down his back and around his waist and up his chest. A line of goose bumps followed the trail she left with her fingers. A new wave of need crashed over her body.

"Now you can see what I see," she said. Her eyes were fixed on his as she moved her body to see around him.

His eyes followed her hands as they touched him, the moment was so intimate that he almost wanted to look away. The connection they felt before was just multiplied and it was more than he was used to feeling with anyone. It was uncomfortable to watch but his eyes were glued to hers in the reflection anyway.

Katherine took her index finger and traced a path along his chest, gently scraping her nail across his nipple and relishing in the response of him sucking in a breath. She smiled a womanly smile.

"See your arms, how they are so strong and defined." She demonstrated her point by moving her hands down his biceps.

Her hands moved up to his shoulders, "And the power of your shoulders, how the muscles bunch and move so smoothly beneath my fingers."

His eyes were as dark as the night; he wanted her so much.

She spread her fingers and splayed them across his upper chest, "I look at your chest and I see the hair and how it tickles my fingers."

His hardness was pressing against his trousers and he knew she could see how he was affected by her touch and words. It didn't matter, nothing mattered except him and her right now.

"Do you see how I see you? Very strong and sexy," she purred from behind him. "I assure you, Mitch, you ARE that interesting."

"No," he said breathlessly. "I only see your eyes and they tell me you want me as much as I want you."

Katherine smiled, "Yes I do."

That was all he needed. He turned and picked her up, letting her wrap her long legs around his hips and loving the feel of her.

They made their way to the bed, giggling about being clumsy and falling onto the bed in a heap of limbs.

Katherine propped herself up on her elbows and looked at him over her, "I don't want to leave in the morning." She said the words quietly, wondering if he knew how badly she wanted to be with him.

"Good," Mitch nipped her shoulder with his teeth, "I don't want you to leave in the morning."

Smiling the womanly smile, Katherine thought about what she wanted. Wanting him was easy, showing him how she wanted him was a little more complicated.

Mitch didn't want to talk anymore. He wanted to possess her, body and soul. His hand came up and cupped her cheek, his thumb rubbing gently against her soft skin. Her eyes closed and she moved into his hand, the small gesture letting him know she enjoyed his touch. When her lips sucked his thumb into her mouth, his breath caught in his throat. Oh God, she lightly nipped the pad of his thumb with her teeth.

Their eyes watched one another, just as they did in the mirror's reflection earlier. It was like each was studying the other and memorizing the response. It was probably the most erotic thing Katherine ever experienced and she wasn't about to waste the moment.

"Make love to me, Mitch," she pleaded.

Mitch smiled, "Yes, ma'am."

He sat up, pulling her onto his lap. He cradled her in his arms and kissed her tenderly. There was more than just having great sex, there was making your lover know you think they should be cherished. He wanted to let Katie know she was important to him. His hand held the back of her head as he kissed her lips, her neck, and her shoulder.

Mitch left a trail of sensation as he kissed her skin. Without thinking about it, her hands came up and her fingers dove into his hair. The feeling of his short hair as it caressed her palms combined with the awareness his lips created were riveting.

Katherine let out a sigh, "Ahhh," she whispered.

Her response was his undoing. He brought her around to straddle him. The wispy fabric of her dress spilled around them like a cloud. The straps fell from her shoulders and skimmed across her upper arms. Her hair was half pulled out of the complicated twist and curls she had done for the wedding. Her eyes were bright, her cheeks slightly blushed, and Mitch thought she was the sexiest mess he'd ever seen. And she was here, with him, tonight.

The kisses quickened until they were both breathing hard. Katherine's hands went to his waist and undid the buttons of his dress trousers.

Mitch managed to unclasp the back of Katie's dress and pulled down the zipper slowly, the sound of little metal teeth coming apart made his skin tickle with anticipation.

Not wanting any barrier between them, Mitch stood, taking Katie with him, so he could push down his trousers.

Katherine smiled against his lips; she could hear the frustration in his breathing so she helped him slide down the fabric, pushing her feet lower to help pull the fabric down over his tight butt.

Mitch could feel her smile but wanted to bury himself in her until he wiped that smile off of her face and replaced it with need. Once the pants were low enough, he sat back down, cupping Katie's bottom in his hands. He felt the slip of fabric she called underwear beneath his fingers. With very little effort, he tore the fabric away, pulling it up between them and dropping it behind her.

Well, Katherine thought, he was a man of action and determination. The same could be said about her. She reached between them and grabbed his hardness with her hand. The contradiction of the power of his need with the softness of the skin beneath her fingers made her think of all sorts of things but none of them ladylike.

Panting, Mitch was close to letting go. Katie's holding him in her hands made his body scream with want. She touched him boldly, somehow knowing, what would bring him the most pleasure.

"I want to be in you," Mitch said through gritted teeth.

Between tasting her lips and feeling her manipulations with his erect shaft, he was using every ounce of control to stave off his release.

Katherine smiled, "I want you in me," she replied and lifted herself up and slid onto his maleness in one quick move.

Mitch sucked in a breath, "Oh, Katie, you feel so good."

"Not as good as you feel inside me," Katherine whispered into his ear, "you fill me so completely."

If she didn't stop talking like that, he was not going to be able to hold off his climax. Without responding he grasped her hips and started moving her to create the most sensational friction between them.

Katherine threw her head back in surrender. He was moving her how he wanted, using her body to bring them both release. The movement was a luscious combination of heat and wet and she felt the climb of awareness her body strived to reach.

Mitch could feel her body tightening as it reached for the peak of her desire; his was screaming for the same but he wanted to please her before succumbing to his own needs. Keeping one hand on her hip, guiding the movements of her hips on his, he reached around and cupped her breast with the other hand. Taking his fingers, he squeezed her nipple between the two fingers and moved them slowly. Her eyes flew open and looked into his. He saw the wave of release as it crashed over her body. She bit her lower lip, embracing the feelings her body released, and his climax pounded through him.

There was something so scrumptious about being held in a man's arms while the sensations of sexual release covered your body. It was like finding the most complete form of yourself in another. Katherine watched Mitch as he settled down from his wild climax. It was like watching a feather as it slowly descended to the ground; very quiet, soft, and entrancing.

When Mitch was able to open his eyes, they met with Katie's sparkling green ones. She was smiling a wicked smile and looking very smug.

"Well," Mitch said, "my sweet, Katie, you are incredible."

Katherine smiled, "I don't think so, and it's you and I together that make it incredible."

There was no way he could argue with that. He nodded and kissed the tip of her nose.

Katherine stretched her arms above her head, realizing she still had her dress on. It was pulled in all directions, exposing the breast he tantalized to drive her over the edge of madness. She would never be able to wear it again without thinking of her and Mitch making love. It was a good memory.

"Now, young lady," Mitch said softly, "let's go to bed so I can regain my strength."

Katherine smiled and nodded, "Alright."

Chapter 9

The next day, Mitch woke up to a bright room and complete silence. Sitting up quickly, he felt a brief moment of panic. He thought maybe he dreamed the night before. Maybe Katie hadn't come back to his room with him and maybe she hadn't stayed the night and made love with him over and over again.

He looked around the room and saw the paper on the pillow beside him. Reaching over, he brushed a hand down his face and smelled her perfume. He read the note and smiled. Lord, even her handwriting was adorable.

Mitch,

I didn't want you to think I ran off again. I wanted to do some sketching. Don't forget, we have a brunch and gift opening at twelve.

Katherine

Mitch looked at the clock; it was ten thirty. He got up to get ready and go find his lady.

Sitting on the beach, Katherine let the ocean breeze flow over her. The sensation of sitting here was very serene. When she came down, she wasn't sure what she would draw, only that she needed to sketch something. For her, creating was like an addiction. Sometimes the desire just overwhelmed her and she had to do it.

She was sketching a child playing in the sand when she felt someone behind her. He skin tingled and her pulse sped up. The response was to one person only. She smiled and looked up to see Mitch standing over her.

"Good morning," she said, lifting her hand to block the sun from her eyes. He looked gorgeous in his khaki shorts and blue shirt.

Mitch knelt down in the warm sand, "Good morning to you," he said softly and kissed her on the lips.

The kiss was like a spark to tinder; if he tried it would turn into a full blown fire. He knew her response was the same but they were on a public beach and had someplace to be so he wouldn't follow through with his desire. Instead, he looked down at the sketch she had half laying on her lap.

Katherine followed his eyes to her drawing. "I'm just doodling."

"You realize," Mitch said as he sat down on the sand beside her, "that your "doodles" are better than most people's masterpieces."

His compliment made her feel warm. "They just keep my mind from thinking too much."

He looked over to study her. She was getting tan from sitting out in the Hawaiian sun the last few days. Her hair practically glowed as the breeze made it dance around her face and neck. But when he really looked at her, he could see there was something in her that seemed 'unsettled.' Maybe because he sensed the same thing in himself.

"Why does your mind think too much?" he asked. The comment made him wonder about the mystery that was Katie.

That was a difficult question for Katherine to answer, "Sometimes, I just get overwhelmed and art calms me down." She looked away briefly. "I know it sounds flaky, like I have some issue, but it's just what I feel."

Not being artistic, Mitch was sure he didn't understand. That made her feelings no less valid. She seemed so self-assured but then she said something that made her seem very vulnerable. The contradiction only intrigued him.

Mitch took her hand in his, "I can't say I understand, but we all feel what we feel, Katie."

Not wanting the conversation to be too serious, Katherine shoved her papers and pencils into the bag she grabbed from her room. "Well, let's go to brunch." She stood and held her free hand out to Mitch, "All that sex last night made me hungry."

Mitch grabbed her hand and stood. Katie's mention of the word sex unnerved him for some reason. He followed her back to the hotel, wondering why he was being so sensitive.

The brunch was held at one of the restaurants in the hotel. The group was seated outside on a large lanai so everyone could enjoy the beautiful weather.

When Katherine walked over she noticed Eryn and Chase seated closely in one corner. They looked like they were sharing a secret that only lovers shared. She looked over her shoulder at Mitch and knew she had her own secrets. The feeling completely warmed her insides.

Mitch smiled at the look of satisfaction Katie shot him over her shoulder. Was she thinking of the night before when they wore each other out with their lovemaking? Lord knew he wasn't likely to forget it any time soon. They slept in each other's arms. He fell asleep with his hand resting on her thigh, on her breast, on her neck and he would wake up wanting her so badly. Now he was becoming aroused thinking of all the places they touched and kissed.

"Katherine," Victoria Fredricks called when she saw her daughter.

Mitch watched Katie visibly stiffen when she heard her mother. He followed Katie as she made her way toward the table where her parents and a few others were sitting. The Katie he just spent the night with was now gone and was replaced with a much more formal version of herself. He wasn't sure how he felt about that.

Katherine sat down and smiled at her mother but she wasn't in the mood for conversation. She just wanted to enjoy the food and Mitch's company. She could feel him stand beside her and felt better knowing he was there.

Mitch was smiling at Mrs. Fredricks as she spoke to her daughter and he wondered what the deal with Katie and her parents was. He noticed a few things over the last few days but he and Katie didn't talk about that stuff. A movement out of the corner of his eye made him look over to see Chase waive him over.

Bending down, Mitch whispered in Katie's ear, "I'll be right back."

Just the closeness of his lips to her skin made Katherine tingle. She smiled and nodded. When her eyes returned to her mother's she wondered if her mother knew what she and Mitch were doing. If the knowing look her mother shot her was any indication, her mother knew exactly what she and Mitch were doing. She didn't seem upset by it though and that surprised Katherine.

Chase met up with Mitch and hugged him, "Thanks for being my best man."

Mitch smiled, "Thanks for asking me." He was glad his friend looked so happy.

"We're going to sit down to eat but I wanted to thank you again before we took off." He looked back at his new bride, "Eryn and I are taking off for Kauai this afternoon."

Mitch was reminded how lucky Chase was. He got to spend the next week holed up in a tropical bungalow with the woman he loved. Lucky son of a gun! His eyes automatically sought out Katie. She looked so stiff, sitting there talking to her mother.

Chase watched his friend watch Katherine and wondered if the guy knew he was a goner, "When are you headed back to the mainland?"

"What? Oh, in three days." Mitch answered absently. He needed to get his head off of Katie and into the conversation with Chase.

Chase nodded, "Are you going to plan on visiting again soon? I hear Katherine is planning on spending Christmas here this year."

Why was Chase talking about something nine months away? "I really hadn't thought about it."

"Hey, Mitch," Eryn said as she walked up to where the two men were talking. "How was your night?"

Mitch heard the innuendo in the question, "It was probably as good as yours was," Mitch said dryly but winked.

Eryn smiled, "Lord, I hope so." She leaned up and kissed him on the cheek and walked over to where Katherine was sitting.

Yep, Mitch thought as he watched Katie warm when she saw Eryn, there was definitely something between her and her parents. He was pulled from his thoughts by Chase clapping him on his shoulder and walking toward the table they were sitting at for the brunch.

A few minutes later, everyone took their seats and brunch was served. The food was good and the conversation was lively about the wedding and reception the night before. Pictures were passed around and people were laughing and the ahhhs started.

Mitch did what was expected but his thoughts were preoccupied with Katie. She looked so serious and the only thing he wanted to do was take her upstairs and make her look free like she did the night before during their lovemaking.

Katherine made the appropriate comments during the brunch but was disappointed that she wasn't sitting next to Mitch. She figured that was her parents' doing but she wouldn't say anything. She learned early on when to speak up and when to just let things be. Her plummeting thoughts were stopped when she was handed a picture.

She studied the picture as if it was a piece of art. It was of her and Mitch dancing at the reception. The look on their faces was what made her hold the photo for a while. They looked so focused on one another; as if no one else existed. She looked up to see her mother smiling at her knowingly again.

Emma leaned over to peer at the picture Katherine was holding and sighed, "How long have you two been dating?" she asked.

The question startled Katherine as she looked at Emma, "We're not," was her quick answer.

"Well," Emma said, "if you're not dating and he's looking at you like that, then you need to be." Emma gently squeezed

Katherine's shoulder, as if giving her encouragement then went back to speaking with Abi and a few others.

Chase and Eryn were starting to open up gifts and the room seemed to be closing in around her so Katherine excused herself and quickly walked out onto the outer deck.

Mitch watched Katie get up and walk away from the crowd. The look on her face concerned him so he excused himself and walked out after her.

Katherine was trying to get her bearings when she felt someone behind her. Without looking, she knew it was Mitch. She could smell his cologne, feel his heat; she just knew he was near. That was just as unnerving as the picture she was handed inside.

"Are you okay?" Mitch asked softly from behind her. They were within view of the other guests so he didn't touch her.

Katherine shrugged, "I'm fine." She was lying but what was the point of telling him the truth; she was confused and frustrated and had no idea why.

She was anything but fine but he wouldn't argue with her. "Would you like to take a walk down the beach?"

Katherine looked at him for the first time and her breath hitched, he looked so wonderful and warm and welcoming and she wanted nothing more than to just walk into his arms. But she wouldn't. She didn't answer, only shook her head no.

Mitch nodded, "Okay, I'll see you inside later then." What else could he say?

"Okay," Katherine nodded and tried to smile but it never quite made it to her eyes.

She stood there and watched him re-enter the room. There was laughter and congratulations and love in there but she was standing out here and watching, like she always did, from the sidelines.

Mitch went to the bar and ordered a beer. It was after lunch and perfectly acceptable to get drunk. He wasn't driving so what the hell? He was sitting there and sulking when he noticed Abi Rochelle come up and sit beside him. He was reminded of Katie's asking for a tour of Crash Crew.

"Hey, Gunny," Mitch said to Abi.

Abi was well on her way to getting drunk and only lifted her glass in a mock salute before swallowing it in one full gulp. "Master Sgt," she said in a slightly slurred voice.

Okay, Mitch thought, someone else who wasn't feeling so cheerful. He could relate. "I don't want to intrude on your clear intention of getting wasted here," he moved closer, "but I was wondering if I could bring Eryn's cousin, Katie, er Katherine, over to Crash Crew on Monday for a tour. She's curious about our job."

Nodding slowly, "No problem, Master Sgt," Abi lifted her newly filled glass in a toast then proceeded to down it again.

"Not to pry," Mitch leaned over, "but you're putting those down pretty quickly."

Abi nodded, "Yep," another drink, "I was systematically dumped this morning and I feel like drowning my sorrows."

Ouch, Mitch thought. Been there, done that. Poor girl. "Well, we'll drown our sorrows together then," he motioned for another beer from the bartender.

Katherine could see the gift opening part of the brunch starting to die down so she came back in and sat down near Eryn. Emma was kind enough to make the lists of gifts and who gave them but Katherine was going to take care of getting everything in order for Chase and Eryn as far as the thank you notes. She gathered up all of the information and looked around for Mitch. Her heart dropped down into her stomach when she saw him at the bar. His arm was around the shoulders of the other bridesmaid, Abi.

Mitch was listening to Abi spew about the jerk who dumped her after six months of dating. He was a Class A jerk if her comments were any indication. Mitch was trying to show support and felt like he was doing a good job. He looked over to see Katie on the other side of him and smiled, God she looked so beautiful.

"Hey, Katie," Mitch said brightly. The alcohol was definitely lightening his mood.

Katherine was mad, "Hello," she said coolly.

Abi realized very quickly, even through the alcoholic haze, that this didn't look good. Katherine was upset and, apparently, Mitch couldn't see that. "Um, Katherine, Mitch was just listening to me go on about my recent ex-boyfriend."

Mitch awkwardly removed his arm from around Abi's shoulders and dug into his wallet for some cash to cover his bar tab. After throwing some bills on the bar he got up and guided Katie to a nearby corner.

"It's not what it looks like," he said. The room was swaying a little so it was hard to focus.

Katherine knew, logically, that what he and Abi said was true but that didn't stop the stab of jealousy from rearing up into her chest. "I know that, Mitch."

Mitch took her hand into his and brought it to his lips, "I was feeling rejected by you and she was dumped and I was just listening to her let out her feelings."

Rejected? Damn it, she thought. Now the jealousy was replaced by shame, "I'm sorry that you felt that way, Mitch. I was just feeling a little confused about things here."

He tried to focus on her but it was tough with the alcohol making his head swim, "What things?" he asked.

"Katherine," Marcus Fredricks said as he came up behind his daughter, "we're going to be assisting Tom and Beverly in taking the gifts over to Chase and Eryn's house then we're going to do some sightseeing."

Mitch watched Katie's father firmly place his claim on his daughter. The man didn't even have to speak directly to him to make him feel like he wasn't good enough. Anger, slow to boil, was stirring around in his gut. He looked at Katie and watched the confident woman he met only days ago become an obedient child right in front of him.

Katherine looked at Mitch, hoping he would ask her to stay but knowing he wouldn't. Her father made his proclamations and everyone towed the line. That was how it always was.

Mitch watched Katie walk away with her father and wanted to kick himself for his behavior. He knew better than to drink and act stupidly when all he wanted to do was spend time with Katie. His eyes met with Chase's and he knew his friend knew full well what he was going through at the moment.

Katherine helped to gather up the gifts and rode in the car with her mother and aunt to take them over to Eryn and Chase's house in Kailua.

Apparently her father's way of helping was to go golfing with her Uncle Tom and his friend Ben. She was mad about what she viewed as his deception to get her away from Mitch. She was even madder at herself for falling in line and not standing up for herself.

Victoria Fredricks looked over her shoulder into the back seat and watched her daughter look absently out the car window. She felt bad for Katherine and knew Marcus was interfering with their daughter's budding romance with Mitch. She was reserving her judgment to see if this was just a short term affair or full-blown love. Katherine was like her father in that an observer never was completely sure what either of them was thinking.

Always the buffer, Beverly Fredricks hated to see her niece look so forlorn. "Katie," she purposely used the nickname to lighten the mood, "did I tell you how I was responsible for getting Chase and Eryn together?"

The question catapulted Katherine out of her pity party and into the moment, "I don't believe I was told about that," she replied.

"Well," Beverly said, "you see I knew that Uncle Tom was sticking his nose in where it didn't belong," she shot an empathetic look at her sister-in-law. "The men in our family tend to be dictators."

Katherine couldn't help it, she snorted. The sound drew a pointed look from her mother but she didn't care; her aunt was completely right.

Beverly smiled, "Well, after Paul died, I could see how badly Eryn was hurting and knew that Chase could help her heal."

Katherine leaned forward, "How did you do it."

She made a turn down the road to Eryn and Chase's place, waiting to answer until she parked in the driveway and got out.

She popped open the trunk and grabbed some bags, motioning the other two ladies to follow her.

After placing the bags in the spare bedroom, Beverly walked into the kitchen and leaned against the counter, "I did something I shouldn't."

Katherine was surprised, her aunt was always so nice and easy-going.

"I put my nose in and found out where Chase was stationed and if he was still single," She smiled at the shocked look on both her niece's and sister-in-law's faces, "well if he wasn't it wouldn't work."

Katherine nodded, anxious to hear the rest of the story.

"Then I called up someone I knew and pulled some strings to, let's just say, help along Eryn's orders to get her to where Chase was." She walked to the refrigerator and pulled out a pitcher of lemonade.

Katherine was amazed at the audacity, "How did you know they would end up together?"

Beverly handed Katherine a glass of lemonade, "Oh, I didn't."

Almost choking on the lemonade she was trying to swallow, Katherine cleared her throat.

"You see," Beverly lightly touched Katherine's arm with her hand, "when two people are really in love, time and distance don't really matter."

Victoria sighed, "You always were a hopeless romantic."

Beverly shot a look at her sister-in-law, "Let's see, Vicki, you've been married how long?"

"Thirty-five years," Victoria said proudly.

Nodding, Beverly walked over to her, "And does Marcus still make you feel, even for the slightest of moments here and there, like he did when you first fell in love?"

Katherine was interested in her mother's answer. They never discussed how her parents met. She sipped her lemonade, waiting for her mother to respond.

Victoria sighed again, "Yes, he does." She looked at her mother, "Your aunt is right, Katherine. I love your father as much today as I did when we married, probably more."

It was a relief to hear her mother say that she loved her father. The bigger revelation was to hear the way her mother said it, as if she'd just fallen in love with him. The last couple of days were an eye-opener to see her parents differently. She smiled at her mother.

"So now you know who was really behind it all," Beverly winked at her niece, "but don't feel obligated to share that with Eryn or Chase."

Katherine chuckled. She wondered why her aunt felt the need to tell her the story at all but, in the end, it was a nice thing for her to do. And, of course, it all worked out beautifully for Eryn and Chase. She thought about her and Mitch and wondered if things were different, if they would stand a chance at a relationship. She'd have to think on that for a while.

Mitch sat by the pool at the hotel and sulked. He watched Katie leave with her family, then Eryn and Chase took off to start their honeymoon, then everyone else seemed to have somewhere to be. He was alone and didn't have a clue what he wanted to do. So now, an hour later, he was sitting by the pool still clueless.

Katherine tried to call Mitch's phone. Eryn was kind enough to forward his number to her phone before she and Chase left for Kauai. No answer. Damn! She wanted to see him, to talk to him about this whole business. They slept together and now things needed to be clarified.

She went to his room and, having no answer, decided to go downstairs to see if he was in one of the bars or out at the beach.

Mitch had enough of the sun and people. There was only one person he really wanted to be with and she was somewhere else. How did this whole thing happen anyway? He thought he'd fly to Hawaii for Chase's wedding, have a good time, then fly back to Virginia. Simple. But now he was waiting on a woman who, in one minute, seemed as in to him as he was in to her, then the next, wanted nothing to do with him. It was damned exasperating.

He was stomping through the lobby on his way to the elevator, lost in his thoughts about his situation when he saw Abi Rochelle by the front desk. He walked over to talk to her about that tour of Crash Crew.

"Abi," Mitch called when he saw her turn away from the desk and start toward the doors.

"Master Sgt," Abi replied. Her head hurt from her earlier binge on alcohol. A friend was picking her up and driving her back to the base.

Mitch smiled, he knew she was feeling the not-so-lovely effects of alcohol. He put his hand on her shoulder and started walking with her outside.

Katherine exited the elevator and immediately saw Mitch coming in the far side of the lobby. She started moving toward him when she saw him moving away from her. She followed him with her eyes until she saw him go over to meet up with Abi. If the stab of jealousy wouldn't have been so deep, she would've turned right around and went back up to her room. But having that much of a reaction made her stop to think about why she was feeling it at all.

Mitch set up the meeting for Katherine with Abi, waved her off, and went back inside. He was just inside the doors to the lobby when he saw Katie. She was standing against a pillar, staring at him. The look on her face was unreadable. He smiled automatically. Even with his feelings in an uproar, the sight of her made him happy.

"Hi," he said when he was close enough.

Katherine looked at him, his eyes shone warmth and he seemed happy to see her. That was enough to heal her chafed feelings for now. She smiled and took his hand. She didn't want to talk just yet.

Mitch was puzzled, she didn't say anything but took his hand and led him to the elevator. They road up the elevator and got off on a different floor than his room was on. They must be headed for her room. He was intrigued.

Still silent, Katherine led Mitch to her room, used the key to enter, and walked in. She waited for him to pass her then hung the Do Not Disturb sign on the door handle.

There was no mistaking her intentions in Mitch's mind. She wanted what he wanted; them together, alone.

Katherine stood before him, not touching him. "I missed you."

The words warmed him from the inside out. "I missed you too," he replied and leaned down to kiss her.

It was like slipping into a warm bath; she settled into the kiss, her hand instinctively moving up his arms to his shoulders.

Mitch tasted her and wanted more, so much more.

Katherine didn't want to waste time kissing when there was so much more they could be doing. She pulled her hands down and slipped the straps of her dress off her shoulders. The fabric slid to the floor; the coolness of the air conditioned room creating ripples of goose bumps on her flesh. Her face was on fire since she was kissing Mitch, her tongue swirling around his. She would nip at his lip with her teeth in an effort to get more of him.

Mitch put his arms around her waist, loving the feel of her skin against his palms. It was soft and smelled of flowers and the ocean. He lifted her so he could have her flush against him.

When he lifted her, Katherine felt cherished. She would never tire of him picking her up as if she weighed nothing at all. He held her against him and she could feel his heart as it beat as erratically as her own did. Her hands were in his hair and her elbows on his shoulders to hold her in place.

He wanted to devour her, she tasted so damn good. Her tongue danced with his and tempted him beyond belief. Holding her like this, anything was possible. His breathing ragged, he tried to find his way to her bedroom so he could make love to her properly.

Katherine smiled against his lips; he was fumbling with her in his arms and trying to find his way through her hotel room. It was laid out a bit differently than his was. She didn't say anything, just kept kissing him and touching him, his hair, his neck, his ears; she wanted to memorize everything about him.

Finally, the bed, he thought. Reluctantly, he pulled his head back far enough to look into her eyes. The slanted rays of the late afternoon sun came through the window and illuminated her profile. She looked almost magical, a glowing aura surrounding her beautiful body.

Katherine watched him watch her and she wondered what he saw. "What would you like?"

The words alone aroused Mitch but the way she said them, very softly and seductively, made his body find a whole new level of awareness. She was offering herself to him. It was profound and he felt his chest tighten with something akin to pain.

He didn't answer and Katherine wondered if he didn't understand her question. "I think I would like to please you, sir."

Did the woman not know that her words were pushing him further into sexual ecstasy? "I want you," he finally said breathlessly.

"Yes," Katherine slid onto the bed and scooted back on her knees. His hands were in hers, "But how do you want me?"

Katherine brought his hand up to her lips and started kissing his fingers. She liked the reaction so she took a finger into her mouth and suckled it.

Mitch was captivated by watching her mouth on his finger. His body demanded that he appease its needs so he tugged her toward him, wrapping his other hand around her waist.

"I want you every way I can think of," he kissed her softly, "then I want to start all over again." His eyes were set on hers.

Looking at him, Katherine knew he was serious and she was all too happy to accommodate him. "Alright."

With a set determination, Katherine set to work trying to figure out all the ways they could possibly want one another. It was going to be a very long and enjoyable afternoon indeed.

Chapter 10

Katherine stretched, her body ached in places she never would have thought before meeting Mitch. The man did things to her that were meant for trained acrobatics. Smiling, she turned over and found the other side of the bed empty. Strange, she didn't remember hearing anything.

Getting up, she found Mitch's t-shirt and slipped it over her head before leaving the bedroom. She walked out toward the living area of her suite and found him sitting on the sofa. He was looking out the window; the Honolulu city lights the only illumination in the room. They created moving shadows over his form. She stood there just watching him.

Mitch woke up and saw it was still dark outside. Why did he wake up? He didn't want to disturb Katie so he went out into the living room and sat there staring at nothing. The last couple of days played through his head like some long movie trailer and it was driving him nuts.

Katherine couldn't stand there and watch him look so serious; it made her feel bad for some reason. Pushing away from the door frame, she went farther into the room and made her way to him. He looked up into her eyes when she stopped in front of him.

"Hey," Mitch said softly. He pulled her gently into his lap.

Katherine slid onto him and snuggled into his embrace. She didn't say anything; she just wanted to feel him hold her.

They sat there for a long time, just looking out at the city. Each wondering what the other was thinking and too afraid to ask.

Morning light poured into the room, waking Mitch. He was still on the sofa holding Katie in his arms. A smile played across his face when he looked at her. She looked so small and content in his embrace. It would be easy to just stay in the room and make love all day but he promised Katie he'd take her on a tour of Crash Crew and he wanted them to go out and have some fun. Gently, he moved to stand, taking her with him.

"I don't want to wake up yet," Katherine mumbled.

Mitch smiled, "But we have things to do."

One eye opened, "We do?" She used her sly tone in the hopes he would take her back to the bedroom and make love to her.

He set her down at the threshold to the bathroom, "We do but not that," he smiled at her pout, "we'll do that later."

Somewhat appeased, Katherine opened both eyes fully, "Okay, so what would you like to do?"

Mitch had to fight his body and resist what it wanted to do. "I am going to my room to shower and change and give you time to do the same here." He checked his phone, "I'll meet you in the lobby in an hour okay?"

Did that man want to torture her? She was officially on vacation now since she was done with her maid of honor duties. Ugh! She sighed and nodded.

Leaning down, Mitch kissed her on the tip of her nose. "I'll see you then." He grabbed his room key and his phone and left.

Katherine smiled as she got into the shower a few minutes later. She was still wearing his t-shirt when he left and decided he wasn't getting it back. It smelled like him; male and sexy.

Mitch was waiting in the lobby almost an hour later when he saw Katie come off the elevator. She smiled but it looked forced. He saw her father get off the elevator with her and figured he was the reason for her tense expression. Crap!

Walking over, Mitch stretched out his hand, "Mr. Fredricks, how are you this morning, sir?"

Marcus appreciated the man's manners even if he didn't appreciate the fact that he was seeing his daughter. "Fine, thank you."

No response, again with the intimidation, Mitch thought. Well the man may be used to others following his directives but Mitch had seen bigger and badder during his time in the Corps. The only reason he gave the man so much leeway was because he didn't want to upset Katie. Their time together was short and he wasn't going to let her father, or anyone, ruin it.

"Are you ready?" Mitch asked Katie.

Nodding, Katherine was stressed. Her father got on the same elevator and just assumed she was spending the day with him and her mother. Of course no invitation was issued, it was just a foregone conclusion in his mind. But being the attentive and obedient child for years was a hard habit to break.

Marcus looked at his daughter, "I thought you were joining us today?" His brow furrowed.

Mitch stepped closer to Katie and took her hand in his. He didn't miss the obvious look of disapproval from her father, "Sir, Katie has agreed to join me today in a tour of Marine Corps Base Hawaii and some sightseeing. We'll be with Abi Rochelle; you met her at the wedding."

Katherine looked from her father to Mitch and back again. Had someone just told her father no? She was astounded and, apparently, so was her father because he didn't even have a reply.

"Have a good day, sir," Mitch said. He took Katie's hand and led her outside toward the parking lot.

Katherine was silent on the way to the car. Chase left his jeep at the hotel for Mitch to use for the remainder of his stay. They got in and Mitch made his way easily through the Honolulu traffic. It was only after they left the city and were on the H-3 toward the base that she decided she could speak.

She looked over at Mitch, "Thank you."

He reached over and put his hand over hers on her thigh. "You're welcome."

"No one ever really stands up to him," Katherine said over the wind whipping through her hair.

Nodding, Mitch smiled, "I figured." He looked back at the road, "With rank or position, sometimes people forget they're the same as everyone else." He squeezed her hand, "It never hurts to remind them once in a while."

She couldn't help it, she laughed. "Oh my, I wonder what he said to my mother or my uncle."

A shot of worry ran up his spine, "Are you mad that I bulldozed him?"

She shook her head, "Oh no, he definitely needed that reminder."

Relieved, Mitch laughed. He flipped on the lights so they could go through the tunnel that ran through the mountain.

Once they passed through the tunnel, they had a spectacular view of the valley below. They could see the base in the distance. It was stunning to see and Katherine wondered why she didn't notice it earlier. Probably because she never took the time, she scolded herself mentally.

Mitch drove the road that lead to KBay (Kaneohe Bay Marine Corps Base) and smiled. It was like coming home, going through the gates. The sentries waved him on and he nodded in response.

They drove past the Lodge at Kaneohe, past the statue of the raising of the flag at Iwo Jima, and down the main road that led through the base. He would point out things he thought Katie would find interesting. She nodded and he wondered if she was just being polite. It didn't really matter because he liked sharing things with her. He knew a fair amount even though he wasn't stationed here. Chase and Eryn had told him some things over the last year and the rest he knew from being here for a conference a few years back.

Katherine listened intently on what Mitch was saying about the base but it wasn't what he was saying as much as the fact that he was talking. Their relationship, such as it was, was based mostly on sex so they really never talked about their real lives. She liked the sound of his voice as he described life here. She could hear the pride he had in the Marine Corps. It was so easy to just listen and relax.

Mitch pulled into the Crash Crew parking lot and put the jeep in park. He told Abi they would arrive about eleven and they were a few minutes early. Not wanting to interrupt the regular duties the Marines carried out, he thought they would do a quick tour while most of them were at lunch and then they would treat Abi to lunch afterward at the Staff NCO Club.

He got out of the jeep and went around to help Katie out. She turned and looked at the Crash Barn so he started in with his explanation of the building and the surrounding area. He pointed out the Air Traffic Control tower nearby and the layout of the hangars. Then he started toward the building, his hand on her lower back to guide her.

They entered the Crash Barn and Katherine noticed the offices right away. The one marked OIC was first on the right so she assumed that was Eryn's. She experienced a rabid curiosity about her cousin's work environment and hoped to talk Abi into giving her a peek. They passed a sign that said Admin, one that said Supply, and another that read NCOIC.

"They currently don't have an NCOIC since Chase retired so Abi is filling in for both Chase and Eryn's position while they're away. She may be a little busy." He explained as they worked their way down the hallway.

Next there was a room labeled Mess but it was really a lunch room. Katherine wanted to ask but decided it would sound silly. Finally there was an office with a sign that read Crash Chief. She stopped and waited to see what Mitch would do.

Mitch knocked and waited for the sharp, "Enter." He opened the door slowly and smiled. "Hey, Gunny," he said.

Abi sighed, "I'm sorry, Master Sgt." She rose from behind her desk and came to the door to greet them, "Please come in."

Katherine followed Mitch into the office and was surprised by the hug she received from Abi right away. When she pulled back she could see something was bothering the woman. Mitch probably thought it was work related but Katherine knew that look. Abi was upset and it was personal.

"Is this a bad time?" Katherine asked. She didn't want to burden Abi. She was such a nice woman, even if she was a little too close to Mitch the day before at the hotel. Katherine didn't hold a grudge.

Abi waived her hand, "No, not at all." She absently straightened the papers on her desk, "I believe I owe you a tour."

They walked back out into the hallway and started to back track the way she and Mitch entered just a few minutes before. Abi gave a more thorough explanation of the jobs and the people and Katherine listened intently.

Abi was kind enough to let her peek into Eryn's office and she poked around for a few minutes. She noticed the pictures on Eryn's desk and smiled. One of Chase, of course, one of her and her parents at her boot camp graduation, and even one of her and Katherine from years earlier over summer vacation. Her cousin was a kind person.

Katherine asked a few questions and Abi answered them patiently. They walked into the actual bay that held the fire trucks and Katherine peeked into each one, asking questions about them. Mitch would answer a few but really let Abi lead the tour. Katherine would listen to them talk between them about work-related things and found she respected Mitch's obvious passion and knowledge about his chosen field.

They went into some offices that were on the far side of the bay that held the office of the Truck Master and even went upstairs into the TV room designed for the crash crewmen to relax in and finally the Section Leaders' offices. There was so much more to the operation of Crash Crew than she knew and she was quite proud to know how important her cousin's job and those who worked with her was.

At the end of the tour she hugged Abi tight, "Thank you so much for taking time to show us around and answer my incessant questions."

Abi smiled, "It really was my pleasure." She shook Mitch's hand and turned back to Katherine, "You better send me the info on your show."

Chuckling, Katherine nodded, "Of course, a deal is a deal."

"Would you like to join us for lunch?" Mitch asked Abi.

Abi shook her head no, "Thanks, but no, I've got a ton of stuff to do."

Mitch helped Katie into the jeep and went around to get into the driver's seat. Katie looked like she was serious. "Is everything okay?" he asked her before turning on the jeep.

"No," Katherine said, "I just know that Abi was upset by something."

He was puzzled, "Really?"

Katherine shook her head in disbelief, "Apparently, a woman can recognize it more than a man."

He didn't doubt that for a minute. "Should we go talk to her?" He wasn't sure what they should do.

"No," Katherine said, "she'll let us know if she needs someone to talk to."

As they pulled out of the parking space, Katherine made a mental note to call Abi later in the day to make sure she was okay. A woman sometimes just needed to talk to another woman.

Instead of going back toward the main part of the base, Mitch decided to take a detour toward the beach. They had to cross the airfield to get to it which he thought Katie would like.

The area was gorgeous, Katherine thought. Even though this was a working military base, it was surrounded by the lush landscape native to the islands. They drove around the airfield and wove around to a beach nestled behind a deep grove of trees.

Katherine slipped off her sandals before she got out of the jeep. The beach was small and deserted. Trees grew up only feet from the water so it was almost hidden. Mitch took his shoes off and joined her on her side of the jeep.

"I wanted to take you for a walk before we went to lunch." He took her hand and brought it to his lips to kiss it.

Smiling, Katherine nodded, "Okay." She wouldn't deny him anything, especially if it meant they could have some time alone.

They walked about twenty yards down and followed a path that lead to the water. The breezes were stronger here and Katherine had to hold her hair in her hand or it would start blowing everywhere. She didn't consider that when they left this morning.

Mitch wished Katie would just let her hair go; he loved to watch it blow freely in the breeze. It was reckless and reflected just how he felt when he was with her. He was relieved when they didn't see anyone else around. After walking a bit, he sat down on the sand and pulled her down with him. He tucked her in front of him, gently pushing her hair in between their bodies so it wouldn't annoy her.

"Thank you," Katherine said, touched that he would be so considerate.

Mitch kissed her shoulder, "My pleasure."

His attention made Katherine's body stir. Just feeling him behind her made her feel safe and aroused and even confused. The feelings she was experiencing made her happy and scared all at the same time. She couldn't say anything to him since she didn't know what it all meant.

They sat there on the beach, not really saying anything, for a while. Mitch's stomach was getting ready to growl so he started to move. "C'mon."

Katherine watched him stand and was happy to go with him but a part of her wanted to just stay here, just the two of them. She smiled, "Okay."

Once back in the jeep, Mitch took her back through the base and exited through another gate. He explained that they were just a few minutes from Kailua and he wanted to take her to a restaurant there.

Mitch swung the jeep into the parking lot of a popular local restaurant Chase and Eryn raved about. He'd been to the location in Honolulu but this one was the first and, everyone said, better. He hoped so because he wanted to impress Katie.

They were seated quickly and Katherine looked around. It was a local place and sparsely decorated, allowing the natural beauty of the area to entertain patrons. It was comfortable and the smells were heavenly.

Once they ordered lunch, Mitch reached across the table and took her hand in his. "So tell me about yourself."

Katherine shrugged, "There is absolutely nothing about me that is interesting." She meant it to sound flippant.

His eyebrows raised, Mitch cocked his head, "I don't believe that for one minute, Katie."

She absolutely loved it when he used her nickname, "Believe it, I work all the time and run around." She played with her napkin, "It's not at all important, not like what you and Eryn do."

What? He was shocked by her statement. "I'm not saying what we do isn't important, Katie, but everyone's job is important."

Spoken like a true gentleman, Katherine thought. She squeezed his hand and smiled. "You are sweet."

"Oh, don't say that," Mitch crinkled his brow in pretend shock. "When women say that they mean, 'your nice and all but let's be friends,' and my heart gets broken." He punctuated his dramatics with a fist to the chest.

Katherine laughed, "I think it's a little late for us to be "just friends", Mitch." She rubbed her fingers across his hand, "Unless you have sex with all of your friends that way."

Mitch shook his head, "I do not." He smiled but couldn't help but be bothered again by her use of the word sex. Was that all this was to her? He should ask her but it sounded needy.

Their food arrived and they each dug in. The place was known for steaks so they each ordered one. The calamari was spectacular and they took their time eating, chatting about the islands and the food.

Katherine excused herself to the ladies room while Mitch paid the check. It was a lovely lunch but they never really did talk about her. What she did back home in New York and what her life was like. He was genuinely interested in everything about her but she was, admittedly, evasive.

As they walked out of the restaurant Katherine looked over at the beach across the street, "Is that Kailua Beach?" she asked.

"I think so," Mitch answered.

She started walking toward the road rather than the jeep, "Would you mind if we walked it a while?"

Mitch shook his head, "No, I have no plans."

"Let's go." She smiled like a child. It sounded like fun and she desperately needed that.

They crossed the street and made their way down to the sand. Now this was a beach Katherine thought. The sand was fine and white and warm between their toes. They walked hand in hand for a while, watching the beach goers and commenting here and there about the scenery.

After a while Katherine realized she needed to say something. "I'm a private person, Mitch."

He nodded, "I kind of figured but I would hope that since we've been rather close over the last four days that you would think you could trust me."

Smiling, Katherine walked closer to the water. The cool liquid covered her feet when the waves brought it in over the sand. The feeling was calming and she liked feeling that way.

"My life is chaotic," she said dryly. "It's in New York so it's always busy."

She wasn't exactly revealing, Mitch thought, but it was a start as far as he was concerned. "Okay," he said and drew it out to encourage her to say more.

They stopped and he pulled her up against him. He wanted her to look into his eyes.

Katherine felt like he towered over her; she looked up and felt the warmth of the sun and the warmth of his gaze on her. It made her want to open up. "It's silly."

"How can you say that?" he asked. "I've seen your drawings. Hell, the one of me made me hard just looking at it." He didn't want to say it but the words spilled out.

He was fantastic! "Really?" she purred.

"Really." He said and claimed her lips with his. They were warm and tasted a little salty from the sea air. His hands came up and wound their way into her hair, holding her to him.

His kiss was heavenly, lifting her up into a cloud of desire she wanted to stay in forever. No one else existed, just them. That was, until a wave of water came crashing over their legs and almost swept them off their feet.

Katherine squeaked and ran up the beach, Mitch's laughter trailing after her. She looked at him with a mischievous gleam in her eyes and started running after him.

They ran around the beach like kids, playing in the water, splashing one another, then running away from the invading waves.

Sometime later, Katherine ran up the beach until she found a patch of grass to collapse on. She plopped down unceremoniously, her chest was heaving from running around, but she was extremely happy.

"What?" Mitch said as he came up to her, "Are you tired?"

She nodded, "Yes, you wear me out!" She fell back onto the grass, her arms outstretched.

He laughed at her looking so spent, "Well, I am a trained professional so I'm used to rigorous exercise. I guess you aren't."

His mocking tone made her wonder what kind of revenge she could enact.

Mitch could see the wheels turning and knew she would get even for his smart aleck comments. He actually looked forward to it.

"Well, now I'm sandy and sweaty." He reached down and grabbed her hand to pull her up. "Let's go back to the hotel and shower."

She tried to look shocked by his suggestion, "Together?"

Laughing again, he asked, "Is there any other way?"

"None that I can think of at the moment." She tried to look demure but her knowing smile betrayed her.

They walked back to the jeep and made their way out of Kailua and back towards Honolulu a few minutes later.

After parking in the hotel parking lot, Mitch helped Katie out and they went into the lobby. The place was certainly bustling now. With all the activity, it took them a few minutes just to get to the elevator and even longer to wait to get on.

"My room or yours?" Mitch whispered in her ear.

She smiled, "We'll stop by yours to pick up some of your things then let's go to mine." She felt so sneaky with the way they were talking.

Their whispering added a new level of awareness to their actions. The focus was now on the more basic need of making love. The elevator finally arrived and they got in, grinning like naughty children.

Minutes later they were finally in Katherine's room again, kissing, touching, pulling at clothes. It was like they hadn't made love in ages as opposed to just hours earlier.

They wanted each other so badly that they never even made it to the bedroom, instead they fell to the floor in the sitting room and made love right there.

It was primal as Katherine settled her ready body over his and rode him fast to reach the wave of desire she knew they would raise together.

Mitch watched her find her climax and relished in the sight of her muscles tensing and the fast hiss of air she released from her lungs as the last vestiges of her orgasm settled. He slowly got up off the floor and picked her up. He was only just getting started with showing her how much he wanted her.

Katherine could feel the slickness of their skin as he carried her to the bed. It didn't matter that she just came and it was overwhelming; her body wanted more of him. She would gladly take as much as he was willing to give. As soon as he laid her down on the bed, she pulled him down to her, not wanting them to be apart.

He started kissing her face, her lips, her cheek, her forehead, then he worked his way down her body. Her shoulders were next to receive his attention, his tongue sliding over her skin and tasting her. He made his way down to her breasts, taking one protruding nipple into his mouth and suckling.

The feelings he was bringing out of her were mind blowing. Her body was reaching for release again and she knew she would find it with him.

"Mitch," she whispered.

He brought his head up from his attention to her breast so he could see her, "Yes, Katie."

His breath whispering across her skin made her blood boil and skin tingle, "I want you," she said through gritted teeth. "Please, I want you inside me."

The sound of Katie begging him to love her was more than he could resist. Without answering, he lifted himself up and guided his hardness into her core. She was tight and wet and sheathed him with her need.

He started slowly, working his way into a faster rhythm to draw out her pleasure. It was difficult because his own body was screaming at him for release but he was determined to hold off until he tipped her over the edge of madness one more time.

"Yes!" Katherine yelled, "Yes!" She was feeling the building wave of climax skirting through her body.

With one last thrust, they both tumbled over into their climaxes.

Minutes later, laying wrapped in one another's arms, Katherine was watching Mitch. His eyes were closed but she knew he wasn't sleeping. He was enjoying the afterglow of their sex. She was exhausted too, but didn't want to stop looking at him.

She wanted to memorize every bit of him. She liked to do that so she could pull out the image later on when she was back in the reality of her life. This would be a lovely reminder of her time here in Hawaii when she met a handsome man who made her happy.

Mitch opened his eyes to see Katie looking at him. She wasn't focused on him though, she was miles away.

"Hey," Mitch whispered, "you look serious."

Reality could wait a while longer, "I'm sorry," she said and kissed him.

Her body fit perfectly against his which made him feel strong and protective of her. He wanted to just stay in bed with her but they should probably get out so they didn't get hurt with all this physical activity.

He sat up against the headboard, pulling her with him. "I forgot to ask you," he said as he finger combed her hair. "When are you going back to New York?"

So much for putting off reality. "I fly to LA on Thursday for a few meetings, then I get back to New York on Saturday." She looked up at him, "You?"

He was let down for sure, "I fly out Wednesday; I have to be back to work on Thursday."

"Well," Katherine said as she sat up, "what should we do between now and then?"

Mitch thought that was a loaded question for sure. "I should, at least, take you sightseeing so you can say you did something touristy."

Katherine nodded, "That would be wise," she was trying to look serious but failing miserably.

Mitch thought she was sweet, "Okay, young lady, where would you like to go for dinner?"

The man should be sainted for referring to her as a "young lady." She kissed him again. "I don't know, let's find out."

She jumped out of bed and ran into the living area to sit down at the desk. She was stark naked but it was her hotel room so she didn't care. She pulled up the internet on her laptop and started looking at restaurants.

Mitch watched her as she sat there looking intently at the computer screen. She was bewitching, sitting there naked, her hair spilling over her shoulders in a curtain of gold. Even though they just made love, he found his body stirring with want.

Katherine scanned the options and motioned Mitch over. "I've made some selections," she kissed his hand when he placed it on her shoulder as he came up behind her.

After a few minutes of debating what they were in the mood to eat, they decided on a quiet local place. Between kisses and touches, they somehow managed to get ready and actually left the hotel an hour later to walk to the restaurant.

Chapter 11

The night was balmy and Katherine was glad they decided to walk to the restaurant. Honolulu was bustling even on a weeknight so there was a lot to see. She always liked living in a city, preferring the noises and conveniences to the country.

Although, truth be told, she never really lived in the country since her father was always assigned to Embassies in large cities. She always thought it was fun to visit museums and go to the theater. Holding Mitch's hand, she mentally wandered as they walked through the streets of Honolulu and dodged tourists waiting in lines for restaurants or clubs.

After a few blocks, the city center gave way to shopping centers and smaller clubs. The restaurant they picked for dinner was tucked in beside an enormous hotel.

They walked in and were greeted by a young hostess with gorgeous long hair and a beautiful smile. Katherine studied the woman's graceful movements as she seated them and wondered if she could remember enough later to sketch her. She smiled warmly as the hostess handed her a menu. Once she and Mitch were left alone, she looked around the room.

Katherine noted that it was warm and welcoming, done in muted Hawaiian décor accented the rich woods of the tables and bar. The staff wore the flowered attire so well known in Hawaii which gave them a laid back appearance.

"I see you thinking again," Mitch said from behind his menu.

Katherine chuckled, "Always."

Slowly, Mitch put his menu down on the table and took her hand in his. "I'll tell you what, young lady," He kissed her fingers, "why don't you take a vacation from your thoughts for a little while and focus on enjoying yourself."

From anyone else, Katherine was fairly certain she would have felt patronized. But from Mitch, she knew he meant it. Of course, he probably had no inkling of the fact that she constantly stood in her own way of doing that.

Katherine smiled at him across the table, the need to touch him was taking over her will, "I will definitely try." She watched his lips as they tenderly touched her skin, making it tingle.

Looking at her, Mitch was breathless. She was beautiful all the time but the soft lighting in the restaurant gave her a waif-like appearance.

Their server came over and asked if they were ready to order. Katherine shot Mitch a salacious smile and placed her order. She'd heard great things about the local seafood so she decided to try it. He ordered steak with a side of seafood and a good bottle of wine.

"You know your wines," she said as the server took their menus.

Mitch smiled. "There are certain things a gentleman should know and wine is one of them."

Katherine cocked her head, considering his statement. "What else should a gentleman know?"

"Well," Mitch took snagged her hand with his fingers again, absently rubbing his thumb along the back of her hand. "He should know wine, have a decent understanding of current world events, ALWAYS hold a door open for a lady, know when he's had enough to drink," he creased his brow trying to remember more.

Smiling, Katherine took a sip of the ice water on the table, "And where did you learn these pearls of wisdom?"

Mitch smiled slowly, "From the smartest person I know, my mom."

Katherine's eyes widened. "Really?" She was shocked that it wasn't some reference to a men's magazine article he'd read at some point.

"Yes really," Mitch leaned over and tapped her nose with his finger, "I am not a mama's boy or anything like that but the woman whipped me into shape long before the girls came into the picture."

Katherine wanted to meet this woman. She had a ton of questions.

He shook his head slowly and said quietly, "No."

"No what?" she asked innocently.

Mitch sighed, "I don't give out my mom's number."

Katherine was torn between laughing and slapping him for being so protective. The comment made her somewhat uncomfortable because it said that there were other women who asked. And, it wasn't like she was a stalker or had a criminal record… but…she was having sex with the woman's son so that could be an uncomfortable situation. She came to the conclusion that he was justified.

"Okay," Katherine said and took another sip of her water.

The server returned with their wine. Opened it, poured a little into a glass for Mitch to taste and left them quietly.

Mitch felt like he was being duped, "That's it?" he asked.

Nodding, Katherine put the glass back down and neatly folded her hands in front of her, "Mitch, you have a right to privacy for yourself and your family." She smiled, "We're lovers now but it's obvious that we wouldn't meet one another's families under these circumstances. The only reason you met my parents was because of their relationship to Eryn and their invitation to Eryn and Chase's wedding."

Anger started to build up in Mitch's gut. He heard the words. Katie definitely sounded calm and rational, and yet it felt like she just insulted him. What the hell!

Katherine could sense his tension. She knew she said something that upset him. "I apologize if I've offended you."

Her apology only made him madder, "I didn't ask for an apology, Katie, I'm a big boy. You've made it plain that this is just sex."

The intended jibe hit its mark with precision and now Katherine was getting upset. "Perhaps we should let it go and talk about something else." She stiffly picked up her glass and took a sip of water.

The last thing Mitch wanted was to argue with Katie, even if her flippant attitude ticked him off. Their time together was short enough; there was no use in wasting it acting like an ass. "I'm sorry, sweetheart," he placed his hand over hers again. "You're right."

Their food arrived, and Katherine thought it was perfect timing. She couldn't understand where the conversation turned wrong but now was not the time to dissect it. They were having a lovely dinner and she didn't want to be the one to spoil it.

Mitch started to eat but his appetite was obstructed by the lump in his throat. He felt awful about his comments. It looked as though Katie was having the same problem.

"Listen." He scooted his chair closer to hers and took her chin in his hand. Their faces were inches apart, "I want to be with you for every second until I get on that plane and I don't want us to argue over something silly." He kissed her softly.

Anger melting away through her toes, Katherine placed her hands on either side of his face; she smiled when he drew away, "I agree."

Taking a deep breath, Mitch took a drink of the wine and poured Katie a glass, "It's pretty good."

The rest of the meal turned out to be very pleasant. They moved along neutral subjects, each of them wanting to avoid the earlier tension. Once the check was delivered and Mitch handed their server his credit card, Katherine excused herself to the restroom. She washed her hands and looked at herself in the mirror.

She looked the same as she always did, long blonde hair with highlights of light brown and red, a slender frame, and yet, there was something a little different in the reflection. Since a public restroom was not the place to delve into her own psyche, she left to rejoin Mitch.

Once they left the restaurant, Mitch held her hand while they walked down the sidewalk. Katherine was relieved. She really didn't want to spend what little time they had left here in Hawaii arguing. The walking did them good too, it let the food settle and gave them time to people watch. Honolulu was very lively at night and Katherine indulged in trying to see everything and everyone.

"Let's go in there," Mitch pointed to a club up the street. There was a group of people around and the music was pretty loud.

Katherine smiled, "Okay."

They walked up and got in fairly quickly. The music was pretty loud so it was tough to hear someone talk, although everyone looked like they were having a good time. Mitch wove through the crowd to the bar and ordered drinks for them.

Katherine was amazed at the people on the dance floor. They moved so gracefully and looked carefree.

Mitch handed her a drink, "Would you like to dance?"

Shaking her head quickly, she smiled, "Oh no." She pointed to the floor, "I can't do that."

Laughing, Mitch guided her to a nearby table that was just vacated. "Me either, but I'd try it for you."

The man was so sweet. "Thank you." She meant it.

They sat down and watched people for a while, commenting here and there about the music or dance moves.

"Is this how it is in New York?" Mitch asked her.

Katherine chuckled, "It might be for some but this isn't how I choose to spend my time."

She was very cryptic with her answers, she never explained. It made Mitch wonder about her life there again.

Katherine looked down into the melting ice in her glass. She felt like they were still a little "off" from their conversation in the restaurant. She wasn't very good at working things out and it frustrated her. She looked over to see Mitch watching her. He was handsome with a slight smile on his face like she fascinated him or something. It aroused her and made her curious at the same time.

"What shall we do tomorrow?" Katherine asked. She wanted to stop feeling so uncomfortable about his studying of her.

Mitch felt the words like ice water on his body. He did not want to think about leaving yet. "Whatever you want," he answered.

She lifted her hand and placed it over his. "I want you," she said loudly so he could hear her over the music.

His body responded immediately, a couple of words from Katie and he was lost in a storm of desire. "I want you too, Katie."

To hear Mitch say the words was more than she could fight. Her body started pulsing with need. "Then why are we sitting here?"

Mitch thought the woman was smart, "No idea, let's go."

He moved so fast that Katherine started to giggle. It was like telling a kid they could finally have candy. Honestly, she felt the same way. It was far more interesting to see what they could do in the hotel room than sit here in a loud club and watch others.

The trek back to the hotel was short but they stopped to steal a kiss along the way. They were trying to stave off the need each of them felt rising up inside. A lovely tree provided a moment's seclusion a block from the hotel. Katherine pulled Mitch behind it and kissed him madly. Her hands wove through his hair and held him close as her lips assaulted his. She couldn't remember feeling so physically needy around a man.

After being kissed thoroughly, Mitch smiled and opened his eyes. "Lady, you are quite the kisser."

Katherine blushed, "It's easy when you have such a good partner."

"C'mon," Mitch said lowly. He wanted her in the room and naked as fast as possible.

They were engrossed in one another as they entered the lobby of the hotel. So much so that they didn't see Katherine's father until he was right in front of them.

"Katherine," Marcus Fredricks said directly. He watched his daughter as she came into the building, her arms wrapped around Mitch. The site did not make him happy.

It was like a bucket of ice water being thrown onto Katherine's skin. She pulled away from Mitch and absently ran her fingers over her clothing.

Mitch watched Katie's dad and felt the anger stream through his body. He wasn't sure if he was more upset by the man's tone or Katie's response to him; she pulled away as if she was embarrassed that they were together.

"Father," Katherine said softly.

Mitch watched the exchange between father and daughter and he didn't get it.

Marcus cleared his throat, "I expect more out of you."

Being chastised in a hotel lobby when she was over thirty years old was a bit much for Katherine to take in.

"What!" Katherine shouted. The sound of her raised voice shocked her as much as it shocked her father. He stood there, speechless.

Mitch didn't say anything, he wanted to see how this would play out.

Closing her eyes, Katherine sighed, "Dad," she tried to remain calm, "I'm an adult on vacation."

Marcus tried to interject but stopped when his daughter raised her finger to stop him.

"If I want to spend time with someone who makes me happy, then I'll do it." She pursed her lips together, smiled tightly, then grabbed Mitch's hand and walked to the elevator, leaving her father in the middle of the lobby staring after her.

The ride up to her room was quiet. Katherine didn't dare speak, she was too keyed up from the embarrassing scene with her father. Never, in all of her life, did she ever raise her voice to him. It felt good and scary all at the same time.

Mitch watched Katie out of the corner of his eye. Perhaps he should have interjected but in the short time he'd known Katie, he sensed that she needed to find her own footing; especially where her parents were concerned.

Katherine unlocked her hotel room, walked in, and waited for Mitch to enter, then she pushed him up against the door. Her lips sought his, for comfort, for reassurance, for release. His response was quick which only drove her desire. She pulled at his shirt so she could feel his skin with her fingers.

This Katie was different, Mitch realized as he allowed her access to his body. This Katie was a little wild.

Katherine wanted her lips to taste every part of him. She was finally able to free him from the shirt and started kissing his shoulders. The muscles rippled under her lips.

"Mitch, you are so beautiful," Katherine whispered against his skin.

Her comment humbled him enough that he pulled away to look into her beautiful eyes, "You are beautiful, Katie," he leaned down and kissed her gently, "so beautiful."

The kiss deepened immediately. Neither of them could contain the want they felt. Mitch swept her up into his arms and walked her to the bedroom. If there was anywhere in the world he'd rather be than right here with Katie, he couldn't think of it. She made him feel alive.

Being laid down gently on the bed, Katherine felt cherished. His eyes were dark with need, and reflected her own. She ran her hands up and down his arms as they held her gently. She shivered when he lifted his fingertips up to brush a strand of hair from her face.

"Mitch," she looked up into his eyes, "why do I feel this way when you touch me?"

The question aroused him even more, "I don't know, Katie," he smiled. "I feel the same way as soon as I look at you, or touch you, or feel you."

Katherine didn't want any more words. She reached up and pulled him down to kiss her and relieve the aching she felt in her body and in her soul.

Katherine ran her hands up and down his back as he made love to her with his lips. She pulled at his pants and got them off, along with her own dress, in record time. When she was stretched out naked beneath him, her chest heaving in anticipation, she looked up at him and wanted to always remember this moment.

Mitch entered her warmth and was lost in a whirlpool of need and sensation. He would never be able to describe the enormity and complexity of his feelings, nor would he ever want to. They were private, like his feelings for Katie, his alone.

They made love until they were exhausted. They slept entwined in one another's arms, waking only to make love again. It was magical, being so in-tuned physically to one another. They anticipated each other's needs and were only sated when the first rays of sun peeked up over the horizon.

The phone ringing brought Mitch to the surface of consciousness. His body craved sleep but the damn phone just kept ringing. He opened one eye and saw Katie sprawled out on the bed beside him. Smiling, he grabbed for the phone, hoping not to wake her up.

"Hello," he said, hoarse from sleep.

Marcus Fredricks didn't care if he woke the man up, this was important. "Mitch, this is Marcus Fredricks," he said in a clipped tone that demanded attention.

Mitch sat up straighter. Oh great, Katie's dad. "Yes, sir," he returned.

"I'd like to meet with you to discuss my daughter," Marcus stated.

Shaking his head in frustration, Mitch took a breath, "That's fine, sir." He knew it would be no use to explain to the man that his daughter was a grown woman and it would certainly be no good to explain that she was next to him in bed.

Marcus nodded in satisfaction, "Let's say a half hour in the lobby."

Mitch looked at his phone for the first time, "Yes, sir."

The line went dead and Mitch pushed the disconnect button.

"My father, right?" Katherine asked from her side of the bed. She opened her eyes and saw Mitch looking tense. Only her father could prompt such a reaction first thing in the morning.

Mitch nodded and smiled, "Yep."

Katherine sat up, pulling the sheet with her. She didn't know why she wanted to cover up, the man had seen every inch of her.

Smiling, Mitch took her hand and brought it to his lips, "He's just posturing, it's a guy thing."

Frustrated, Katherine stood up, "No!" she started pacing, "It's him just, just trying to control my life!"

Mitch was a little confused. If this thing between them was just sex, as she kept saying, then why did her father's reaction bother her?

"Well, I have to go and meet him in twenty-five minutes so I'm going to go down and get ready." He got up and started looking for his clothes.

Katherine was panicked, "Are you coming back?"

Her tone had Mitch stopping to turn and look at her. He saw fear in her eyes and walked over to her, "Katie," he kissed the tip of her nose, "this is not a big deal."

She was not convinced about that but she appreciated the fact that he didn't seem intimidated by her father. Over the years, her father was most likely the culprit in the demise of most of her relationships. It basically made her resistant to starting anything with anyone.

Mitch got back down to his own room a few minutes later and jumped in the shower. He shaved and dressed in some khaki shorts and a red polo shirt. It was a bit casual but he didn't care.

As the elevator doors opened twenty minutes later, Mitch saw Marcus Fredricks sitting at the far end of the lobby. The man would probably be imposing to most guys but Mitch saw him for what he was, a bully. He started towards him and stopped only when he spotted Eryn's dad coming toward them from the other direction.

"Tom," Marcus said to his brother, "what are you doing here?"

Shaking his head, Tom Fredricks sat down beside his brother.

Mitch decided there was no use in trying to avoid the two men, he walked up to where they sat extended his hand to each of them. "Mr. Fredricks, General," he said formally.

"I'm just here as a brother," Tom Fredricks said.

Mitch nodded and sat down across from them. He looked pointedly at Katie's father, "You wanted to speak with me, sir?"

Marcus nodded, "Yes," he stole a quick glance at his brother then looked back at the young man, "I'd like you to stop seeing my daughter."

Trying not to laugh, Mitch cleared his throat, "Is there any particular issue you have with me, sir?"

Marcus was surprised at the question since most of the young men he warned off just obeyed. "Not really, I just don't believe you are the right man for my daughter."

Well, Mitch thought, at least he was honest. "Well, sir, I have to say that I remember your brother having a very similar conversation with Chase a decade ago and that turned out badly." He looked at Tom Fredricks, hoping he hadn't insulted the man.

Marcus looked at his brother, "Is that so?"

Tom Fredricks nodded, "Yes it is." He wasn't proud of the fact that he interfered with Chase and Eryn's relationship years earlier.

"But besides that," Mitch said calmly, "sir, with all due respect, your daughter is an adult and fully capable of deciding who she would like to spend time with." He tried to keep his voice even, "She has expressed to me that this is a short term relationship and hasn't said she wanted to continue seeing me after she leaves Hawaii so hopefully that alleviates your concerns." He didn't even wait for Katie's father to answer, he got up, nodded to the men and left the lobby. He decided he needed a walk on the beach to clear his head.

Tom Fredricks smiled as he watched Mitch leave the lobby. His eyes returned to his brother and he had to fight back laughter at the look of absolute rage that radiated from Marcus.

"That man," Marcus Fredricks said through gritted teeth.

Tom placed a hand on his brother's shoulder, "Just put you in your place, Marcus."

Marcus looked at his brother's delight in the situation and wanted to punch him, "It's not funny, Tom."

"Of course it's not," Tom started, "for you." He put his hands up when his brother made a move toward him, "If Chase would have said that to me when I was ballsy enough to run him off, I would've been pissed, but then I would've respected him for it."

Katherine was upstairs in her parents' suite trying to get information out of her mother. Surprisingly, Victoria had no idea her husband was downstairs "warning off" Mitch. She told Katherine that had she known in advance she would never have let her husband go down. It was humiliating for their daughter and he should be ashamed of himself for his behavior. She tried to comfort Katherine with her words.

"I'm so sorry, my love," she said to Katherine as she pulled her close.

Sinking into her mother's embrace, Katherine fought back tears, "I like him, Mother." She dared not say anything else.

"Sweetheart," Victoria set her daughter away from her so she could see her face, "anyone within a ten mile radius can see that you like him."

248

Smiling, Katherine nodded, "I suppose." She walked to the window and looked down to the beach; people wear playing and acting carefree.

Victoria came up to her daughter, "Don't let anyone, especially your father, decide who you want to be with for you."

Katherine nodded, "You're right." She took a breath, "Besides, he's leaving tomorrow and this will all be done."

Victoria watched her daughter leave and knew that her daughter was going to hurt tomorrow. She may think this was "all done" but it was really only just starting. She just prayed that Katherine was smart enough to see what Mitch offered her and was willing to go after the happiness she deserved.

Mitch strolled along the beach for a while. He was pissed at the audacity of Katie's dad but even more upset at the fact that he was leaving tomorrow and would probably never see her again. 'So why are you out here walking along the beach instead of with her, you ass!' he said to himself.

Katherine saw him walking toward her on the beach. She got worried when he didn't answer the door to his room and she didn't see him or her father in the lobby, so she went outside and started looking around for him.

She watched him move and was absorbed in everything about him. The way he moved; so assured. The way he looked; as lost in his thoughts as she was most days. She stood there and smiled until he was close enough and noticed her.

"Hey," Mitch whispered when he noticed Katie standing in front of him. Without thinking, he took her into his arms and kissed her.

His touch warmed her from the inside out, Katherine reveled in the feel of his lips on hers. She was relieved that he didn't seem upset about the spectacle her father made.

Katherine held him tight, "I'm so sorry about my father," she whispered into his ear.

Mitch pulled away and looked at her face, she was so beautiful, glowing in the sunlight. "I'm not afraid of him," he tried to sound casual.

"I'm so glad," she responded. She followed his lead as he started walking back toward the hotel.

They walked around the massive building to the parking lot where Mitch parked Chase's jeep. Katherine had no idea where they were going and didn't really care as long as she was with him. She got in without a word and buckled up.

The drive through Honolulu was a little slow as the work week traffic congested the freeway. But, once they were clear of downtown, Mitch took the Hwy Sixty-One exit. The highway split through the southern part of the island and took them up through the Koolau Mountains. Chase told Mitch about the drive and said it was beautiful so he thought Katie would like it.

An hour later, Mitch saw the sign he was looking for and pulled off the highway. It was considerably cooler up here since they were in the middle of the mountains, but the views were spectacular. He pulled into the designated parking area and went around to help Katie out.

"Where are we?" Katherine asked.

"The Nu'uanu Pali Lookout," Mitch said. "Don't ask me to repeat that either, it won't happen."

Katherine chuckled, "Okay."

They walked down with the other sightseers and walked up to a wall. Before them was a view of the windward side of the island and it was breathtaking. Katherine grabbed her phone and snapped some pictures. She wasn't the tourist type normally but this was something she wanted to remember. It was a panoramic view of lush greens that travelled to the ocean in the distance.

Mitch watched Katie more than the stunning landscape in front of them. In his mind, she was much more fascinating to look at. It was windy so her hair was being freed strand by strand by the winds blowing up against them. Strands of the spun gold whirred around her head in mesmerizing dances.

Awareness of Mitch's eyes drew Katherine out of her scrutiny of the valley below. His eyes created a trail of heat on her skin with their intensity. She smiled but didn't look at him, "What are you looking at?" she asked.

Mitch smiled, "At you."

She finally turned to gaze into his eyes, "At me?"

"Yes," Mitch whispered and pulled her into his arms. After a minute, he turned her so he was to her back and they could look out at the expanse of island before them.

Katherine could feel him around her and felt very safe, "Why?"

Mitch rested his chin on the top of her head, it was warm from the sun, "Why not?"

She was becoming frustrated, "Why are you answering my questions with questions?"

Mitch didn't dare laugh, she'd hit him for sure, "Because I like getting you riled up." The truth was always the best.

She appreciated his honesty, "Well, that's something."

Her voice was deadpan and he laughed. "Come on now," he turned her so she was facing him again, "I'm just teasing you, Katie." He kissed her, "I love looking at you."

The honesty in his eyes moved her. "Thank you."

"You are welcome." He leaned down and captured her lips with his. The sensual movement of their lips together excited her.

Reluctantly pulling back, Katherine smiled, "Well, let's eat, I'm hungry."

Mitch released her, "You are a very intuitive woman, Katie." He turned and grabbed her hand, "I'm famished."

Hand in hand, they walked back up to the jeep. Mitch helped Katie into the vehicle and walked around to hop in the driver's seat. It didn't escape his notice that she leaned over to catch one last glimpse of the scenery before they turned back onto the highway.

After a lunch in Kailua, Mitch and Katherine walked along the shops there. Katherine explained that she had to do some shopping for her assistants and a few friends in New York. He nodded but wanted to forget that they would have to face the real world too soon.

Once the gifts were bought, they decided to head back to the hotel. Mitch's flight was leaving early and he needed to pack.

A feeling of dread started to seep into in Katherine's chest. This was not at all what she expected to feel like when they parted ways. Walking back to the jeep, she stole glances at Mitch and wondered if he felt the same way.

Mitch walked along side Katie and knew she was thinking of tomorrow and them separating. He could hardly think of anything else. For him, saying goodbye was part of his job. Being in the Marine Corps for this many years, he stood in airports dozens of times and watched his mom cry or his sister tear up because he was leaving. But this was the first time he could remember having real reservations about it.

Chapter 12

Mitch parked the jeep in the hotel parking lot but didn't make a move to get out. The atmosphere between them was becoming tenser as the day went on.

"Listen," he turned to face Katie, "I don't want to worry about tomorrow and the fact that I have to get on that plane and leave you." He took her hand and brought her fingers to his lips. "I'd rather just spend every minute I can with you until then."

Katherine smiled and nodded but couldn't shake the feeling of trepidation. She just didn't want to be away from him. Instead of saying what she felt, she just nodded and murmured, "Okay."

They grabbed the bags of souvenirs and went into the hotel.

A few minutes later, Mitch got off on his floor. He wanted to get packed and get the gifts situated before they made plans for the rest of the day. The truth was, he was relieved when Katie nodded in agreement. He needed a few minutes to get himself together.

Entering the room, he thought it was like any other room except that this was the room that Katie shared with him. Come to think of it, they'd only made love in hotel rooms. Smiling, he took his stuff into the bedroom and started packing.

Katherine got into her room a few minutes later and plopped down on the sofa. Not very ladylike but there was no one here to tell on her so she didn't really care. Mitch was a few floors down packing and she was up here pouting. She stood and walked over to the window hoping the amazing view of the ocean would ease her mind.

She felt like one of the waves coming toward shore. Little did it know it would crash against the sand and be obliterated. Is that what would happen to her tomorrow? Would it be fine when they said goodbye or would it be like crashing into nothingness?

The phone ringing caused her to put her maudlin thoughts on hold as she went over to answer it. The caller ID said a number she didn't recognize. "Hello?" she asked.

"If this is Katie Fredricks, then I'm your date for the evening," Mitch said lightly.

She couldn't help it, she smiled. "This is she and I sure hope so."

Mitch threw his clothes into the suitcase. "I'm almost done here, I'll be up in a few minutes if that's okay with you?"

Katherine smiled, "Yes, I'll freshen up."

After hanging up, Mitch threw the rest of his stuff in the suitcases he brought and took out some clothes in case they went out for dinner this evening. He checked his laptop to make sure his flight itinerary was good and checked in on line.

The knock at the door had Katie running, she was smiling when she threw it open, thinking it was Mitch. Her smile fell away when she saw that it was her father instead.

"Katherine," Marcus Fredricks said stiffly.

Katherine nodded, "Father, would you like to come in." Years of training in the art of being a good hostess had her asking before she thought about it. Mitch would be here any minute and she did not want a repeat performance of this morning.

Marcus entered the room, his hands pinned to his sides; he was not good at this sort of thing. "Katherine, your mother insisted I come to your room and apologize for my behavior with Mr. Frinnel earlier." He lifted his chin defiantly, "Although I feel justified in my actions, I am the only one who does."

It was so tempting to laugh but Katherine used her resolve to keep from doing so. Her father was most certainly uncomfortable and wasn't used to apologizing. But she couldn't let him suffer either, she let the incident go earlier when Mitch reassured her he wasn't upset about it.

"I accept your apology," she said and stepped forward to give him a quick kiss on the cheek.

The interplay between them was certainly strained but Marcus was glad she forgave him. He didn't want to deal with both his wife and daughter being upset with him. "I know this is only for the duration of your stay here so I need not have worried."

His comment brought Katherine to a standstill. "I'm sorry?" she asked.

Marcus cleared his throat, "Mr. Frinnel said that you made it clear you were only seeing him during your trip here in Hawaii so I will let this go."

The man was insufferable. "Father, would it have mattered?"

"Would what have mattered?" he asked his daughter.

Katherine started pacing in front of him, "Would it have mattered had I said I intended to keep seeing him after my vacation?"

"Well," Marcus blundered, "I," he wasn't sure what to say.

Katherine walked back to the door and opened it, "I guess it doesn't matter now," she waited quietly for her father to leave.

He wasn't sure what he did but he was pretty sure his daughter was still upset with him. He walked through the door as confused as ever. The women in his life could make him crazy.

After watching her father leave, Katherine shut the door forcefully and walked back to the sofa. That's what Mitch told him? She wanted to be upset with Mitch but knew it was not fair. She never said anything about them seeing one another after this. Maybe that's what he wanted? There was only one way to find out.

Mitch was walking down the hall to Katie's room when he saw her father coming toward him. Oh, this should be good. "Mr. Fredricks," Mitch said and nodded to the other man in acknowledgement.

Marcus stopped, "Mr. Frinnel," he stuck his hand out.

Surprised, Mitch shook the other man's hand, "Have a great day, sir."

Nodding, Marcus let go of the younger man's hand. "You too."

That was a little weird, Mitch thought as he continued on to Katie's room. He knocked and waited. When she answered, he could tell she was upset.

Mitch came into the room, "I just passed your dad in the hall."

She nodded, "Yes, he came to apologize for this morning and his behavior with you."

Mitch's eyebrows raised, "Well that was nice of him."

Katherine cocked her head, "Do you mean that sarcastically?" She couldn't tell.

"No," Mitch said slowly, "are we going to argue?"

She couldn't help it, she had to laugh now, "No," she walked to where he stood and put her arms around his neck, "we are most certainly not going to argue."

He kept his eyes open so he could watch her as he leaned down to kiss her. Her lashes slowly closed and rested on her smooth skin. Her lips met his and all rational thought left his brain.

The kiss took on its own life as they stood in the middle of the sitting area of her hotel suite. Hands began moving over skin, slowly removing clothing. Sighs were shared as lips traveled over skin and found new places to taste. The light from the sun came through the windows and warmed their skin as they explored one another. Mitch only left her briefly to get a blanket from the bedroom. He laid it down on the floor in the sitting area and knelt down.

"Are you going to join me?" he asked Katie. She was so gorgeous, her clothes tugged every which way, her lips red from his kisses.

Katherine gave him her hand, "Of course," she whispered as she knelt down in front of him.

They made quick work of removing the rest of their clothes. They settled into each other's arms to slowly make love.

Katherine touched him and felt giddy with need. He made her feel everything. The sensation of his lips on her skin, the way he held her to him, it was as if he was protecting her from the rest of the world. Her chest felt tight and free at the same time. The contradiction confused her. Reluctantly, she pulled away, but only far enough so she could look into Mitch's eyes.

"Are you okay?" Mitch asked. She moved away and he wondered if she was upset.

Katherine looked at him, searching his eyes, "Why am I so sad and so happy at the same time?"

The question threw him. She wanted answers but he couldn't be the one to give them to her. "I feel the same way," he whispered and bent to kiss her shoulder.

Katherine cradled his head against her, "You feel so good," she all but purred.

"So do you, Katie," Mitch said against her skin. "I want you so much."

The words calmed her fears and that would have to be enough for now. She moved so she was laid out on the blanket in front of him. "Please," she reached for him, "make love with me."

Mitch nodded, a ball of emotion filling his chest. He was as confused as she was but, right now, all he could do was show her all he felt. He ran his palms up her legs relishing in the softness of her skin against his. Moving her legs, he knelt between them and positioned himself to enter her softness. He looked into her eyes as their bodies joined and let out a breath. She was heaven here on earth and made his body sing with want.

Katherine watched Mitch above her, loving her body, looking lost in the passion they created between them. It was awe-inspiring to see him look at her as if she were the last drop of water. She understood his need because hers was the same.

She was having trouble focusing as his movements sped up. Release was clawing at her belly, wanting to be let free, but she wanted to wait as long as possible so they could tumble over the edge together. His breathing was becoming more ragged, just like hers. She couldn't contain the pent up orgasm any longer; it rushed over her in a wave of bright light.

"Yes!" Katherine called out.

Mitch was right behind her, his climax at the precipice of insanity, "Yes, baby," he said.

He followed her into the mindless madness their bodies reached. Afterwards, they snuggled up together on the blanket on the floor, holding one another as their minds and bodies settled.

Mitch absently ran his fingers down Katie's arm. Her skin was soft and inviting. He smiled into her hair, its tendrils tickling his nose. His other arm pulled her closer to him. There were things to talk about but right now he only wanted to feel her next to him.

Katherine turned over so she was facing him, absently pushing her hair back out of her face. "Thank you," she said to Mitch, a smile playing on her lips.

"No, thank you," Mitch replied. He kissed her lips and lingered for a moment.

Katherine sat up, not worrying about covers, he'd seen every part of her so what was the point of covering up now? "I want to sketch you," she said as she ran her fingers through his hair.

Mitch turned over onto his back, his arm was behind his head for a pillow. "Why?"

"Because I want to," Katherine responded. She didn't know why, only that she wanted to draw him.

As Mitch lay there watching her, he couldn't deny her this. "Sure, why not," he said softly.

Katherine got up quickly and ran to get her sketch pad and pencils. She sat back down unceremoniously and started to sketch, her hands flying across the page.

Mitch studied her as she drew him. She was sitting there naked, still flushed from their lovemaking, and drawing him. He felt exposed, wondering what she saw when she looked at him. And his body was starting to stir again. He wouldn't be embarrassed because wanting Katie was like breathing to him now.

Katherine did the sketch quickly and with just the pencil. It required more shading but it was how she wanted this one to look. The other one of Mitch was done with charcoal and seemed rougher. This sketch took shape quickly. When she put the last mark on the paper, she looked up to see Mitch with his eyes closed. He'd fallen asleep. Putting the paper and pencil aside, she lay down beside him and watched him.

His chest rose and fell rhythmically with his deep breathing. She wanted so badly to touch the little hairs there she knew would tickled her fingertips. But she needed to let him rest. Instead, she just studied him with her eyes, wanting to commit every inch of him to memory before he left tomorrow. That would have to be enough.

Mitch opened his eyes to see the sun low in the sky. The shadows in the room were deep. It took a minute for him to realize where he was. Once he looked over to see Katie sleeping softly beside him on the floor, he was slammed with the feeling of desperation. He was desperate to touch her, he was desperate to feel her, and he couldn't shake it.

Sensations ran through her body as Katherine stretched in sleep. The feelings were wonderful, touches on her skin, warm breath against it. She woke up in increments, finally feeling the full force of intense need Mitch brought out in her. When she opened her eyes, she could see the top of his dark hair, his lips were exciting delicious sensations against her flaming skin. His touch brought her to the highest level of awareness. She could feel her own body waking up from sleep, little by little, as each part of her tuned into her need for him. She smiled when he lifted his head and looked into her eyes.

"I want you," Mitch said softly.

She didn't want to talk so she ran her hand alongside his cheek and nodded. For right now, words weren't necessary.

Mitch trailed kisses up her belly, over her luscious breasts, and found the place at the base of her neck that drove her crazy.

It was knowing that little secret about Katie that made him want her even more. He knew some of her secrets and wanted to take the time to find them all.

Katherine sighed, her body drowning in a pool of physical needs. It made her want to be stronger, better, please him every way she could. She put her hands around his neck and used her body to flip them over. Now she was on top and in charge. She looked down to see a smug smile on Mitch's face. She wanted nothing more than wipe it away and replace it with a frenzied need. Her fingers trailed up his sides, leaving awareness in their wake. She leaned down and tasted the skin just below his ear.

When she pulled up, the look of smugness was replaced with the intense look she wanted to see. Katherine stared down at his chiseled features, wanting to bring him everything she could physically.

Watching Katie watch him was unsettling. It was like watching someone at an art gallery, staring at a painting and trying to figure out what the artist was trying to convey. It was a silly comparison and yet, it seemed about right when he thought of Katie. She was all about sensations, textures, and experiences. He wanted to give her all of that and more.

Katherine's hair slid down and made a blanket over Mitch's tanned skin. She usually hated that it was in the way but now she was mesmerized by the additional sensations it made when it slid over her skin. She moved so she could take him inside her. Sliding slowly, she wanted to feel every millimeter of movement between them. Her body was ready, accepting him until she was astride his hips. Taking a moment, she threw her head back to just feel him as he filled her completely.

Mitch lay beneath Katie and watched in amazement as she moved over him slowly. His body was on fire, only shadowed by the feelings in his chest as she made love to him. Her hair fell over her shoulder, covering one breast, the tips of the golden strands sweeping across his chest. Her skin held a sheen of glistening from their lovemaking; he wanted to feel everything she was willing to give him and so much more.

Katherine threw her head back and her hands grabbed Mitch's. She moved her fingers so they were entwined with his and leaned back. The slight shift in position made her belly burn with excitement. She picked up speed, reaching for the apex she knew they would bring to one another.

"More!" Katherine yelled.

Mitch was moving beneath her, his hips thrusting up as her moved forward. Faster, faster, he kept saying in his head. They were so close now. He could feel her hard nub of desire as it slid down him. The friction was hot and slick and rocked him to the core of his being.

At last Katherine was swept over the edge. The trip down was no less moving than the climb up as far as she was concerned. It was like a feather drifting slowly to the ground after being shed from a bird in flight. She could feel her body softly come down to earth.

Mitch watched her and wondered how he could enjoy just looking at someone so much. She was a piece of art all by herself. Her emotions were plainly written on her face, satisfaction of a woman who'd just been loved. It made him feel strong.

Katherine looked over to see Mitch studying her. "Hello there," she whispered.

He couldn't resist, he leaned down and kissed her softly, "Hello there," he whispered back.

The light from the city was now pouring into the windows. Katherine looked around to find her phone. She pushed a button and the screen illuminated her face. "It's already eight?" She couldn't believe it. Why did the time fly so fast when they were together?

Crap, Mitch thought. "Really?" He asked.

Katherine showed him her phone and frowned. "Are you hungry?"

He could see the change in her, it was subtle, but he could see the tension starting to take root in her features. He was upset about their time growing shorter too but life had to start up again. They couldn't stay here on vacation forever, no matter how much they wanted to. Of course, he was really only speaking for himself; he shouldn't use the word they because he wasn't sure how she felt.

"Mitch?" Katherine asked. He was lost in thought and didn't answer her question.

Mitch looked over at Katie, "I'm sorry, baby." He kissed her lips. They were so soft, he wanted to just feel them on his for the rest of the night.

Katherine sat up, absently pushing her hair over her shoulder, "Are you hungry?" She didn't want to ask the questions that were plaguing her mind right now.

His stomach answered for him, its rumbling filling the quiet room. "Sorry," he said sheepishly.

She smiled and stood, "I am too, don't worry." She held her hand out to him and took it while he stood.

Katherine walked over and flipped on a light, its glow filling the room. She dug up the room amenities folder and sat down on the sofa.

It was so easy to watch her, Mitch thought as he grabbed his shorts. He joined her on the couch and handed her his t-shirt.

Sliding the shirt over her skin, Katherine loved that she could smell Mitch on the fabric. He sat beside her, his mere presence giving her comfort. They paged through the menu the hotel offered and debated over a breakfast or dinner appetite. They each settled on their choices and Katherine called downstairs to place the order.

Mitch walked into the bathroom to splash water on his face. He looked up into the mirror, the droplets of water running down his skin. Here was a man who'd been just completely made love to and he was damn happy about it too. He heard Katie hang up so went back into the sitting room.

Katherine was sitting on the sofa and watched him walk toward her. He was so tall and handsome. A pretty clichéd observation but she didn't care. "They'll be here in twenty to thirty minutes," she said as he sat down and took her into his arms.

"Okay," Mitch said.

She leaned back into his arms and sighed. "Are we going to talk about what neither of us wants to talk about?"

There it was, the opening both wanted but didn't want. He leaned forward and kissed the top of her head, "I suppose."

That was not a good sign, Katherine thought. She turned to face him. "Tomorrow is coming whether we want it or not." It was a statement, nothing more.

This woman could sum it up for sure. "I realize that, Katie, and I want to talk to you but it's tough because I'm not sure what you're thinking."

She nodded, "Is it because you told my father that this," she gestured between them, "was only while we were here in Hawaii?"

For some reason, her saying it pissed him off, "Yes!" The word was stated sharply and he stood. He walked to the window, not saying anything for a few minutes, then he turned back around, "Isn't that what you said?"

She couldn't deny it, "Yes I did," she whispered. Tears were fighting their way up but she would not let them spill, even though it hurt not to.

Mitch's only consolation was that she looked as miserable about them parting as he felt. But still, neither of them said the words. "Well, what do you want?"

Her rational mind was saying, end it now, but her heart was yelling for her to tell him they'd make it work somehow. She'd been around Marines her whole life, she knew they came and went to new duty stations. She knew that there were no bases in New York. And she knew that she wasn't sure she would want to live anywhere else but New York because that's where her life was.

Mitch watched her internal battle. She was thinking it through like he was; the options, the obstacles. Lord knew he kept pouring over them in his own mind as well.

"I think," Katherine said as she stood and walked toward him, "that we both know tonight is our last night and we should just be together." She put her hands around his waist and stepped closer.

Her words hurt but he understood. He put his arms around her and laid his head on hers. Even if this was it, he wanted her to be with him for every minute of it. They'd both smart from it but that was part of life. "Okay," he said against her hair.

There was a knock at the door and Mitch went to answer it. He took the tray from the waiter and gave the kid some money with extra enough that the kid smiled like it was his lucky day.

They set up the food on the small table in the sitting area and ate slowly, each debating on what to say or do afterwards.

Katherine finished eating, leaving most of her meal on the plate. The hunger she had earlier seemed to have left her. "How's your meal?" she asked Mitch.

He was having the same problem, "It's fine," he answered.

"Let's not do this," Katherine said shortly. She was getting frustrated and hated feeling it.

Putting his fork down on the plate quietly, Mitch stood and walked back over to the window, "I know," he said while looking out the smooth glass.

What did she say? There wasn't anything she could say, "Do you want to go back to your room?" She stood and walked up behind him. He didn't answer her. "I want you to stay with me but I understand if you want to go."

Did she understand? Mitch wondered. She was awfully calm about all of this. Maybe she didn't feel how he felt? Like tomorrow was going to be tough because they wouldn't be together. He turned around, "No, I'd like to stay here with you."

His answer settled Katherine's heart. "Good," she said quietly.

Without saying anything more, Katherine took him by the hand and led him to the bedroom. They would make love every minute they could until he had to go.

Morning light broke into the room and Mitch opened his eyes. He was exhausted physically from being up most of the night with Katie but he felt great. Smiling, he looked over to see her nestled against him. She was warm and smelled like summer. Knowing he had an early flight, he looked over at the bedside clock and grimaced. He had to get up and going if he was going to make his flight.

Katherine felt movement and opened her eyes. Once her vision cleared, she saw Mitch sitting beside her on the bed. He was dressed and his hair was still a little wet from the shower. How did she sleep through him getting up?

"What time is it?" she asked.

Mitch smiled, "It's early but I need to catch my flight in about an hour."

No!, she yelled on the inside, "I know," she murmured into his arm as she clung to it.

Mitch smiled, "I left all my contact numbers on the table by your laptop. My work, cell, and home. You call me whenever you want to." His words caught in his throat.

Katherine looked up into his face, he was smiling but it was purely for show. She knew it and he knew it. "Okay."

Mitch shifted slightly so she could sit up. He looked into her sleepy eyes, "Thank you, Katie, for giving me so much."

The words made her throat tight and her chest hurt. She couldn't speak so she only nodded.

He kissed her softly, his hands running down her arms one more time. "I'll wait to hear from you," he whispered and got up to leave.

Katherine laid there in bed for a few minutes letting the weight of their separation settle over her like a wet blanket.

Mitch went up to his room to get his bags. He showered in Katie's room so he only had to throw on some deodorant and cologne and he was off. He went down to the lobby, his steps heavy, and checked out with no issues. The staff was smiling and wished him a safe trip and all he could do was nod. He took a shuttle to the airport, listening to the other passengers carry on conversations about their Hawaiian experiences.

Getting through the line at the airport was easy, he was already checked in and took his bags over to the security check line for baggage. After dropping the bags off, he turned to head toward the security gate for passengers when he heard someone yelling his name.

"Mitch!" Katherine yelled when she spotted him in the airport terminal.

Two minutes after he left, she couldn't think of anything except being with him for just a little longer. She washed up and threw on clothes and tried to catch him in the lobby but the shuttle had just left. She grabbed a cab and chased after it like some crazed lunatic. Now she was calling across a crowded room for him and smiling like an idiot.

Mitch walked over, "What are you doing here?" he asked.

She didn't answer, only pulled him to her. She kissed him desperately, as if her whole life depended on their lips together. When she pulled away, she laughed at the shocked expression on his face.

"I needed to say goodbye properly," Katherine murmured.

He laughed, "I think that was great." He pulled her into his arms and held her tightly.

Katherine looked up at him, "I know you have to go," she nodded to the security line, "but I will be calling you, Mitchell Frinnel, and you better answer the phone when I do."

Mitch's world was now right, "I'll answer, Miss Fredricks, but don't wait too long." He smiled and kissed her one last time. Her lips tasted sweet and he wanted to feel them again, soon.

He stepped back and cupped her face in his hands, staring into her eyes, telling her everything with them he couldn't say with his lips. Another quick kiss and he turned to go.

Katherine stood there in the airport and watched him go, torn between laughing and crying.

Chapter 13

Los Angeles was rainy when Katie landed there Thursday afternoon. The weather matched her mood perfectly. She was here for work but couldn't seem to clear her mind. After Mitch left the day before she went back to the hotel and got her things in order for her flight.

She called her assistant, Suzanna, who thought she'd dropped off the face of the earth because she hadn't called the office in days. There were a million things to take care of for work and, for the first time, Katherine was just not that interested in doing them. This new Katherine was not someone she was familiar with and she didn't really like her.

The car service picked her up at the airport and took her to the hotel she would be staying at the next two nights. It was upscale and the staff was fantastic but she kept comparing it to the hotels she stayed in with Mitch. She got ready for her dinner meeting and wondered if the food would be like the meals she and Mitch shared. After applying her makeup and doing last minute checks of her appearance, she chastised herself for her behavior.

She arrived at the five star restaurant and met with one of the investors who backed her new line, a Mr. Harold Werstead. The meal was fine and the conversation revolved around business so it was easy to participate in it. She brought out the sketches she started in Wyoming and waited for the response.

"These are different," Mr. Werstead said as he poured over the drawings. "Definitely edgy but I like them."

Katherine was relieved. She was still relatively new in the world of clothing design so having investors was important to get her business off.

Harold set them aside and smiled. He was a man in his late fifties, widowed, and looking to find things to distract him. A friend introduced him to the young Miss Fredricks last year as a possible investment opportunity and they hit it off right away. She was young, ambitious, and talented. He had money so it was a good match. For a while he thought they may hit if off personally but he found out quickly that the lovely Ms. Fredricks was all business. That he could definitely understand and admire. Now he looked at her more as a daughter. Unfortunately, he and his late wife never had children so he supposed he was missing that part of himself.

Putting her hand over his, Katherine smiled, "I'm glad. They are really different but I like them."

Harold started asking about fabrics and accessories and Katherine was blown away. The man did his homework. She always liked him and sincerely appreciated his investment in her business but was somewhat surprised at the friendship they developed since meeting. He was a sweet man and she respected him.

Two hours later they were leaving the restaurant. Harold turned to her, "Thank you, Katherine, for meeting me here in LA. I won't be back in New York for another month or so."

Katherine leaned up and kissed his cheek, "It wasn't a problem; you were on my way from Hawaii." She smiled at his look of shock. He knew she wasn't keen on traveling. "My cousin was just married and I was in the wedding."

Harold nodded and guided her toward their waiting car, "I see, how was it?"

"Beautiful," Katherine said as she got into the car. The cool, leather seats felt good against her skin.

Harold got in after her and said something to the driver, "And?"

Katherine didn't understand the question. "I'm sorry?"

"Katherine, I'm much older but I know a thing or two." He winked at her. "You met someone."

She was surprised by the bluntness of his statement. They never really talked about their personal lives. "Yes." She wouldn't lie because he was a friend.

His eyebrows raised, Harold was intrigued. A woman kept things close if she wasn't sure what was happening with a man. Katherine never struck him as a woman who didn't know EXACTLY where she was going and with whom.

"He's a Marine stationed in Virginia," she said as she looked out the window. The city streets passed in a blur.

Harold laughed, "It's the uniform," he patted her hand, "it gets the girls every time."

Katherine laughed, "Among other things."

Interesting indeed, Harold thought. Well, he'd tortured the poor woman long enough so he changed the subject back to the new line.

When Harold dropped her off at her hotel, she was relieved. It was a productive and enjoyable dinner but she was eager to be in the privacy of her own hotel room.

She walked into the dimly lit room and thought of her time with Mitch. She wished they were here together, making love. Without thinking, she picked up the phone and dialed the number for his cell.

Mitch was finishing up some paperwork for work when his cell phone went off. He'd been working at home since he left Crash Crew in an effort to keep from thinking about Katie. He looked down to see the number on his caller ID and smiled.

"Hello, Katie," Mitch said quietly when he hit the accept button.

Katherine smiled, "I didn't know if you'd still be up. I didn't think about the time difference when I called."

He smiled, "It doesn't matter, you said I better answer and I did."

Laughing, Katherine sat down in an overstuffed chair and slipped off her heels. "Did I wake you?"

"No," Mitch answered, "I was still up working on stuff I missed when I was on leave."

Work was something she could understand, "I'm trying to get my own work back on track as well."

He nodded, "Vacations are great except when you get back and figure out you still have to do the work."

"Exactly," Katherine chuckled, she absently rubbed her feet, "What are you wearing?" she asked in a sultry voice.

It was impossible to not adore her, "I'm wearing my flight suit," he responded.

She pulled her feet up and tucked them under her, "What about under that?" she asked, accentuating each word.

His body was responding, damn it, "Ms. Fredricks, are you flirting with me?"

The hum in her nerves was more than just flirting, "I'm missing you."

Her statement put his body into overdrive, "I'm missing you too," he whispered. "I keep thinking of you in my arms and in my bed."

"What does your bed look like?" Katherine asked.

Mitch thought for a moment, "It's a big king-sized bed with an intricately carved headboard in mahogany."

She sighed, "It sounds very comfy."

"It would be more comfortable if you were in it with me," he said softly.

His words made her smile again, "I wish I was."

He tried to control his libido because it was going full speed and he needed to get off the subject of her in his bed. "How's your trip in LA going?"

Katherine was plopped back into reality, "Fine."

Again, she kept her answers short. She never elaborated on it. "I got back here to chaos," he said.

"Is everything okay?" Katherine asked. She was interested in his work. Eryn told her a bit about their jobs and she learned some when they visited Abi in Hawaii but she wanted to hear about his daily routine.

Mitch started to explain about some issues he had at work. He never went into too much detail because he would never embarrass one of the Marines under him and he thought it was all too boring for Katherine. He was surprised when she asked more probing questions about his job and his experiences.

Just listening to Mitch talk made her feel better. It was like she was unsettled and now hearing him put her on an even keel. It felt good on one hand but she was upset by it on the other one. Why did she need him to make her okay? She'd done quite well on her own up until now.

When Mitch stopped talking, he waited for Katie to say something, "Are you there?" he asked.

"Oh, yes, I'm sorry," Katherine answered, "I was just thinking how your voice lulls me."

"Not exactly what a guy is used to hearing but I'll take it as a compliment," he smiled.

Stifling a yawn, Katherine, wished he was here with her. "I should get to bed."

An invitation, he thought, "I will be right over."

Katherine snorted, "I wish."

"You do, huh?" Mitch asked. He liked baiting her.

She rubbed her hand up and down her arm, "I do." She whispered, "I wish you were here with me, your hands on my body, and your lips on mine."

Definitely interesting, Mitch thought. The woman turned him inside out. "I wish that too, Katie."

Her body keyed up, Katherine knew it was time to end the conversation. She would not have phone sex. "I'm hanging up now."

Damn, Mitch thought, "Okay. Call soon."

"I will," Katherine said then hit the end call button on her phone.

An hour later she was tossing and turning in bed and wondered why she discounted the phone sex option. All she could think about was Mitch and what he could do to her body. She replayed every bit of lovemaking they shared in her mind and wondered if she would ever be lucky enough to get that experience again. After several more hours of tossing, she finally drifted into a restless sleep filled with dreams of Mitch.

Friday was a clear day in Los Angeles although the sun did nothing to lift Katherine's spirits. She was slated to spend the day with some fabric vendors. Clothes were defined by the fabrics they were cut from and she always took that part of her design process seriously. There was a new line coming out in two months and she wanted it to kick some serious butt.

At lunch time, Katherine found herself with a few minutes to spare before her next meeting. She decided to call Eryn and see if her cousin would answer. She and Chase were scheduled to get back to Oahu that morning. She dialed the number while sitting at an outside bistro.

"Hello there," Eryn answered on the second ring.

Katherine smiled, "So how is married life treating you?"

"Well," Eryn said between dodging Chase's arms, "pretty good, we just got home a few minutes ago."

A small niggling of envy shot up Katherine's spine, "Good, how was the trip?" She almost asked "how was the honeymoon" but didn't want to embarrass herself or her cousin.

Eryn cleared her throat and slapped at her husband's wandering hands, "It was productive."

Giggling, Katherine shook her head, "I'll bet." She did not want to know details, "I will let you go, I just wanted to check in with you and thank you and Chase for including me."

Eryn thought that her cousin was about the nicest person on the planet. How could they not include her? She was one of the few true supporters of their relationship, a decade earlier and now. Eryn only wished they lived closer so they could see one another more.

"You are very welcome, thank you for the dress, I've gotten a ton of comments on it." She was studying some of the pictures from the wedding while she was talking. Chase found something else to keep him occupied for a few minutes. "You may want to get into the wedding dress business."

Katherine coughed, "Uh, no." It was very simple.

Eryn laughed, "Well, cousin, I hear from a little bird that you and Master Sgt. Frinnel spent a lot of time together after we left." She felt compelled to tease Katie a little bit.

She knew it would happen eventually, someone would bring up her and Mitch, "We did."

"That's it?" Eryn was appalled. "I get nothing else here?"

Katherine didn't want to hear it, "You spent time with a guy for the last week so you'll get nothing from me."

"Whatever," Eryn said. She waived Chase over when she saw him come in the front door with their suitcases, "we're married now."

Mouthing 'thank you' to her server, Katherine lifted her glass of iced tea and sipped. "We spent time together until he left on Wednesday." She knew that Eryn was a master interrogator so she might as well volunteer something.

Eryn was relating the information to Chase, "And?"

Katherine was confused, "And what?" she asked.

Rolling her eyes, Eryn tsked, "Are you guys an item now?" Why did some people fight it so hard?

"An item?" Katherine returned. "Eryn, we don't even live in the same state." She looked at the lunch the waiter just set down and didn't have any appetite now. Darn Eryn for getting her thinking about Mitch. "We met up for our vacation and now we're back to our real lives."

Listening to Katie, Eryn didn't believe a word of what her cousin was saying. She may be saying the words but there was no meaning behind them. Interesting news indeed. She and Chase discussed the couple briefly during their honeymoon; how both Katie and Mitch needed a distraction and maybe they were each just what the other needed.

Katherine didn't want to talk about this anymore, she was getting upset. "Listen," she said tensely, "I have another meeting soon so I'm going to let you go and eat my lunch."

One thing about Katie, she certainly spoke her mind. Eryn could appreciate it. "I know. Call me soon, okay?"

"I will," Katherine smiled, "Bye." She hung up quickly before she felt the guilt of cutting her cousin off. She looked at her watch and decided that she'd better eat something and get going.

The afternoon flew by with negotiations on prices between Katherine and the vendors. It wasn't normally the designer who did that but it was a deal Katherine made with herself years earlier. She would be involved in every aspect if she was putting her name on it.

Once back in her hotel room, she looked over her messages and voicemails. She had a couple of offers for dinner with acquaintances she knew here in LA and common sense told her to get out and enjoy her time here before she flew back to New York but she just couldn't seem to do it. Instead, she ordered room service and sat on the bed eating a salad and channel surfing on the television.

Saturday morning Katherine boarded the flight home to New York with a mixture of feelings. She was relieved to be heading back home; it was always nice to sleep in her own bed. Plus, she could really focus on work. Maybe she wouldn't fixate on Mitch so much.

When the plane touched down, Katherine took a deep breath and went to face her life. The airport crowd was manageable and she found the escalator that led down to baggage claim quickly. She pulled out her phone and turned it on to see she had at least a dozen messages waiting.

Stepping off the escalator, Katherine scanned the crowd of people waiting to meet the deplaning passengers. She finally found her assistant, Suzanna, winding through the throngs of people, a smile pasted on her face. She clicked her phone off just before meeting up with Katherine.

"Welcome home," Suzanna said breathlessly, "I have a car waiting for us and someone will get your luggage." She prided herself on taking care of her boss. It was a full time job for sure.

Katherine smiled, "That's okay; we'll get it quick."

Suzanna stopped, "Okaaayyy," she looked at Katherine curiously but didn't comment.

The two women walked over to the baggage claim carousel and waited for Katherine's bags to come off. Once they retrieved the luggage they headed out to the waiting car. The driver smiled and took the bags to the trunk while the ladies got in.

The car service was a good one, the seats were clean and smelled like leather. Katherine settled in and stared out the window. She could see the New York skyline in the distance...home. So why didn't she feel like it then?

Suzanna pulled out several folders, "Okay, we've got contracts for the new line in the first one." She handed it to Katherine, "The lease on your apartment is up for renewal so please look that over and sign it. I'll get it back to your building super." She dug through her bag, "Ah, and here are your messages."

Katherine took the stack of papers and set them on her lap. She went back to looking out the window as the driver pulled out into the airport traffic.

"Is something wrong, Ms. Fredricks?" Suzanna asked her boss. In the three years she worked for Katherine Fredricks, the woman never stopped. A car ride was spent doing things she didn't have time for at the office. Now she just sat there, staring out the window.

Placing the appropriate smile on her face, Katherine turned to her assistant, "No," she touched Suzanna's arm, "I'm just worn out from traveling."

Okay...Suzanna thought...that was weird. Ms. Fredricks was all go, no quit. Her phone rang and she answered it, her boss' behavior would have to be analyzed later.

The car drove them straight to the office where Suzanna directed the driver to take Ms. Fredricks' bags to her apartment.

The women got off the elevator on the fifth floor of a major downtown building. Katherine smiled when she saw the shiny sign that said Katie Fred Designs on the wall. Seeing that sign always reassured her that she was successful.

As she walked into the office, her staff stopped and started clapping. Katherine smiled and said hello to people as she made her way across the large loft space to her office. Before Suzanna could follow her inside, she turned to face the young woman.

"Suzanna, can you give me a few minutes?" She smiled, "I need to make a phone call."

A stunned Suzanna recovered quickly, "Of course, I'll be at my desk when you're ready." She slowly walked over to her desk area, clearly in shock by her boss' behavior.

Katherine entered the office and threw her purse onto the nearest chair. She always loved her office. It was huge, bigger than the first apartment she rented here in New York. One side of it was dedicated to the business end of Katie Fred; it held her desk and all the necessary office equipment a businesswoman needed. The other side was dedicated to her designs. She had four drafting tables with designs on each of them in varying degrees of completion. She was starting the new line before she left and basically turned away from it when she drew her new ideas in Wyoming.

The thought of that immediately brought Mitch to her mind. She didn't really have to make a call but now she wanted to. She got out her phone and looked up his work number in her contacts. She knew Eryn worked from seven thirty to four thirty most weekdays and assumed Mitch's hours were along those lines. Then she remembered it was Saturday and he probably wasn't at work. Her staff worked Saturdays when they were prepping a new line.

"Hello," Mitch answered absently while reviewing a work roster for the next week.

Just hearing his voice made Katherine fumble. "Um, Mitch," she said quietly.

Mitch dropped the paper, "Hey there," he said softly.

He could make her smile so easily, "Hi." She sat down at her desk and played with the pens laying there. "I wanted to let you know I made it back to New York." She sounded so ridiculous, like a little lost puppy.

"I'm glad," He smiled into the phone, "I was going to call you tonight to make sure."

Knowing he was going to call her made her breathing hitch. "Really?"

He was confused, "Yes, really," he leaned back in his chair, "you don't believe me?"

Oh Lord, she was sounding so pathetic, "No, I was just surprised."

Still confused, "You shouldn't be surprised, Katie." He leaned forward again and stared out the window of his home office, "I miss you."

Hearing the words from him was a balm to her frayed nerves. "I'm sorry, I was just frazzled from the trip and trying to get back to work here."

That sounded like the Katie he knew, "Okay then."

There wasn't much else to say so she sighed, "Okay then, I'll let you go."

Mitch was really at a loss now, "Okay, have fun."

"I will, thank you," Katherine said formally and hung up the phone. She was just sounding ridiculous. He was a man, not the 'be all, end all' of her existence. She'd do well to remember that. She turned back to her desk, "Suzanna, could you come in here please."

Two weeks later Mitch was sitting in a meeting at the Crash Barn and not paying attention to any of it. It was a department head meeting to discuss some upcoming projects and the holiday schedule for the fourth of July. The airfield would be closed so most of the crew had an extended weekend. He should be in on the discussion but kept looking at the clock hoping the meeting would end.

After another half hour, the meeting concluded and he walked out of the conference room knowing little more than what he knew going in. He got back to his office and was glad his Admin clerk was taking notes to type up a bullet point summary. His Officer-In-Charge wouldn't be too pleased if he wasn't up-to-date on the daily operations.

He sighed as he sat behind his desk Mitch found himself thinking about Katie at the oddest moments. It was becoming an issue and he didn't know what to do about it. He called her twice and she never called him back. Although their last conversation had him wondering what was going on. She sounded so unsure, almost scared, on the phone and he wanted to reassure her he was there for her.

He picked up the phone and dialed the number he knew by heart. "Can I speak with Warrant Officer Johnson, please?" he asked the clerk who answered.

Eryn Johnson just walked into her office and picked up the phone, "Warrant Officer Johnson here," she said formally.

"What the hell is going on with your cousin?" Mitch all but yelled into the phone.

Not knowing how to respond, Eryn plopped down in her chair. "Okay, Master Sgt, I'm going to give you a moment to compose yourself and speak to me in a more respectful manner."

Mitch wanted to kick himself. "I'm sorry, Eryn." He was acting like an ass.

Trying to stifle a laugh, Eryn tucked her lips in. "I accept your apology, Mitch." She made sure her office door was shut. "Now what kind of insults were you spouting out about my cousin?"

Mistake number two, Mitch thought. "I wasn't trying to insult you or Katie, I've just called her twice in the last couple of weeks and she isn't calling me back."

Oh, now the picture was becoming clearer. Her cousin's MO during this time. "She's getting ready to launch a new line, she's probably swamped." Eryn said. It was always tough to reach Katie around this time.

"What line?" Mitch asked. Now he was really confused.

Eryn's brow crinkled, "Her new clothing line."

Mitch was becoming really frustrated, "What clothing line, she's an artist or owns a dress shop!" He all but yelled.

A feeling of dread worked up Eryn's spine. "She didn't tell you she's a clothing designer?" She asked although she already knew the answer.

"NO!" Mitch stood up and started pacing in front of his desk, "She sketches and draws and stuff like that." Why did he feel like the ground was coming out from under his feet?

Eryn leaned forward and closed her eyes, this was just about right where Katie was concerned. The woman never gave up anything. "Just do me a favor, look up Katie Fred Designs when you get home." She took a deep breath. "Then call us at home tonight if you have any questions, okay?"

Mitch tried to calm down; he felt like a jackass for speaking to Eryn this way. It wasn't his normal attitude and he was ashamed. "I'm sorry, Eryn."

"It's okay, Mitch." She pinched the bridge of her nose, hoping to keep the impending headache at bay.

They hung up and Mitch sat back down at his desk and wondered why he was so twisted up.

Later that evening he went into his office and sat down at the computer. He typed in Katie Fred Designs into the search engine and waited for a response. Almost immediately, articles popped up on the screen. After reading a few of them, he came across the link that took him to the Katie Fred Designs home page.

Once the page loaded, he was shocked to see the picture of Katie pop up on the screen. Of course, she looked different. She was more sophisticated than the Katie he met on the plane and spent time with in Hawaii. He read about the beginnings of her business. How she was the daughter of an Ambassador who struck out on her own in New York.

Mitch sat back and stared at the screen. He wondered if he really knew anything about Katie and was mad as hell.

Katherine was still at her desk in the office when the phone rang. She didn't answer it during release time but she glanced over and saw it was Eryn. Smiling, she picked up the phone. "Hey there," she said.

"Don't you 'Hey there' me, young lady!" Eryn said loudly. Chase spent the afternoon trying to calm her down but it was no use. By the time they got home it was late in New York but Eryn didn't care.

"Uh oh," Katie said smiling, "what did I do now?" She thought maybe she forgot a birthday or something.

Eryn paced the floor in the living room of their house and glared into space, "You neglected to tell Mitch what you did and who you are."

Her cousin's tone said it all. "I didn't neglect to, it just didn't come up," she said defensively.

Eryn shook her head, "NO!" She knew Katie too well, "You just didn't say anything because to you, it's no big deal." She started crying, "But you don't keep that from someone you're seeing or sleeping with, Katie!"

Katherine's heart started pounding, "How mad is he?"

"I don't know, it was enough of a shock to find out you weren't just an artist," Eryn held Chase's hand trying to get strength from him, "but he's pissed you haven't called him back."

What? Katherine didn't remember seeing any calls from Mitch. She looked around her office and didn't even know what day it was. "Are you mad?" Katherine couldn't stand it if Eryn was mad.

Eryn swiped at the tears on her cheeks, she hated crying but she was mad. "I am but I'll deal. It's just that he's a friend, Katie," she smiled at Chase who was looking worriedly at her, "He's the reason Chase and I are together and that means something."

Katherine hated letting anyone down but she especially wasn't going to upset Eryn. "I'm very sorry; I'll call him."

They talked for just a few minutes more and hung up feeling like they were okay.

Pulling up her caller ID log in her phone, Katherine scanned the numbers. Sure enough, there were two missed calls from Mitch. Should she call him now? It was late but maybe he was up. She wouldn't sleep until she tried to make it right. She dialed the phone.

Mitch heard his cell ringing and looked over at it. He saw it was Katie and couldn't answer it. Maybe it was petty but he was still pissed at her for her omission. Turning away from the phone, he tried to sleep.

Katherine hung up once his voicemail picked up. She didn't have a clue as to what she should say to him so she didn't try. It would just make things worse. Picking up her jacket, she walked slowly out of her office, wondering if she just made a big mistake.

Chapter 14

The spring morning was muggy and mirrored the oppressed feeling in Katie's chest. She was in the car on her way into the office when she dialed Mitch's cell number again. If she thought about it, she wasn't sure he would pick up now either. He'd called her twice and she didn't call him back. She deserved a little bit of that back.

"Frinnel," Mitch barked into the phone. He was cranky from lack of sleep and he was just finishing his coffee when his cell went off.

Katherine sighed, he picked up at least, "Mitch, its Katie."

Standing in his kitchen, Mitch tried to calm himself. He really needed to check the caller ID before picking up. "Hi," he said flatly.

"I'm so sorry," Katherine started, "I don't think about my job, I just don't talk about it." She started to explain.

Mitch couldn't listen to this, "We slept together!" he shouted.

Katherine sat there in the car and listened quietly. "I know but I don't share those things easily," she stated calmly.

His patience was gone, "We're not talking about a secret here, Katie; you're plastered all over the internet." She tried to speak but he stopped her, "It's not that you don't share those things easily, it's that you don't share them at all." He shook his head, "If you didn't want to be with me once you were back in New York then you should have just said so."

"No!" she yelled, and shook her head at the cab driver when he turned, "Mitch, please."

What could she say to make this okay? "Please what?"

Katherine felt defeated, "Nothing." It was clear. "I understand your point of view and I won't bother you again." She hung up the phone and put it in her bag.

Mitch looked at his phone, not sure what just happened. Why did he feel like HE was the one who did something wrong here? He put the phone on the counter and went up to take a shower and get ready for work.

Katherine arrived at work and looked awful. She was fighting back tears and didn't want to be there. Unfortunately they were only six weeks away from the release of her fall line and she needed to be there. She rode up the elevator and tried to forget about the conversations with Eryn and Mitch. He was right to be angry but she didn't intentionally mislead him. She didn't tell people much.

"Good morning," Suzanna said and handed Katherine a cup of coffee.

Katherine nodded and took the mug from her assistant. She turned to go into her office but stopped and turned back around, "Suzanna, am I secretive?"

Suzanna stood there for a bit, trying to figure out how she should reply, "Um," she looked around for anyone to help her but none of the other staff was nearby, "you don't say much." Feeling the truth was the best, she nodded, "The only personal information I know about you is what's on your website."

At least she was honest, Katherine thought, "Thanks." She smiled and went into her office.

A few days later, Eryn was sitting at the breakfast table when Chase came in from his morning run. They normally ran together but Eryn was fighting a cold so she didn't feel up to it. She smiled when her husband came in. "Good morning," she smiled up at him and waited for a kiss.

Chase smiled, "Good morning, Gunner Johnson." His standard greeting for his wife. He used the term they used to use to address warrant officers years earlier.

"How was your run?" she asked.

He walked over to get a bottled water out of the refrigerator, "Good," he took a swig, "I forgot to tell you, I talked to Mitch yesterday."

"What!" Eryn stood quickly and walked over, "What did he say?"

Chase shrugged, "It's more like what he didn't say." He took another drink, "He didn't even mention Katie."

Eryn rolled her eyes, "I knew it!" She went back and plopped back down, "She shut down." Chase sat down next to her and took her hand in his, "That's what she does. It's like she doesn't think she's worth it or maybe she just can't trust."

This was not a situation they would figure out any time soon and he didn't want to get into the middle of it. He let Mitch know he was there for him and he'd always be thankful for Mitch's input about Eryn. Chase especially didn't want to have Eryn be upset about this.

"I guess they're adults and need to figure it out." She looked over at Chase, glad that she knew he loved her. "I just hope it doesn't take them ten years to get there."

Chase kissed his wife, "I think they're a little smarter than we are, my love." He got up and pulled his wife with him into the bathroom. If he played his cards right, she might conserve water and shower with him.

Mitch did an inspection of the trucks in preparation for a visit of the squadron commander next week. The week was dragging on and he would be happy when it was over. A couple of days away from everyone would do him some good. Being professional and not biting off everyone's head was wearing on him big time.

"Master Sgt. Frinnel, you have a phone call," came on over the PA in the truck bay.

Great, Mitch thought as he went back to his office, another person he had to speak to...great! His movements were rigid as he picked up the phone in his office, "Master Sgt. Frinnel," he barked in a clipped tone.

"You will not use that tone with me, Mitchell," Aly Frinnel said sternly to her son on the phone, "I've changed your diapers."

He couldn't help it, he smiled. His mom calling him at work was a little unusual so his mind went on full alert, "Is everything okay, Mom?" he asked quickly.

Aly wound the phone cord around her finger, "Yes, yes, everyone here is fine. I'm calling to find out about the woman you were seeing while you were in Hawaii."

Damn! Over the years Mitch knew his mother possessed some pretty wicked powers of observation but this was good, even for her. "Not sure what you're talking about." He'd try the dumb act if it got him out of this conversation.

Knowing her son was trying the good old avoidance tactic, she shook her head. The man may be a Marine but she was a mother; there simply was no comparison. "Mitchell Frinnel, are you lying to your mother?"

Her fake consternation made him smile again. "No, ma'am," he answered, feeling chagrined.

"Good," Aly Frinnel said. "Call me this evening and we'll have a real conversation. I'm sorry I bothered you at work." She hung up quickly not giving him time to make up an excuse to not call her.

Matt Frinnel looked at his wife, "Was that really necessary?" he asked. Usually he didn't interfere with his wife's plan of parenting but Mitch was their oldest and he was a well-adjusted and successful one at that. They didn't need to pester him with things.

Aly walked over and kissed her husband of over forty years, "Yes, Matthew," she only used his given name when making a point, "it was."

Mitch hung up the phone and wondered why the women in his life were giving him such a hard time.

Later that night, he called his mom. Of course he called her after he had two beers to relax and came up with a reasonable explanation for his so-called relationship.

He let the phone ring four times and was about to hang up when his mother answered, "Hello, son," she said brightly.

Yeah, yeah, he thought. She's being nice now... "Hi, Mom."

"So are we going to beat around the bush or are you going to tell me about the woman who had you preoccupied while in Hawaii?" She played with her water glass absently while she waited for his answer.

Nothing about this conversation was starting off well. "First of all, I'm not beating around any bush, and second of all, who told you about a woman?"

Aly shook her head, "Please, Mitchell," she only used his given name when she wanted to make a point, "I called Chase and Eryn to give them our best wishes and Chase slipped up about a young lady and you spending time together."

Leave it to Chase to throw him under the bus. He was probably diverting attention away from himself during the conversation. Mitch reminded himself to beat Chase to a pulp the next time he saw him. "Mom, she was a guest at the wedding and we spent a couple of days sightseeing together."

This was a joke, "Mitchell Frances Frinnel!" She put her hand up to silence her husband since he was about to interject, "If it were just that then Chase wouldn't have even mentioned it." She took a breath, "I'm sure he's kicking himself for saying what he did."

Mitch could agree with that. "Mom, we were seeing each other while on vacation and now it's done." He didn't want to have this conversation anymore, "It's done, okay."

"Okay, Mitch," Aly Frinnel said softly. "I'm sorry I pestered you about it. I'll let you go and we'll talk again over the weekend. Shelley will be here with Rob and the kids."

He nodded, "That's fine, Mom, say hi to Dad. Love to you both, bye." He hung up the phone quickly and went back to the kitchen to get another beer.

Matt Frinnel stood in the kitchen of their home and gaped at his wife. Never had he seen her back down from a "talk" with one of their kids. He was shocked! "What was that?" he asked his wife.

Aly swiped at a stray tear, "That was the sound of our boy having his heart broken," she said softly and walked through their house and upstairs to their bedroom.

New York in summertime was exciting, the hustle and bustle of the city along with the heat created an almost frenzied atmosphere. There were tons of parties, picnics, openings, and other social gatherings to attend. Being an up and coming designer, Katherine was invited to more functions than she could attend and relied on Suzanna to limit her schedule so she could work her normal twelve to fifteen hours a day.

Between her grueling schedule at work, her exercise regimen, and regulated sleep, Katherine kept herself mind numbingly busy. The days flew by and she didn't have to think about Mitch. Every time he entered her consciousness, an ache started in her chest and she hated every minute until it passed.

But here she was, at yet another boring cocktail party trying to avoid questions about her new line and trying to not look as miserable as she felt. One of her oldest New York friends, Liv, came over to see her.

"You look absolutely thrilled," Liv said as she handed Katherine a martini.

She took a large sip and let the cool liquid run down her throat. "I am, of course," Katherine answered.

Liv kissed her friend's cheek, "Only two things make me look as morose as you do right now; lack of money or a man." Her mouth twitched at Katherine's expression. "I know you don't have a lack of money so it must be a man."

Katherine rolled her eyes, "Me?" she took another drink, "Never!"

Interesting, Liv thought, "Well, that's what they said about the Titanic and the Stock Market and they both sank so I'm thinking you have too."

Laughing, Katherine looked around. She was so rusty at socializing, she was surprised she could carry on a conversation. No wonder she buried herself in work. Liv was a friend and she deserved the truth. "I have, I think."

"You think?" Liv asked. Not what she expected her no-nonsense friend to say. "You're not sure?"

That was a loaded question in Katherine's mind. "That would require about four more of these," she gestured with her glass.

Liv smiled, "I can arrange that, my dear." She motioned for a server to come over.

Two hours and more than four more martinis later, Katherine was stumbling up the steps to her apartment in the Nolita district. She moved here because of the vibe and because it was just east of Manhattan where her office was based. The building her apartment was in was converted from an old business into apartments. She unlocked the door and entered her apartment.

Her "home base" was warm and bright. A bank of windows covered the far wall and offered a great view of the city street below. The furnishings were an eclectic mix of comfort and funk. It was not at all like her office because she needed to decompress here. Right now she was flopping down on the couch and wondering why she didn't drink more often.

She felt numb and she liked that...a lot. She didn't worry about the new line, she didn't worry about her parents and pleasing them, and she didn't worry about Mitch. Well, not really anyway. He still sat there, in her subconscious, and haunted her dreams.

She picked up the phone and pushed a button, not caring that it was late. Her head swayed a bit as she waited for the line to connect.

Mitch was just falling asleep when his cell went off. He growled, not wanting to be disturbed. This time he did check he caller ID and saw it was Katie. What the hell? He hit the connect button, "Katie?"

"Yes," she said loudly, "Mitch, it's me, Katie."

Okay she didn't sound like herself, "Are you okay?" he asked. He sat up in bed to try and shake the sleep from his head.

Katie cleared her throat, "Yes, I'm perfectly fine, thank you for asking." Her words started to slip a little. "I wanted to call you and say that I don't blame you for being pissed at me. I'm wound tight and repressed most of the time."

He had no idea how to respond to her declaration, "Okay?"

"Well, except with you," she said quietly, "With you, I just got to be me. And the sex, well the sex was fantastic." She fanned her face, thinking about them naked in bed pushed the temp in the room through the roof, "Where did you learn all of that?"

It was no use, he had to laugh. "Katie, you drunk dialed me, didn't you?"

Katherine nodded, "Well, of course," she sighed, "I would never be brave enough to call you and beg for your forgiveness if I wasn't plastered."

Mitch wiped his hand down his face, she was certainly something. "Well, I appreciate that. Now why don't you go to bed and call me in a few days."

"I don't want to do that, I want you to come to New York and make love to me like you did in Wyoming and Hawaii." She was almost pleading.

His body reacted of its own accord, "Katie, I would if I could but New York is too far away for me to get to now." He felt like he was speaking to a child.

Katherine sighed, "I know that," did he think she didn't know that? "I was just hoping is all."

It was really hard for him to be pissed at her when she was like this. He sucked in a breath, "I'll tell you what," he did some math, "If you want me to come up there, you call me in a few days and we'll set a time."

"Really?" Katherine asked excitedly.

He laughed, "Yes really."

She hopped up from the couch and did a little dance in her living room, "Okay, I'll call you, I promise."

"Okay, you go to bed now, okay." He wondered how he ended up talking to a drunk Katie.

Katherine stopped dancing, "I will, I promise." She kissed the phone and made a large muah sound into it. "Goodnight, Mitch."

"Goodnight, Katie," he said and hung up the phone.

An hour later he was still snickering about the phone call from Katie. Of course now he was also thinking about her asking him to come up there and make love to her. No normal red-blooded guy would be able to resist that request.

He drifted off to sleep with thoughts of him and Katie making love. It was nice to dream of them together.

Katherine woke up the next morning, her head pounding with every beat of her pulse. Maybe drinking wasn't such a good idea after all. She picked up her phone and looked through her recent calls. She saw she called Mitch, she was hoping that was just a dream and she didn't really call him while she was drunk and practically beg him to come to New York and make love to her.

Now she was mortified. How could she have done that? What did he think of her now? Did he think she was some crazy woman? Well, it couldn't be any worse than what he thought of her before, right? Too many questions before she had coffee and aspirin in her system.

An hour later she felt somewhat human again and called Liv. "Good morning, you bad influence," she said to her friend.

Liv laughed, "You were a willing victim so it doesn't count." She ordered another coffee from the waiter at the coffee shop she was sitting at.

"We'll do it again soon," Katherine said smiling, "but let's do it after the new line is out. I can't afford recuperation time."

Liv loved Katherine, she was a genuinely nice person and a good friend, "No problem, I'll find other willing victims in the meantime." She nodded her thanks to the waiter, "I'd better get an invite to your big shindig."

Katherine jotted down a note, "No problem." She hung up the phone and shook her head. She really needed to get out more and be with people who made her happy. Life was too short to just work and not participate.

Two days later, she couldn't remember why she said she couldn't just work. There was too much to do. The final selections for the line were made but there was some issues with fabric coming over from Spain and then some of the fittings weren't right. Last minute things that drove Katherine crazy but were a necessary evil of the business she was a part of.

She was in her office and asked Suzanna to get some sketches out of her bag so they could look over some of the details when she heard Suzanna gasp. She turned around to see Suzanna gaping at a drawing and wanted to crawl into the nearest hole. She knew it was the sketch of Mitch she drew the last day they were together in Hawaii. Walking over and trying not to embarrass her assistant or herself, Katherine quietly took the sketch from her assistant's hands and placed it in her desk drawer.

"So that's what's been going on with you," Suzanna stated before she could help it. It was not in her nature to be so outspoken with Ms. Fredricks.

Is that what everyone thought now? First Liv and now Suzanna. Was she that transparent? It didn't matter because it was none of their business. This was work and that's what they were doing.

A few hours later, her staff gone, she sat at her desk and pulled out the sketch. She laid it on her desk and studied it. He was gorgeous! It was of him lying on the floor, his arm behind his head, and him looking at her with want in his eyes. How could she not want him? Everything about him drew her in. She picked up the phone and dialed his number.

Mitch was stretching out for a run when his cell phone went off in his bag. He picked it up and smiled when he saw Katie's name. "Hello there, are you sober?" he asked smiling.

Embarrassment engulfed her, "I was hoping you'd forget about that."

"Well, your drunken call saved your butt," he sat down on a nearby bench, "I couldn't help but be taken in by your slurred demand that I come up there and make love to you."

Oh Lord, she did not say that...did she? "I'm so sorry."

He couldn't deny he liked her being embarrassed, "Don't be, it was sweet."

She shook her head, "I can honestly say I've never done that before."

"What?" Mitch asked, "Called a guy drunk or begged him to make love to you?"

Oh his teasing was doing the trick; she was bright red, "Either of those things," she said in frustration.

Mitch could tell she was getting upset so he decided he was done with torturing her. "Katie, it's fine." He waived hello to one of the guys from work. "I do have to ask one last thing though."

She was almost afraid to ask, "What is that?"

"Well, do you still want me to come up there and make love to you like we did in Hawaii?" He asked the question slowly, he wanted her to know he was serious.

Looking down at the sketch she did of him, there was only one answer. "Yes, Mitch."

He smiled, "Good." He had a thought, "Eryn mentioned your new line and I saw something about it on your website. Do you want me to come up then?"

The question threw her. She didn't answer right away because it was crazy when they launched a line. What if she couldn't spend time with him? But then he asked so did that mean that he didn't want to spend a lot of time with her? But then why would he consider coming to New York at all?

"You're thinking again," Mitch said quietly.

She was unsure, but then nothing in life was a sure thing right? "I like to consider it, analyze and," she took a breath, "I'd love you to be here then."

Mitch was relieved, he almost expected her to say no. "Good."

Katherine was scribbling a note for Suzanna. "Okay, I'll have my assistant, Suzanna, send you all the information." She didn't know what else to say, "And, Mitch?" she asked him shyly.

"Yes, Katie," he said her name smoothly.

She smiled and touched the drawing of him, "I can't wait to see you."

Mitch hung up the phone and thought that maybe his Katie was still there. He hoped to see her when he was in New York.

A few days later an envelope was in Mitch's mailbox. He saw the stamp for Katie Fred and opened it right away. When he pulled out the contents, he was wondering if he bit off a bit more than he could chew with this visit. The envelope contained programs and itineraries. Some lanyards with passes on them that said "back stage" and finally a note. He assumed it was Katie's writing. It said, 'I can't wait to see you.'

He put the papers back in the envelope and filled out his leave request. It would be tricky if a lot of other people were taking leave but he was pretty sure the dates would be approved. But whether he and Katie were able to spend time together remained to be seen.

Katherine was in a planning meeting with Suzanna and a few of her other staff members when her phone rang. She saw it was Mitch and answered, which caused a reaction within the meeting's attendants. She was not known for answering her phone during meetings. They really looked shocked when she got up and stepped out of the room.

"Hey there," she said quietly into the phone.

Mitch smiled, "Hey there, I got your information today."

She was worried it would be too much for him, "Are you able to come?" she asked, holding her breath for his response.

"I'll be there, Katie," he answered.

Relief washed over Katherine like a spring shower, "Great, I have to go but I hope we'll talk before you get here."

Mitch smiled, "Yes, we will."

"Bye," Katherine whispered and hung up quickly.

She went back into the conference room and sat down. The looks of astonishment were so priceless she laughed, "Okay, okay, let's get back to work."

Katherine was able to talk to Mitch a few days later and they figured out his flight itinerary. She was nervous but she gathered up the courage to ask him if he wanted to stay with her at her apartment. They both knew this was a very big deal for her and she was thankful again when he said he would stay at her place. The new line was finished and they were just putting the finishing touches on the shows and parties that accompanied the release.

As the days passed, Katherine wasn't sure if she was more nervous about the new line or about Mitch coming to New York. She heard back from Eryn's friends, Emma and Abi since they received invitations to the show she promised at the wedding. Neither could attend due to work or personal conflicts and she was a little sad about that. Eryn was fighting off another cold so she and Chase decided not to fly in either.

Now it was a week away and she could barely sleep from all the excitement. There was an expectation and it was unclear if it was about the clothes or about herself. She would find out soon enough.

Chapter 15

Two days before her new clothing line was to premier, Katherine woke up feeling ill. She did not usually get sick so this was something she wasn't prepared for. Even with her exhausting schedule at work, she always made time to exercise and eat right. Maybe the stress of everything was just taking its toll. She decided to call in to Suzanna and ask her to bring some things to the apartment so they could work from there. She didn't need to spread anything at the office when everyone was working so closely.

Suzanna arrived an hour later, a worried look on her face. She watched Katherine take the papers she requested and sat down, "Are you okay? You don't look good," she asked.

Katherine smiled, "I'm sorry you had to come over; I'm just under the weather so I'll be fine."

"I have some calls to make to confirm vendors for the party and we're setting up the lighting today at the salon." Suzanna scanned her planner. "I can stay here if you need me though." She was worried about her boss.

Getting up to get another cup of tea, Katherine shook her head, "No, I'm fine, really," she shooed her assistant out, "you go take care of the millions of details you're good at taking care of."

Suzanna wasn't completely convinced but she left the apartment assuring Katherine that she would be back with some lunch in a few hours.

Setting up shop in the living room, Katherine scattered the multitude of papers before her, trying to figure out where to begin. This was the time she always had the most reservations. Just before a new line was revealed there were all the second guesses, the worries about how people will receive it, if she was as good as some said. She poured herself into her career and loved the creativity, just not the whole marketing and publicity aspects that were necessary to be successful.

An hour later she was laying on her couch, a cool cloth on her forehead. The room was spinning and she decided it was time to call someone. She phoned a friend who was a doctor and he was kind enough to come over.

"Hey, Greg, come in," Katherine called from the sofa when she heard the knock.

Greg Phillips entered the apartment and smiled. He met Katherine through his wife a few years earlier and they were all friends. She never asked him the tedious "you're a doctor" questions and was always very respectful so when she called his office, he came over as soon as he could. He took one look at her on the couch and his brow furrowed.

"I see we're under the weather today." He was trying to keep the atmosphere light.

Katherine rolled her eyes, "Just a little." She hated seeing a doctor. Another necessity she just didn't want to contend with.

Greg disregarded her sarcasm, "Let's take a look here."

He sat down and took her temperature, asked some questions, and asked her to give him a urine sample he could take back to his office. Katherine dutifully answered the questions and wrote down what he said so she could ask Suzanna to pick up the necessary medications. She thanked him a while later and was happily munching on saltine crackers to soothe her upset stomach when Suzanna came back.

"How are you feeling?" her assistant asked when she placed the bags from a local bodega on the kitchen table.

Katherine was upright at least, "A little better I think," she peeked into the bags, not sure if she was up to eating real food yet, "a doctor friend came by and told me to get a few items. Can I ask you to pick them up for me?"

Suzanna took the list quickly, "Yes, I need you well for day after tomorrow, okay?" She was usually not the bossy type but sometimes even the boss needed to be "handled."

Nodding, Katherine smiled, "Sure, I'll be fine."

After Suzanna left, Katherine was finally able to get to work. She signed the appropriate documents and scanned some correspondence she wanted Suzanna to change before sending. Luckily her staff was awesome and the details for the show were well in hand. By the afternoon she felt a lot better and was even able to get down some of the deli lunch Suzanna dropped off.

The sun was setting low in the sky when her cell phone rang. She was going over some last minute details and was so engrossed in her work she jumped when it rang. She picked it up and smiled.

"Mitch," Katherine said smiling.

Mitch cradled the phone on his shoulder, he was making dinner and didn't want to call Katie too late, "Are you busy?"

She got up and walked to the kitchen to get a bottled water out of the refrigerator, "No, I was getting ready to stop for the day."

"How's it going?" He didn't know anything about clothing except that he went into the store and bought what he liked.

Smiling, Katherine sat down at the bar that separated her kitchen and dining room, "Almost done."

Mitch shook his head, the woman never gave anything away, "Okay, are you still okay to pick me up at the airport? If not, I can always find a ride you know. If you have things to do, I understand."

His consideration was very sweet, "I think meeting you at the airport is the most important thing I have to do tomorrow."

When she said things like that, Mitch remembered why he was so crazy about her. "Well thank you," he didn't really know what to say, "I'm glad you think so."

Now she was at a loss, "Well, I'll be there."

"Okay," Mitch said, "I'll see you then."

Katherine nodded, she was feeling funny in her stomach again and didn't want to be sick while on the phone, "You have a good night and I'll see you tomorrow."

Mitch hung up but didn't feel very good about the conversation. She was distant again and he wondered if this was the real Katie.

The next morning, Katherine woke up early. She wanted to make sure her apartment was ready and get some work done before she went to meet Mitch at the airport. Was he really coming here to see her? She couldn't remember every having a date for one of her previews and she was sure there was never a man who stayed at her apartment. She wanted to call Eryn but it was still in the middle of the night in Hawaii. She would just have to deal with her worries by herself.

The morning flew by in a flurry of activity. Most of her staff was running designs over to the showroom area they rented. She wasn't the only designer having a show so there was chaos everywhere. She managed to get through a conference call with Harold and the other investors and felt confident they would be happy.

Suzanna came into her office just after lunch, "Time for you to go to the airport to meet Mr. Frinnel," she looked at her watch, "his flight is on time."

Katherine grabbed her purse and started walking out, Suzanna hot on her trail. "Okay," Katherine said, "we're going back to my apartment to drop off his bags and then we're going to meet you at the showroom to make sure the catwalk and lighting are set up right."

Nodding, Suzanna made some notes, "Did you want me to make some dinner reservations for you?"

She hadn't thought of that and was upset that she didn't. "No," She threw over her shoulder to Suzanna as she got on the elevator, "we'll figure it out."

As the elevator doors shut, Katherine couldn't help but notice her assistant's knowing look. Well, she was right. If Katherine had her way, Mitch Frinnel would spend a lot of time in her bed and they would just order in.

Mitch deplaned at JFK airport and walked toward the departure area. He didn't want to check a bag but he brought a suit for tomorrow's premier so he needed at least a garment bag. Nerves were starting up when he started down the escalator that led to the baggage claim and pick up. They hadn't discussed where to meet so he wasn't sure where to look for Katie.

He made his way to the baggage claim area and waited for his flight's baggage to come off the conveyor belt. He just pulled out his phone when he heard a voice behind him.

"You said you would answer my calls," Katherine said when she was mere inches from Mitch's back.

He didn't turn around. "I'm only supposed to answer calls from a certain lady."

Katherine smiled, "Well isn't she lucky," she all but purred.

Finally, he turned around. Standing before him was a gorgeous creature dressed in a crisp, white blouse, a form-fitting black skirt, and high heels that looked so tall she was only a few inches shy of looking him in the eye. Definitely not the Katie he met on a plane several months ago.

"Hello," Katherine said softly. He was looking her up and down and boy was it erotic.

Mitch took her into his arms and kissed her. His tongue lapped at her lips until she opened them to take him in completely. She tasted like the sweetest thing he'd ever eaten.

Katherine hung on to him for dear life. He took her breath away with one kiss. Good Lord, what would he do to her later? She pulled back so she could look into his blue eyes.

"Welcome to New York," she said teasingly.

Laughing, Mitch held her against his side while he turned around to look for his bag, "Well if every man was greeted like that when he came here, you'd have an influx."

It was hard not to smile when he was anywhere near her. "I'll see about talking to the Mayor about that." She squeezed him.

After getting Mitch's bag, they walked out to the waiting car. He threw his bag in the trunk and helped her into the sedan. Then he slid in beside her and pulled her close. She smelled so good, all sunshine.

Katherine gave the driver her home address then turned back, tucking her head into Mitch's shoulders. Having his arms around her made her feel so warm and safe.

They were quiet for a while, just enjoying the time together. Finally Mitch looked down and wondered if she was sleeping because she was so still.

"Katie," He whispered, "are you awake?"

Katherine smiled, "Yes," she looked up into his face, "I'm just trying to enjoy you before we are overrun with my work obligations."

He looked into her eyes and noticed that she looked tired. "You're worn out already."

She appreciated his concern. "This is how it is."

Again, cryptic answers. "Why don't you tell me how it is?" He wanted to know about her. The sting of her omissions were still there between them. He thought it would be nice to say he put it behind him but he wasn't totally sure he did.

"Well," Katherine began. She knew this was part of it, part of opening up. The problem was she spent a lot of years not opening up so it was very difficult. "I came to New York after college in Spain."

He nodded, "Okay."

She absently played with the charm bracelet on her wrist, "I flew to New York with great aspirations of being an artist."

Mitch smiled, "I can see why," he brought her hand to his lips and kissed it softly.

If the man kept that up, she wouldn't be able to talk, much less speak. "I found out pretty quickly that being an artist wasn't going to happen. I didn't have the edginess or the self-promoting acumen you needed to make it successful." She smiled weakly, it was a letdown that still stung. "I got a job assisting a designer to pay my way and the rest is, as they say, history."

Well, it wasn't a completely revealing life story but it was better than he had when he arrived so he would accept it, for now. "Are you happy?"

That was a question she asked herself a lot. "I feel fulfilled most days," she started, "I don't consider what I do as important so I don't see why others treat me differently."

Her outlook surprised him. It made her more endearing. So she was flawed, wasn't everybody? "I guess it's a matter of perspective then, isn't it?"

The man was wonderful, Katherine thought, he could sum it up in one sentence when she had trouble figuring it out for years. "Yes, I guess it is."

Katherine laid her head back against his shoulder. They rode the rest of the way back to her apartment in silence, watching the city of New York pass by.

After dropping Mitch's bags off at her place and a few awkward moments of wondering what to do, they headed off to the showroom Katherine was assigned to for the fashion show.

They walked into a big room and Mitch was surprised. It was organized chaos at its best. People were setting up chairs, placing assigned seating cards, setting up vases of flowers, walking up and down the platform they would use for a runway. It reminded him of getting troops ready for deployment.

Katherine was surrounded within two minutes of entering the door. She held on to Mitch's hand and pulled him with her through the showroom. Suzanna eyed him up but directed her attention to the list of questions she had for Katherine. Some of her other staff members were shouting questions as they passed by.

"Okay," Katherine said loudly and everyone quieted. "First, Suzanna, go."

Mitch was impressed with her leadership skills. She was organized and calm. There were a few little fires but she seemed to put them out with great confidence and ease. He was surprised because it was so similar to how he was during an emergency on the airfield. Katie would say that her job wasn't as important, but how she performed it was very much the same as his.

After Katherine was done answering questions, she looked at Mitch apologetically. "I'm sorry, no matter how well we plan, there are always a million details we forget."

Shaking his head, Mitch smiled, "I don't mind it at all. I get to see you in action."

"Funny," Katherine said to him, "this is such a small part of what I consider my job."

They looked at each other and said, "Perspective," at the same time.

Katherine brought him closer, "Well, I can't kiss you because I'm at work but I'm hoping you'll come up with me to the lighting booth to help me figure that out."

Why did she make the statement sound so sexy? "Of course, lead the way," He held his hand out to her.

They walked behind where the catwalk was set up and found a staircase. It was spiral and went up to a little control booth. He stood back and watched Katie as she talked with the technicians. They were talking with Katie in technical terms which surprised him a little. She really was very versatile in her abilities. Once she seemed happy with the settings, they went back downstairs. Instead of going out to the main floor, they went backstage.

The room held vanities down the sides which he assumed was for hair and makeup. In the middle of the room were clothing racks. They were covered in plastic with the logo he recognized from Katie's website. The racks were pad locked together which made them seem secretive.

Katherine saw the questions in his eyes. "We try to keep the line a secret until the show." She shook her head, "I know, it's ridiculous."

Mitch shook his head. "Hey, I have a pretty good level of clearance."

He was trying to be cute, and succeeding. "Good," she stopped and stole a quick kiss, "then I don't have to have my security detail question you."

"Heaven forbid," Mitch said flatly.

Once they reached the back of the building, Katherine met up with Suzanna one last time. She gave her assistant a few things then told the woman to go home and get some rest. The next day would be a long one.

Mitch followed Katie toward the exit and smiled at her assistant. She seemed nice and very capable in his estimation. Someone came in as they neared the exit.

"Mitch," Katherine turned to him, "would you excuse me for a second, one of the investors just came in and I'd like to speak to him."

He didn't mind, "Sure," he answered and stepped away to give the two people some privacy.

Suzanna walked over to the man who accompanied Ms. Fredricks, "Mr. Frinnel?" she asked. The man made her very curious for a variety of reasons.

"Yes," Mitch turned around and smiled at Katie's assistant. "Please call me Mitch," he looked at her, "Suzanna, right?"

No wonder her boss was gaga over this guy. He was handsome and sweet, "Yes," she looked at her boss then back to Mitch, "I wanted to say that I hope you enjoy the show."

A strange statement, she seemed almost shy, "I'm sure I will, thank you."

"It's just that," She wrung her hands together, "I am a huge fan of the work Ms. Fredricks does and I think she's wonderful." Another peek to make sure her boss wasn't coming back over, "This line is because of you I think."

Another cryptic thing to say. "I doubt that but thanks." He wasn't sure what else to say.

Suzanna looked down at the ground then back up to Mr. Frinnel, "She's very talented but needs someone to make her feel that way."

Now he was getting relationship advice from Katie's assistant. This day was getting stranger by the minute. He felt the girl meant no harm so he let it go, "Okay, thank you."

Nodding, Suzanna walked back to a group of staffers to give them some work directions.

Katherine gave Harold a peck on the cheek then walked back over to where Mitch was standing, "I'm sorry about that," she said.

"Don't be," he looked over his shoulder at Suzanna, "I was just chatting with your assistant."

She smiled, "Suzanna takes care of me most days."

He had no doubt of that, he looked at his watch, "Are you hungry?"

Katherine smiled, "Yes, very."

Mitch had the impression she wasn't really talking about food. "Okay, let's go then."

The meaning was clear to Katherine. "Let's," she said plainly and walked out the door.

They made it back to her place about an hour later. Traffic was a drawback of living in one of the biggest cities in the world. Once they were in her apartment, Katherine absently undid the cuffs on her blouse and rolled them up. She removed her bracelet and placed it on the bar. She walked to the wet bar set up in the living room and looked at Mitch.

"Can I get you something?" she asked.

Seeing her standing there, looking all businesslike in her outfit, Mitch wanted one thing: Her. He walked over slowly, his eyes on hers. Once he was within inches, he reached out and placed his palm gently against her cheek, "Just you," he whispered.

Katherine's heart sped up. Her mouth was dry, her palms were getting damp. With two words, the man could create a frenzy of need within her. She smiled slowly, "I can arrange that." She turned her face into his palm and softly kissed it, the roughness of his skin creating an erotic friction against her lips.

He followed her silently while she led him down the hall to her bedroom. She opened the door and wondered what he thought. The rest of the apartment was done in muted tones but her bedroom was done in bright jeweled colors. Everything was bright. It was done on impulse when she first moved in.

Mitch looked at this room and knew he was right. His Katie, the flirtatious one he met on the plane, was here in this room. He looked around at the play on color and thought it was the most fun thing he'd seen.

"It's crazy, isn't it?" Katherine asked.

He shook his head, "No, it's you." He walked over and stood before her, looking into her eyes.

Katherine looked up at him and wondered what was going on in his mind. His expression was a mix of serious and sly. He didn't say anything, only lifted his hands to undo the buttons of her blouse. She didn't help him, only stood there in front of him.

Mitch pushed the silky fabric back off of Katie's shoulders. Once the garment was free of her arms, it slid to the floor in an almost silent whoosh. He reached around her, putting his fingers on the top of her skirt and felt along the material until he found the zipper tucked on the side. After pulling it down, he pushed it until, it too, was on the floor. Katherine stood before him, in nothing but a lacy bra, panties, and black stiletto heels. She was simply stunning! His eyes moved over her slowly, as if they were his fingers and touching her body intimately.

Standing there, almost naked in front of Mitch, was the most exposed Katherine ever felt. They weren't speaking, they weren't really even touching; he was just looking at her.

"You are," Mitch whispered as he leaned down to kiss her forehead. He lifted his hands and released her hair so it fell in waves over her shoulders, "without a doubt," he kissed her cheek, "the most beautiful woman I've ever seen."

A single tear found its way down Katherine's cheek. Mitch being here, touching her, saying such beautiful words, was too overwhelming.

Mitch saw the tear and caught it with the pad of his thumb before it could fall completely. "Are you alright?" he asked her.

Katherine nodded, "You just make me feel so beautiful," she said trying not to let her voice hitch with the emotion she was feeling.

"Oh, you are, Katie," he slowly lowered his lips down to hers.

The kiss was sweet and sultry and passionate and crazy and every other word Katherine could come up with in her passion addled brain. His lips took hers and possessed them completely. She wouldn't be able to stop kissing him even if she wanted to, which she did not. His tongue touched her bottom lip, sending a jolt of pure energy through her body. With a moan, she opened up to him, her mouth mating with his.

His hands were all over her back, touching, feeling, exploring. Her curves were familiar and yet he felt like they were her secret. He helped her get his shirt off over his head. They fumbled with his belt and pants and laughed as they tumbled onto the bed.

Mitch made his way up the bed, tucking Katherine in beside him. It was slow progress since they became wrapped up in kissing and discovering one another which each movement. A new sensation was created with every shift of position. It was a potent thing, knowing your lover could make you crazy with simply a brush of a hand.

Katherine pressed her body as close to Mitch's as she could. She lifted her leg to wrap it around his thigh, the patent leather of her heel slid up his skin. She smiled wantonly at him and watched as the need skirted across his features.

"I need to be inside you," Mitch growled when they finally made it to the top of the bed.

Katherine nodded as she kissed his neck, "Oh yes, baby."

Just her using the endearment drove his body into a frenzied mix of confusion. His heart wanted to beat out of his chest and his hands ached to feel every inch of her skin.

He moved her thighs apart with his knee and held himself above her. He looked down at her half smile and wondered if she had any inkling of the power she held over him. Her hair spilled around her covering the silky pillow beneath it. With a sigh, he slowly filled her with himself, wanting her to feel every bit of need he held inside.

Yes, yes, yes, yes, Katherine chanted in her mind. This is what she needed, wanted, dreamt about for the last two months. Since leaving him in Hawaii, she felt adrift and now she wasn't alone anymore.

Mitch felt her body stretch out beneath him, her legs wrapping around his middle. The feel of her heels digging into his backside created another level of arousal every time the edge scraped his skin.

In no time, Katherine was ready to tip over the peak of her desire. "Not yet!" she yelled out.

Smiling, Mitch sped up his lovemaking, "Yes, now," he was breathless.

She was trying to fight the urge to give in to the release clawing at her body, "No!" she yelled.

"Yes," Mitch said, "I'll make you come again, baby, just let it go." His teeth were gritted and he was pushing into her so deep and fast, his own orgasm was moments away.

Arching her back, Katherine let the feelings rush over her. Her climax swept her up into a tornado of sensation. Spinning, twirling, and tossing her insides into oblivion.

Mitch saw Katie go over the edge and followed her into the sweet stupor their lovemaking created.

Laying there, tangled with Mitch's body, Katherine could not think of another place she would rather be. Their breathing was ragged, each of them gulping in the oxygen deprived from primal needs their bodies demanded. She turned her head to see him being very still and smiling. His eyes still held the spark from desire.

She reached up and cupped his cheek, just as he'd done to here earlier. "You are very good at this." She had the silliest smile on her face.

Mitch kissed her palm and covered the back of her hand with his. "No," he smiled back, "we're good at this."

"I suppose it is a team effort," Katherine said flippantly.

Pursing his lips, he tried to think of some comeback but his brain was still short-circuited from their lovemaking. He kissed her hand again and lay there in her bed, looking at her and wondering why he waited two months to see her.

They finally got out of bed a while later and Katherine went into the bathroom to freshen up. She washed her face and threw on some more casual clothes. When she came out she heard Mitch moving around in the other room.

She walked out into the living room/dining room area and watched him as he dug through her cupboards. When he noticed her, he stood up and smiled. He held a saucepan in his hands as if it were a treasure.

"Aha," he said loudly, "I knew you had to have one."

Katherine furrowed her brows, "What are you doing?"

Mitch walked over and pulled her to him, "I'm making some dinner. You made me very hungry."

"No need," Katherine said and looked at the clock on the wall. "Dinner will be here in about twenty minutes."

Mitch looked down at her ruffled appearance. She was a woman who looked thoroughly sated. "What should we do while we wait?" he asked.

Pretending to consider the question, Katherine looked around. When her eyes found his again she wiggled her eyebrows. "I have some ideas." Without saying anything else, she led Mitch back to her bedroom. Yes, she definitely had some ideas.

Chapter 16

The morning of her show, Katherine woke up to the sound of her phone. Peeking at her clock, she saw it was only six thirty. Not surprised by the intrusion, but still annoyed, she answered it with a curt, "Hello."

After speaking to Suzanna about a half dozen of last minute issues, she hung up and laid back down. There was no way she'd get back to sleep now. Looking over, she was surprised to see Mitch laying there and staring at her.

"I'm sorry," she said. She hoped they would get some sleep. They were up half the night making love.

He shook his head, "No need to be," he stretched. "I get more of those calls than you think from work."

Katherine was surprised. "Really?" Not that she didn't believe him, she just thought she was the only one.

"Yep," he said and leaned over to kiss her.

Katherine kissed him quickly then tried to get up to get ready when the room started to spin. She was going to lay back down when her stomach pitched. She jumped from the bed and dashed to the bathroom to be sick.

Mitch watched Katie run for the toilet and was worried. It happened so fast. He went in after her and held her hair back while she emptied the contents of her stomach in gut-wrenching heaves.

"Baby," he murmured, "it's okay."

She was crying, "I'm so sorry." She leaned back and sat on the floor. "I think the nerves and the lack of sleep just got to me."

He didn't doubt it, if yesterday was even a fraction of her life, then she ran at a pretty hectic pace. "It's okay." He got up and ran a washcloth under the water in the sink. He crouched down and placed it on her skin. She looked very pale. "Do you think you can get up?"

Mitch helped her up and half carried her back to the bed. He was worried.

Katherine simply didn't have time to be sick. "I'm fine, Mitch," she murmured. She got up slowly and went back to the bathroom to get ready, leaving Mitch in the bedroom wondering what to do.

Eventually they each got ready, Mitch using the guest bathroom down the hall and was upset that the intimacy they shared before was gone. Katherine was all business now as she munched on a piece of dry toast and scanning emails and texts on her phone.

Mitch watched her as he sat at the bar drinking coffee. She had color back in her face but he was still worried. "Can I do anything for you today?" he asked.

Katherine neglected to account for today when they made their plans. She was really thinking about the parties afterwards so didn't give much thought to what he would do while they were preparing for the show. She wanted him with her but didn't want him to feel obligated.

She walked around the bar and waited for him to face her before nestling in his arms. "I want you to come with me but I'll feel bad if you look bored." She didn't want to beat around the bush with him. It wasn't fair to either of them.

"I won't be." He kissed her forehead and was relieved that she didn't feel warm, "I'll help out wherever I can."

Nodding, Katherine smiled, "Okay, deal."

A few minutes later they were in the car on their way into Manhattan. Mitch looked at the sites of the city while Katie spoke with Suzanna. He didn't realize how much went into a fashion show. Not sure he really wanted to know, but it was part of Katie and that made it interesting to him.

When they pulled up in front of the building, he saw photographers gathered outside. As soon as Katie exited the vehicle they swarmed her. He got out right behind her and guided her toward the building, gently making a pathway for her to travel. One of the photographers got too close for his comfort and he had to hold back from punching the guy.

Once they were inside, Katherine let out a breath. "Hey," she turned to Mitch, "you are really good at that." She kissed him. "I need to keep you here to be my protector."

If people weren't already starting to migrate toward her, he would have taken her into his arms and kissed her senseless. He could see Suzanna out of the corner of his eye and knew Katie wasn't his just yet. "I'll be waiting for you." He winked and stepped back so she could talk to her staff.

Two hours later, he found himself doing some last-minute maintenance on some malfunctioning sound equipment and helping the ushers rearrange the seating. It was busy work but it made him feel like he was a part of Katie's team. He would see her intermittently, coming out from the craziness of back stage to take a call or get a drink of water. A few times he wanted to step in and sweep her away, but now wasn't the time for him to play her rescuer; she was an adult and this was her job.

At one o'clock Katherine called everyone together for one last meeting. Everyone on her staff was there as well as the models they hired, and Mitch. "I want to thank all of you for doing such a fantastic job," she started. It was difficult to keep her emotions in check. "This line is different from what we're used to giving our clients and, even though it's a gamble, I think we've done a great job."

Everyone clapped and Mitch looked around him. They all respected her. She was tough but was level-headed and showed respect to them. He saw her a little differently now. When she looked over at him, he winked, and was pleased with the blush that crept into her cheeks. It was only a moment, but it was their moment.

If Mitch thought the day before was nuts, he was shocked by the momentum this kind of event created. After Katherine's speech, everyone scattered to get ready for the show. He brought a change of clothes and got ready in the men's room.

He sure wasn't getting ready backstage with all those women there. He was all about immersion but not to that extent.

A half hour before the show, the guests started coming in. Mostly women but there was a decent number of men here too. He watched them file in, some of them finding their designated seating and some just trying to get a spot with a good view.

Music was playing in the background. A mix of hip hop and more contemporary music to keep the crowd entertained and the energy level up. Mitch stood at the back of the room just to the right of the stage entrance. He wanted to see as much as possible but be available to move if they needed some help with something.

Katherine was in the back pointing, signing forms, and yelling out last-minute orders to her staff. The throng of activity made it tough to think but she did her best. This was her sixth show so she at least knew what to expect. There was bottled water set around the room so people didn't get dehydrated. She watched the models, in their varying stages of hair and makeup, chatting and laughing. She tried to hire regular girls with little or no modeling experience. Her customers could see from the get go that regular girls were able to wear the clothes.

Suzanna gave her the sign letting her know there was fifteen minutes left until they started. She looked around and was disappointed that Mitch wasn't back here. When she noticed all the half-naked girls, she was somewhat relieved that he wasn't.

The lights dimmed and everyone's attention drew to the spotlight at the back of the runway.

"Ladies and Gentlemen," an announcer said, "welcome to the reveal of the fall line for Katie Fred Designs."

Once the first model appeared, the audience began clapping. Then the music started and it was on. Girl after girl started striding out on the long catwalk, showing off the designs. The music changed from loud to mellow and back again, depending on the styles.

Mitch watched in fascination as the models walked down the runway. It was amazing to him how they could pose and turn on the high heels they wore. He didn't think he could do it, be on display for everyone to look at. Looking at the audience, he figured everyone looked pretty happy so he took that as a good sign.

When the last model came out, the music changed again. The announcer came on, "Ladies and gentleman, our designer, Katherine Fredricks."

Mitch stood there and watched Katherine walk out, accompanied by the models. She went to the end of the runway and bowed. His chest swelled when she clapped for the models. He watched her hug some of the girls and walk back down the runway where they all disappeared. She looked really excited and he was happy for her. He waited a few minutes for the girls to change backstage then went back to find her.

Katherine was chatting with some of the girls when she caught sight of Mitch. She excitedly waved him over, "What did you think?" she asked him, bubbling over with adrenaline.

She was so animated and bounced around like a teenager. Mitch scooped her up and spun her around, "I'm so proud of you," he said and kissed her.

The thrill of having a great show was shadowed by the way his kisses made her feel. She hugged him close, reveling in his lips and how they made her feel. "Thank you."

Suzanna came up behind them and cleared her throat, she hated to interrupt a private moment but they weren't done working yet. "Ms. Fredricks, we're going to go over to the hotel now."

Katherine nodded and gave Mitch one more squeeze before letting him go. "Are you ready?"

Mitch wasn't sure if he was but if she was with him, he'd do it. "Yep," he responded and followed her through the crowd of people.

It took almost twenty minutes just to get out of the building. Everyone wanted to congratulate Katie. He stayed quietly behind her, gently guiding them through the mass of people until they were on the sidewalk. He had no idea where they were going so he would just have to follow Katie to find out.

Katherine was thankful for the cool night air. She was becoming claustrophobic walking amongst the guests. She knew they only wanted to wish her well but it was stifling. Usually she dodged them altogether but she could feel Mitch behind her so it was easier to handle knowing he was with her.

"Thank you," she turned to Mitch as soon as they were outside.

He was surprised, "You're welcome but I don't know what for." He was trying to keep it light. This was an exciting night for her and he wanted to keep her spirits light.

This was his first preview so he didn't know how she normally did it. She squeezed his hand in hers, "I hate going through a crowd like that and the only reason I did tonight was because I could feel you right there with me."

He was humbled, "Katie, I'll always be right beside you as long as you want me to."

The words came out quickly, surprising them both. They both looked at one another, not sure what to say.

"Well," Katherine fidgeted, "I suppose we should go to the hotel. There's a cocktail party and dinner there for about three hundred of my closest friends." She couldn't quite tame the sarcasm.

Now was not the time for them to talk so Mitch just smiled, "Okay, lead the way."

The man was so easy on her. She would be sure to thank him later for it. She grabbed his hand and they walked the couple of blocks to the hotel where the celebration was being held.

As soon as they walked into the room, the applause started. Mitch stayed just behind Katie, his hand on the small of her back. It was her night but he was sure going to be right beside her the whole time. Being around her brought out the protectiveness in him. He looked around at the guests and knew he could take any one of them at any time.

They made their way to the bar and took a breather. Katherine ordered a water since her stomach was still iffy and turned to Mitch, "Can I order you something?" she asked him in a suggestive tone.

Mitch leaned in close, "What I want, I don't think we can order here."

Her body was starting to wake with anticipation. "I'll see what we can't drum up a little later," she whispered in his ear.

She was looking over Mitch's shoulder and saw Harold and two more investors working their way toward them.

Mitch felt Katie stiffen and knew their time was done. "You go and mingle or rub elbows or whatever it is you need to do, I'll be fine."

Again, the man was wonderful. "Thank you," she said and kissed him quickly before moving around him and heading for the crowds.

Mitch turned back to the bar and ordered a whiskey. He may need a little liquid ambition to get him through the next couple of hours.

A few minutes later, he was still standing at the bar when Suzanna came up beside him, "Mr. Frinnel," she nodded politely.

"Yes, Suzanna," Mitch responded. The woman always looked just this side of making a run for it.

She took a glass of champagne from a passing tray. "Ms. Fredricks asked me to make sure you had everything you needed."

If he didn't know better, he's swear the woman was flirting with him. Of course, it was definitely hard to tell because of her skittish nature. "I'm fine, thank you," he said as nicely as he could and excused himself.

Mitch walked around the room slowly. He liked to watch people and this was a good occasion to do that. He could tell there was money here. Katie was good and she was probably pricey. It probably stood to reason that she would have very wealthy people around her. He was no slouch in social situations due to his mom's insistent lessons in manners over the years but this wasn't his preferred kind of social setting.

"Mitch?" a lady asked as she passed him.

Mitch looked at the woman, sure she was familiar but not sure where he knew her from.

The woman came over and hugged him tightly, "Mitch Frinnel, you are a sight for sore eyes." She then proceeded to kiss him square on the lips.

He was in shock. It wasn't every day that a stranger came up and kissed him. Although, Katie did that on the plane. He smiled at the woman because of the memory with Katie.

"You don't recognize me," she said with a pouty grin. "I do look a bit different. I'm Kristy Lawson, from Milford High School. I graduated with your sister, Shelley."

Dawning came, "Oh yeah, how are you?" He looked her over, "You've grown up quite nicely, Kristy."

Kristy blushed, "You were always a sweet talker." She took a sip of her champagne. "How is Shelley?"

They walked over to a bench near the patio doors and started talking about his sister and catching up.

Across the room, Katherine watched Mitch being kissed by some woman. She really had no right to be jealous and yet she was. It would be so easy to walk up to the woman and demand that she take her hands off of Mitch. Instead she pretended to be listening to the conversation she was supposed to be a part of.

Mitch motioned to a passing waiter to bring him and Kristy another round of drinks. He was laughing at the things she told him about his sister. Shelley was in for a nice surprise at the next family gathering. He told Kristy about his Marine Corps career and how he was here with Katie. He tried to make eye contact with her a few times but lost track of her in the room full of people.

Three drinks later, he and Kristy were feeling pretty good. Each was trying to one-up the other with pranks they pulled over the years. It was good to talk to someone from back home. He felt less of an outsider in a room full of people who talked fashion. He did wish Katie was here with him to hear all of it because she might like the insight to his upbringing. She prompted him to tell her about his family when they were in Hawaii so he knew she'd be laughing with them now. He looked around once more for Katie and didn't see her but her assistant, Suzanna, was headed straight for him.

"Mr. Frinnel," Suzanna said in a clipped tone. She nodded stiffly toward Kristy.

Mitch smiled, "Yes," he wasn't sure what the woman wanted but he didn't really want to deal with her right now.

Squaring her shoulders, Suzanna looked at him sharply, "Ms. Fredricks was looking for you and asked that I take you to her."

He looked from Suzanna to Kristy, who looked uncomfortable. She wasn't the only one. Gathering his manners he looked over and smiled at Kristy, "Will you excuse me please? It was good to see you." He purposely leaned in slowly and kissed Kristy's cheek. Then he stood and waited for the ever-obedient Suzanna to take him to "Ms. Fredricks."

Mitch followed Suzanna through the main ballroom and out into the hall. They crossed the lobby and he was taken to a smaller room. Suzanna opened the door and waited for him to enter and then closed it quietly behind him.

The room was dimly lit by a few lamps in the corners. When his eyes adjusted to the difference in light, he saw Katie sitting on a settee on the far side of it. He went over to her, smiling. He was relieved they would have a few minutes alone. He wanted to tell her about meeting his sister's friend.

Mitch knelt down in front of her, "Katie, how are you doing?"

Katherine was sitting there with her hands in tight balls of anger. When her assistant came over and told her Mitch was flirting with some woman in the corner, she was outraged.

"How could you?" she asked through gritted teeth.

He was lost, "How could I what?"

Did he think she was dense? "How could you kiss that woman and flirt with her in front of my friends and co-workers?" She stood abruptly and started pacing. "I'm humiliated that the man I came with would openly put his hands all over another woman right in front of me."

What? Mitch stood slowly and took a deep breath, "Katie, I was not flirting with anyone." He started to realize what the shy Suzanna was up to. "Your assistant was flirting with me earlier and-"

"Oh, so now all the woman here are just flirting with you." She fisted her palms. "It must be so tough to be God's gift to women!"

His patience was wearing thin, "Katie, I'm not here to fight with you. I'm telling you, it's not what you seem to think it is."

Katherine's voice hitched. She was determined not to cry, "All I think is that you don't care about which woman you're with."

It was if she slapped him across the face. The comment was so callous that he was at a loss. No response would be appropriate so he decided it wasn't worth trying to come up with one. "You know," he felt a deep sadness, "I never once felt like you were a snob...until this moment." He wouldn't let her respond. "You've got your insecurities, I get it, we all do, Katie." He walked toward the door, "But some of us don't have to resort to childish behavior to deal with them." He opened the door, "Why don't you have your assistant there call your doorman and tell him to let me in so I can get my things out before you get there?" He looked back one last time, regret filling his chest, "That way I won't have to humiliate you anymore." He left the room without another word.

Katherine sank into the nearest chair and cried.

Suzanna quietly entered the room once she saw Mr. Frinnel leave and handed Ms. Fredricks a handkerchief. "It'll be alright. I know you're upset but you should try and get back to the party."

She nodded, thankful that Suzanna was on top of things. She stood and righted her clothes, dabbed at her eyes and went back to the ballroom. She looked for Mitch as she crossed the lobby, wondering if maybe he reconsidered leaving but she didn't see him. The letdown was immense and she tried to shore up her resolve enough to be a good hostess.

"Ms. Fredricks," Kristy Lawson said to Katherine a while later, "I'm a huge fan of your designs."

Katherine felt very uncomfortable. This was the woman she saw Mitch kissing earlier. "Thank you," Katherine said a little stiffly.

Kristy was so happy, "You should have seen my face when Mitch told me he was your escort tonight. I'm an old high school friend of his sister's and we haven't seen one another in years."

The words sank in and Katherine wanted to die. Mitch was right; she behaved childishly earlier. Ms. Lawson was standing in front of her looking expectantly. "I'm sorry," Katherine said, she was embarrassed at being caught zoning out.

"I was just saying," Kristy smiled sweetly, "that you are very lucky to have a man be so devoted to you." She fanned her face, "I'd better watch it or I'm going to start crying."

Not only did Katherine feel like a fool for jumping to conclusions about Mitch's behavior, but now she wanted nothing more than to go to him and beg his forgiveness. She nodded at the nice woman, "Kristy, will you excuse me a moment?" she asked and stepped away.

Dialing Mitch's number, she prayed he would answer. The phone went to voicemail. Damn it! She wanted to scream at her own stupidity. She tried to find a quiet place to leave a message, "Mitch, it's Katherine," she started, "I am very sorry for being such a crazed lunatic. You are right, I was being childish. Please don't leave the apartment. Please stay there, I'll try to be there as soon as I can."

She hoped he would listen to it and be there but there was no guarantee after her behavior. Walking back into the ballroom, she ran into her friend, Greg, and his wife Pam. Not wanting to be rude, she stopped and greeted both of them. "Hello, you two." She tried to sound bright.

Greg looked at his friend and knew she wasn't feeling well. No wonder with all the stress. "I meant to call you earlier but I didn't get the chance."

Pam stepped aside to speak with someone else she knew so Katherine felt comfortable asking him about it. "Is everything okay?"

Looking around to make sure no one was nearby, he leaned in. "It's fine, you're pregnant. Congratulations."

The words fell over Katherine like heavy bricks. She wasn't sure she heard him correctly and looked up into his eyes. He was smiling and nodding, which told her she had heard him right.

The room spun and Katherine heard Greg call out her name before everything went black.

Mitch arrived at Katherine's building filled with rage. She treated him like some kid, embarrassed him, accused him of God knows what, and then left him a sobby apology. No! He wasn't going to take this. Just because she was some hot shot designer didn't mean she could treat people like that. He stomped up to the stoop and nodded to the doorman.

The man recognized him from earlier and opened the door. Mitch smiled his thanks and asked, "Did Ms. Fredricks call ahead to have you let me in?" Just asking the question made him feel small.

"Yes, sir," the doorman answered and handed Mitch the key.

After going up and letting himself in, Mitch went to the bathroom he used earlier to get ready. He then went to the bedroom to get the rest of his clothes that were strewn around the room from their bout of lovemaking the night before. Feeling drained, Mitch plopped down on the bed. Why did it have to be so complicated? He had a good life; he had his career, his family. Sure he wasn't married yet and he didn't have children but that didn't mean he didn't have a good life. Screw this! He was done dealing with the drama. After quickly grabbing his things, he headed to the airport to try and find the next flight back to Virginia.

Eryn was getting ready for dinner when the phone rang. "Hello," she said happily.

"Eryn, it's Mom," Beverly Fredricks said quietly.

That tone never boded well, "What's wrong?" Eryn asked.

Beverly dabbed her eyes, "We're not sure. We are over in Europe with Marcus and Victoria and just received a call that Katherine passed out at a party earlier tonight." She started to tear up again.

"What?" Eryn asked. She talked to Katie last week to let her know they wouldn't be able to make the show and nothing seemed wrong at the time. "What hospital is she in?" Eryn asked her mother.

Getting upset again, Beverly pursed her lips, "That assistant of hers wouldn't tell us anything." She nodded to the questions from her sister-in-law. "We know you've talked to the girl before. Can you call her and get some information?"

Eryn wasn't sure she would do any better but she'd sure as hell try. "Of course, I've got her number here somewhere." She ruffled through the papers on the desk she and Chase shared at home, "I'll call you back as soon as I've spoken to her."

Smiling, Beverly sighed, "Thank you, sweetie. We'll wait for your call."

Eryn hung up with her mother and found the number for Katie's assistant, Suzanna. She never much cared for the woman but Katie swore she was a godsend. Dialing the number, she waited impatiently for Suzanna to pick up.

"Hello," Suzanna said quietly. She didn't want to get into trouble being on the cell phone in the hospital.

Eryn was relieved, "Suzanna, it's Eryn Fredricks." She wasn't sure if the woman knew her married name and didn't care to explain it right now. "I was told that Katherine was in the hospital; can you tell me what happened?"

Suzanna knew Ms. Fredricks loved her cousin so she felt good about letting her in on what was going on. "Yes, she is in the Emergency Room but it looks to be a fainting spell." She looked around, hoping that no press got wind of this, "If that Frinnel guy wouldn't have walked out on her in the middle of her party, I think she would've been okay."

Did she hear the girl right, "Did you say Frinnel, Suzanna?"

Nodding, Suzanna lowered her head so no one saw her talking, "Yes, he was flirting with other women and such so Ms. Fredricks confronted him and he left." She shook her head in disgust, "He was cruel to her and she just couldn't take it."

Wanting to hurt Mitch Frinnel but knowing that was for later, she asked a few more questions of Katie's assistant then asked her to please call when Katie was released so Eryn could speak to her. Suzanna assured her she would then hung up.

"Chase!" Eryn yelled.

Hearing the tone in his wife's voice and knowing it wasn't right, Chase ran into the house, "Are you okay?" he asked, looking her over for injury.

Eryn sat down in the chair, her hands shaking, "I need you to calm me down, sweetie."

He knelt down in front of his wife and held her hands, "What's wrong?"

She proceeded to tell him a story and he didn't like the sound of it one bit.

Chapter 17

Mitch was sitting at his desk at work the following Wednesday when he heard his name paged for a phone call. He picked it up, "Master Sgt. Frinnel here," he used the standard greeting.

"Mitch," Chase said coolly, "I need to talk to you, man."

Sitting up, he could hear something in his friend's tone. "What's up?" he asked.

Chase hated to do it but Katie was family now. "What the hell did you do to Katie?"

Mitch stood up, anger pulsing through his veins. "I didn't do anything to her!" He resented the accusation.

"I remember saying those exact words to you about eleven years ago. Do you remember?" Chase asked, his tone a bit more sympathetic.

Nodding, Mitch answered, "Yes," he had a sneaking suspicion this was leading somewhere. "What's this about?" he asked his friend.

Chase wasn't that good at telling stories but his friend needed to hear this one. "It started out with a phone call..."

Eryn got into the cab as soon as her plane landed in New York. Chase couldn't get time off yet from his job so he stayed behind in Hawaii. Her Crash Chief, Abi Rochelle, flew with her to

New York for support. Abi's parents lived here anyway, Abi told her, but Eryn was pretty sure Chase asked her friend to come and keep an eye on Eryn. She loved that man!

The cab stopped in front of Katie's building and Eryn got out. "Are you sure you don't want to come up?" she asked Abi.

Shaking her head, Abi squeezed her hand. "No thanks, this is a family thing." She gave the cabbie her parents' address, "I have a family thing to contend with myself so I'll try to work that out and I'll meet you at the hotel later."

Eryn waved to her friend as the cab pulled away then turned around. This was going to be fun. She nodded at the doorman and gave him her name.

Katherine was in bed, Suzanna nursing her like a mother hen, and it was grating on Katherine's nerves. The woman acted like Katherine had a terminal disease or something. Of course, it didn't help that Katherine told her staff that the doctors didn't know what was wrong with her. She swore Greg to secrecy so only two people knew about the baby.

She was about to ask Suzanna to run some errands just to get her to leave when the doorbell rang. She could hear voices but didn't know who was here. They needed to be big if they were going to get past Suzanna. The woman gave sumo wrestlers a run for their money.

Katherine looked up to see a very unhappy looking Eryn standing in the doorway of her room.

"What's this?" Eryn asked loudly while pointing at Katherine.

Suzanna was trying to push past Eryn, "I'm sorry, Ms. Fredricks; she barged in."

This was just ridiculous, Katherine thought, "I'm sure she did, Suzanna. She's my cousin." Her patience was dried up.

Eryn looked at the crazy woman smugly.

Suzanna looked somewhat contrite, "You said no visitors."

That was it! "Suzanna that obviously didn't extend to my family." She tried to calm down, "why don't you go and do those errands we spoke about earlier, my cousin will keep an eye on me."

Eryn walked over to the bed and hugged Katie. They watched a, now sulking, Suzanna walk out. Neither said anything until they heard the apartment door close.

Sitting down on the edge of the bed, Eryn hitched her thumb in the direction Suzanna just left, "What's with Attila there?" she asked.

Honestly, Katherine had no clue, "I don't know, but I'm getting out of this stupid bed," she said and threw the covers off of her.

Katherine walked into the bathroom, a curious Eryn following her. She ran a brush through her immensely tangled hair. She could see her cousin's reflection in the mirror and could see the questions.

"I know," Katherine said softly, "I don't know what the hell happened."

Eryn could tell there was a lot more to the story than what the crazy Suzanna relayed to her one the phone. "Why don't we go into the kitchen and I'll make us some tea?" she asked and guided her cousin out of the bathroom.

Pointing to a chair, Eryn silently told her cousin to sit, and she went in search of the teakettle.

Katherine watched her cousin move gracefully around the kitchen. The woman looked like a model most days and yet she was so unassuming. Katherine could see the love permeate from her and was jealous.

"Start talking," Eryn shouted from the kitchen, "I can listen while I'm doing this."

Where did she begin? She decided that Eryn deserved the whole story. Maybe she could provide some insight on what Katherine should do. She started with the scene at Honolulu Airport when Mitch was flying back to Virginia. The story was happy and sad and everything in between. She was embarrassed to talk about drunk dialing Mitch and was shocked with Eryn's response.

"Yeah, I was so drunk I broke into Chase's house and then passed out on him when I asked him to make love with me." She stood in the kitchen, her hands on her hips.

Katherine could think of nothing intelligent to say to that. She shook her head thinking lunacy must run in their family. She continued telling her about their lovemaking the night before the show and how he helped out with the preparations.

Eryn brought in the cups with tea and sat down across from Katie. "Go on," she prodded.

Trying to sound calm, Katherine finally told her about what she saw, the horrible accusations she threw at Mitch, his responses, and then finding out from Kristy Lawson that it was what Mitch said. She looked up trying to hold back the tears.

"And then," she smiled when her hand was covered with Eryn's, "my doctor friend, Greg, tells me I'm pregnant."

Forming an 'O' with her lips, Eryn was speechless. She wasn't expecting that little plot twist. "Well," she finally said, "join the club."

A full minute passed before Katherine got the comment. Her eyes widened, "What?" she asked, her hand going to her throat.

Eryn smiled, "You heard me."

The women hugged and cried. Finally Eryn pulled away and looked Katherine in the eye, "So what are you going to do about it now?" The question was logical in her opinion.

"I have absolutely no idea," Katherine said then laughed. It was either that or cry and laughing sounded so much better.

In Virginia, Mitch was talking to Chase and getting more upset with what he was hearing.

"What!" Mitch jumped up. "Is she okay?" His heart was trying to pound right out of his chest. All rational thought flew out the door.

Chase tried to remain calm. He had his own wife to worry about flying to New York. "I guess it was just a fainting spell but her assistant wouldn't talk to her parents and Eryn was almost hysterical."

Mitch knew that squirrely assistant Suzanna was a pain in the ass! "But she's okay now right?" He wanted to call her.

His friend sounded like him only months ago, all torn up and so deeply in love he couldn't see straight. Chase wondered if Mitch even knew it. "Yes, Eryn flew to New York." He took a breath, "What happened between you two?"

That was the question Mitch was asking himself still; after five days he still didn't know exactly what happened. "Everything was fine. We went to the show, which was fantastic by the way. I didn't have a clue about what it took to put on one of those things."

Chase smiled. He found himself in awe of Eryn all the time so he understood what Mitch was saying.

"Then," Mitch started to get worked up just thinking about it, "I ran into a friend of my sister's from high school and she kissed me." He took a breath, "Then her crazy assistant *summoned* me." He shook his head.

"Wait," Chase interrupted, "this woman kissed you?"

Mitch frowned, "Yes, it was just a friendly kiss." He felt defensive now.

It was becoming a little more obvious to Chase, "Did Katie see that?" he asked. He knew what Eryn would think if it were him.

Shaking his head, "I don't know. Yeah, I guess," he sighed in frustration, "she said something about it when she was going off on me."

Ohhhh, Chase figured Mitch was better with women than this. "Buddy, you don't kiss a woman in front of the woman you love unless she's a relative, a nun, or...well, that's it." These rules were clear.

"What!" Mitch started pacing. "It was a friendly kiss and I never said I loved her."

"Okay," Chase said sarcastically. "And I didn't love Eryn for ten years."

The statement hit Mitch right between the eyes. He sat there only a few months ago and wondered when he would find a woman to make him feel the way Eryn made Chase feel and here he had one. Plopping back down in his chair, he looked around his office blankly.

Mitch cleared his throat and tried to get his breathing under control, "What do I do now?" he asked his friend.

It wasn't Chase's place to answer, "What did you tell me?"

"That was different!" Mitch shuffled papers that didn't need shuffling. "I don't work with her."

Chase nodded, "Is it really that different?"

Mitch hung up the phone a few minutes later. He sat at the desk in his office for a long time and wondered about what he should do.

Eryn left a couple of days later and Katherine felt so much better for having her here. Her friend Abi was going through some family crisis as well so Katherine felt bad for her cousin having to deal with two women. She was now back to work and still accepting congratulations for a successful line. Sales were going well and everyone was happy. Everyone except her.

Suzanna came into the office and stood quietly, waiting for her boss to acknowledge her. She smiled when Katherine noticed her, "Are you sure you should be back to work so soon?" Suzanna asked.

The mothering fit Suzanna was on had to stop for both their sakes. "Suzanna, you are my assistant and a very good one, but you're not my mother so please stop acting like it." She looked directly at the woman, trying to make her point.

The words Ms. Fredricks spoke were hurtful, "I'm sorry I care about you, Ms. Fredricks," she snapped back. "If that awful man wasn't so cruel to you then this wouldn't have happened."

What? Katherine shot out of her chair, "What does Mitch have to do with this?" She had a sneaking suspicion she was not going to like the answer one bit.

"Oh, he was just sleeping with you then flirting with that other woman, what was her name, Kristy?" She threw the folders she was holding onto the floor, the papers inside scattering.

The meaning was getting clearer in Katherine's mind. "You're jealous, aren't you?" she asked very calmly.

Suzanna looked everywhere except at her boss, "No!" she said loudly, "he just needed to go." She sighed, "He was just...too perfect!" she all but screamed.

As her assistant picked up the papers off the floor, Katherine realized a few things. One, Suzanna was very jealous and needed to find work somewhere else. Two, Mitch was honest with her about everything. And three, she needed to figure out a way to let him know she loved him. Absently putting her palm against her belly, she knew there were a few things she needed to work out with him.

A week later, Mitch was no closer to figuring out his situation. He went to work and did well. Their inspections were almost perfect and he was proud of his Marines. It should be enough for him but he found himself tossing and turning at night, dreaming of Katie and wishing she was there with him.

He still hadn't called her. He couldn't. Maybe it was his pride or just plain stubbornness but he just couldn't do it yet. Of course, if this kept up, he would have to see a shrink or something.

He was sitting in his office when his phone rang, "Master Sgt. Frinnel," he answered roughly.

"Mitchell," Aly Frinnel said to her son, "how are you?"

The one statement was a contradiction. She used his given name which meant she was mad but then asked him how he was in a very quiet voice. Something was up. "I'm fine, Mom, you?" He tried to sound normal.

Aly Frinnel smiled sweetly into the phone, "Well, your sister's thirtieth birthday is next week so we're throwing a weekend party here."

Aha, his mother wanted him there. He knew something was up. "I'll put in for a pass and drive up Thursday night, okay."

Mitch wouldn't want to miss teasing his sister for getting older, plus he had some new stories thanks to Kristy. Of course that thought led to Katie. Dammit! He needed to get her out of his mind. Maybe a few days with his family is just what he needed to do that.

She gave a thumbs up to her husband, "Okay, Mitch, thank you." She stuck her tongue out when her husband shook his head at her letting her know she was a sneak, "Shelley will be thrilled."

"Okay, Mom," someone knocked at his door, "I gotta go, love you guys, bye." He hung up quickly and turned his attention to the door, "Enter."

In Delaware, Matt Frinnel was tsking his wife. "Aly, you shouldn't interfere," he repeated to his wife for the hundredth time that morning.

What did her husband expect? "My love," she said sweetly as she walked over to him and hugged him. After forty some years, he still made her feel young and beautiful. "I want our son to be happy." It was very simple.

She'd been worried since their daughter called a few days earlier and told her how an old high school friend ran into him in New York and explained about the woman, the designer, he was seeing. When Shelley heard that, she looked up the woman, Katherine Fredricks, then called her mother. Aly then called Eryn Fredricks-Johnson in Hawaii, who was a good friend to her son, and pumped the woman for as much information as possible. When she learned all she could, she decided her son was just like his father; stubborn to a fault and needed some pushing to get him to see the woman he loved was the one he should be with.

Matt wasn't sure this was the way to do things. "I know, honey, but if this girl is the one for him, it seems odd that they aren't together."

"Matthew," her tone a little harsh, "do you remember what had to happen for us to get together?" It was a long time ago but she still remembered a lot of turmoil before they decided to get married.

Matt shook his head, "It's not the same, Aly," he said and kissed his wife. Partially to quiet her down and partially because he still loved kissing her.

Aly shook her head, "Yes it is." She walked over to the window and looked out at the green yard, lined with trees, and sighed. "It's love."

A week after talking to Chase, Mitch was packing his bags for his trip to see his family for Shelley's birthday. He was excited to see the family. He had two nephews and a niece now and he enjoyed hanging out with his siblings. He would be the only one there without someone but he'd gotten used to that over the years. The last thing he put in his bag was a small heart necklace with a diamond in the middle as a gift to Shelley. His sister was the one he looked out for. Now she had a husband but she would always be his little sister. Zipping up the bag, he decided to go downstairs and have a beer before going to bed. Maybe he would finally sleep.

New York was rainy and the weather matched Katherine's mood perfectly. There was always some down time after a line was released because everyone needed to recuperate from the stress and Katherine needed some time to re-charge and figure out what she wanted to do for the next line. Usually she took a trip to Europe and spent some time there but with being pregnant, she didn't want to travel that far.

Pregnant. The word sounded so foreign to her. She was rational so she knew what it meant but it was still odd. She called Eryn every other day now so they could talk and compare notes. It turned out that their due dates were only a few days apart. That meant that she probably conceived the baby when she and Mitch were in Hawaii just before he left.

Thinking about their time there made her feel happy. Then she would remember the abominable way she treated him at that party and couldn't get over the shame. A few days earlier she realized she'd acted just like her father; demanding and controlling. Wait until he found out about the baby. All hell would break loose.

Her new assistant, Josie, knocked lightly on her partially open door. "Ms. Fredricks," the woman said smiling, "there's a Mrs. Frinnel on the phone for you."

Katherine stared at her assistant and didn't know what to say. She was at a loss.

"Would you like me to ask her to leave a message?" Josie asked when Katherine didn't answer.

Katherine looked down at her desk, not seeing anything, "No, no, I'll take it. Thank you, Josie." She went to pick up the phone and stopped. "Josie, can you please close my door and hold all my calls for the time being?"

Josie smiled, "Yes, ma'am."

Taking a deep breath, Katherine picked up the phone. "This is Katherine Fredricks." She tried to sound confident.

"Hello, Katherine, my name is Aly Frinnel," the woman said. "I hear you've been seeing my son."

Well, Mitch's mother definitely got right to the point, Katherine thought. "Uh, yes, ma'am." What else did she say? "I don't believe we're seeing one another now though."

Interesting, Aly thought. "Would you mind telling me why?"

Direct. Okay, "Mrs. Frinnel, perhaps it would be best if you spoke to Mitch about this."

"My son is a wonderful man, Ms. Fredricks," Aly Frinnel said sternly.

Katherine nodded, "Yes, ma'am, he is." Her palms were beginning to sweat from nerves.

Aly smiled, "Well he's also prideful and stubborn as the day is long." She wouldn't beat around the bush with this woman. "And now I'd like to know what your intentions are with him."

This conversation was one of the most bizarre ones she ever had, "Mrs. Frinnel, again, you should speak to Mitch."

The girl had gumption, Aly thought, and she was trying to be respectful to Mitch, an admirable quality. "Do you love him?"

"Yes!" Katherine said in a breathy voice. Now she was embarrassed. Why did she say that to Mitch's mother? "I'm sorry, I didn't mean to say it like that."

Laughing, Aly decided she would like Katherine Fredricks, "Yes you did, and I'm proud of you for doing so."

Katherine thought the woman could give foreign dignitaries a run for their money, "Thank you. I think."

"Listen," Aly sat down at the kitchen table. "We're having a little party for our daughter this weekend since she's turning thirty. My husband, Matt, and I would love to have you come down and meet everyone."

Now the conversation was really odd. Did Mitch's mother really just invite her to their home? "I..." She didn't want to be rude but it seemed very strange.

No was not an option for Aly Frinnel; all of her children could attest to that. "Delaware is only four hours away. We've got plenty of room here at the house and we would simply love for you to come."

Katherine couldn't face Mitch, much less his whole family. Of course they would be the baby's family now. The baby. What should she do?

"I'm sorry to say but I think Mitch will not be able to make it." Aly thought a little white lie wouldn't hurt.

If Mitch wouldn't be there, maybe it wouldn't be so bad. She would be able to meet his family and see what kind of people would be involved in her child's life later on. She was torn but decided to throw caution to the wind. She'd call Eryn and make sure Mitch's family wasn't a bunch of raving lunatics.

"Yes, Mrs. Frinnel," She grabbed a pen and paper, "give me all the information. I'll drive down on Friday if that's okay."

Aly nodded to her husband. "Sure, we're so excited to meet you, Katherine."

They exchanged information and hung up a few minutes later.

"Aly," Matt used his best "dad" voice. "You lied to that young woman."

She nodded and walked over to kiss her husband, "Yes I did, dear."

Matt shook his head, "What do you think is going to happen when she gets here and Mitch is here too?"

Aly thought for a minute, "Well, I hope my son tells her he loves her and asks her to marry him."

The woman was incorrigible! "And if he doesn't?" There was always that possibility and Matt was concerned that their son would be hurt.

"Oh, Matt," she hugged her husband tight, "if he feels one half of what we feel, then he'll ask."

Matt Frinnel watched his wife walk outside with their dog, Champ, and wondered how she was so sure. Of course she was sure he would love her forever and that was turning out to be true. He walked out after her and wondered if he should call and give his son a head's up. Probably not.

In Hawaii, Eryn Johnson was at her desk when her phone rang. She answered quickly, "Warrant Officer Johnson here." She hoped the call would be quick, she was going to lunch with her husband.

"Eryn," Katherine said nervously, "tell me about Mitch's parents."

Okay that was out of the blue. "Can I ask why?" Eryn's interest was piqued.

Katherine took a drink of water, "Because his mother just called and invited me to their house for the weekend. It's his sister's birthday and apparently he won't be there." She was out of breath when she finished the explanation.

Laughing, Eryn knew Mitch's mother was a lot like her own. Poor Katherine, she wasn't even going to see it coming. As much as she loved her cousin, she knew well and good that Mitch's mom was up to something and she didn't want to spoil it for Mrs. Frinnel. "Okay," Eryn said. "I've only met them once but Chase has known them for years and he's talked about them off and on."

They spoke about Mitch's family and when Katherine hung up with her cousin, she felt better. Maybe it would be a great weekend. She hoped to relax a little. It was nice that Eryn knew about the baby and she agreed with Katherine about meeting Mitch's family either way.

It was dinner time and she was hungry so she called her favorite Italian place and ordered take out. She needed go home and pack. Maybe she would even take tomorrow off and pick up a new outfit for the trip. She had to rent a car anyway so it made sense. Making a mental list, Katherine shut the door to her office and felt good for the first time in weeks.

Chapter 18

Friday turned out to be sunny and clear, for which Katherine was thankful. She wanted to leave early to beat the traffic going out of the city but her morning sickness delayed her a little bit.

She didn't drive much, preferring to use a driver, so it was weird making her way through the streets in a car. Trying to be proactive, she rented the car the day before and used it to do some errands so she wouldn't be so rusty.

Following her GPS, she left the city through the Holland Tunnel and drove into New Jersey, merging onto the New Jersey Turnpike. The ride wasn't bad, a few slow spots due to the early morning traffic but definitely bearable.

After a couple of hours, she decided to get out of the car and stretch her legs. Her stomach was rumbling so it was probably good she got something to eat. She exited at a little town called Twin Rivers and found a local deli. She sat in their small seating area and watched people come and go while eating her turkey sandwich on wheat bread.

Once back in the car, she kept going south. There were small towns and cities sprouting alongside the turnpike. People were driving to wherever they needed to go and Katherine was grateful she decided to make the drive. There was peacefulness in just driving down the road.

She put in a CD of soft rock and listened to the music. She sang along with some songs and smiled when a song brought about a particular memory.

After another hour or so, she turned a west and crossed the Delaware River. Once in Delaware, her nerves started up. What was she thinking coming down here? She was going to a stranger's home. Very unlike her. Of course sleeping with a man after only knowing him for a few hours and having a torrid affair with him while at her cousin's wedding and inviting him to her apartment in New York and getting pregnant were pretty unlike her too. Finding the whole situation funny, she laughed.

She turned onto Highway 301 and started going south again. After a while, the road turned into Highway 1 and led directly to Dover. Luckily she drove around the outskirts of the city so she didn't really have to deal with a lot of traffic. Down here, there were green fields and lots of trees; a far cry from New York. It was pleasant though. She thought Mitch must have been lucky to grow up in such a place like this.

She laughed when she saw an exit sign that announced a town called Little Heaven and was thankful she had a GPS to get her around. It took her off the highway when she saw the signs for Milford. Her stomach started flipping again.

Aly Frinnel was starting to get dinner ready when the phone rang, "I'll get it," she called out. Not that anyone ever heard her anyway. She answered, "Hello."

"Mrs. Frinnel," Katherine said. She was at a stop sign and thought it would be okay to call. "I'm about ten minutes away according to the GPS and I wanted to just let you know." She felt silly calling ahead.

Smiling, Aly started mixing a salad. "Great," she responded in a gracious tone, "We'll see you then."

Katherine smiled, "Okay." She hung up the phone and made the designated turn the GPS told her.

A few minutes later she was driving down a road in rural Delaware and couldn't get over how green and lush it was here. The yards were large and the houses were set back from the road. She found the number Mitch's mother gave her and stopped before turning into the driveway. The house was huge! She stared at it and wondered what Mitch's family did.

It was a large white Victorian with bright blue shutters. There was even a round turret room. Katherine took a deep breath and turned into the drive. She pulled up behind a few other cars and parked. When she looked up she saw a woman come out of the house. Katherine thought she had to be Mitch's mom. She was tall with dark hair and bright, expressive eyes. She was waving to Katherine as she came down the porch steps toward the car.

"Welcome, Katherine," Aly Frinnel said. She walked up to the young woman and gave her a big hug. One should always welcome guests with a hug. It was a rule she stood by through the years.

Hugging Mitch's mother, Katherine wanted to cry. She was absolutely fantastic. She was warm and smelled like daisies. Katherine smiled when she pulled back from the hug and looked her up and down.

Aly shook her head, "You are stunning!" she said and meant it. The woman was gorgeous. She had delicate features and large green eyes that reminded Aly of stories about Celtic princesses.

They walked arm and arm into the house. When Aly showed her into the kitchen and gestured for Katherine to sit at the table. "What can I get you to drink?" she asked her guest.

"Sweet tea if you have it," Katherine answered, "if not, water is fine."

Aly laughed, "Oh, sweetie, Delaware is on the border of the south, really, so we do have sweet tea here." She got out two glasses and poured some of the liquid in each and sat down across from Katherine. They sipped their tea for a few minutes and chatted about Katherine's drive down from New York.

"I'm so glad you came," Aly said and covered Katherine's hand with her own. "I was beginning to think that my son didn't possess the wherewithal to get a lovely woman."

What did she say to that? She had no clue. "Thank you, Mrs. Frinnel."

Aly shook her head, "None of that," she waved her hand in dismissal, "you call me Aly or Mom."

Katherine smiled. How could she feel so at home in a house with a stranger? It was all very surreal. "Okay," she answered and took another sip of her tea.

Getting up, Aly went to the refrigerator. "We're having some barbeque and cold salads for dinner in a bit." She patted Katherine's shoulders. "Why don't I show you where you'll be staying and you can get settled beforehand."

"Okay," Katherine said, "let me get my bag." She got up and went back out to the car. When she grabbed her bag and turned around a big ball of fur jumped up on her, scaring her half to death. "Oh!" she yelped.

Aly came out the front door looking upset, "Champ!" she said sharply, "Get off Katherine!"

The dog got down and sauntered over to the porch where Mitch's mother stood. She was shaking her finger at him and Katherine swore the dog knew exactly what she was saying. He sat dutifully next to her, his white and brown tale thumping on the wood of the porch.

"I'm sorry," Aly said when Katherine walked back to the porch, "he thinks he's the welcoming committee." She turned to open the door for Katherine to enter.

They walked to the staircase and started up toward the second floor. The house was as big on the inside as it looked. Katherine went slowly so she could look at everything. The bannister going up the stairs was solid wood and intricately carved, its smooth wood felt cool against her palm as she walked behind Mitch's mother. The walls were covered with family pictures so she scanned them as she went up. There were a lot of school pictures, a few posed family portraits, and some candid shots thrown in.

Katherine was smiling as she saw Mitch grow up through the pictures on his parents' walls. He was unmistakable, towering over his three brothers and sister in the pictures. There were some awkward stages but he was a great looking boy. She wondered if their baby would look like him.

Aly reached the top of the stairs and turned around to say something to Katherine but stopped when she saw the look in Katherine's eyes. She cocked her head, studying the young woman's features as she stared at a picture of Mitch.

"A handful, aren't they?" Aly asked when Katherine turned to finish the last couple of stairs.

Smiling, Katherine was surprised at the kindness in Mitch's mother's eyes, "I'll bet it was never boring or quiet around here."

Aly shook her head, "Boring? No. Quiet? Certainly not." She walked down the hall of their house remembering when the kids were all here and it seemed almost small. "Matt and I thought we'd go crazy when they all moved out."

That seemed so sad to Katherine. Her own parents never showed any sadness when she went off to college. She knew they loved her; they were just challenged when showing affection to their daughter. She swore she would never be like that with her own child.

Aly came to a door and opened it up to show another set of stairs. "I thought you'd like to be in the castle," she said and motioned for Katherine to follow her.

Castle? Katherine wondered what she meant.

"We bought this house when Mitch was about two I think," She turned on a light and started up the stairs. "He ran around the place so fast, I could barely catch up." They reached the top of the stairs and Aly stepped aside so Katherine could enter the room.

Her breath hitched! It was a gorgeous room. The walls were rounded and there were windows spaced about two feet apart at the front of the room. There was a bed along the one flat wall complete with a lace coverlet. An antique vanity was placed between two windows. It was like entering another century.

Aly smiled longingly, "I finally caught up to him when he got up here and he said, 'Mommy, this is like a castle!' and I cried and knew it was the house for us."

Katherine fought back her own tears. She thought of Mitch as an excited little boy and wanted their child to have that. "What a lovely story," she said to Aly.

Nodding, Aly said, "It is, isn't it." She patted Katherine's shoulder. "I'll leave you to get settled. Come down whenever you like."

She nodded to Mitch's mom and stood there for a few minutes just taking in the room. It was like a fairy tale to her.

She set down her bag and sat on the bed. Running her hand over the delicate lace she wondered how it would've been to grow up in a big rambling house like this. Her apartment in New York seemed so stark and lacking in comparison.

A few minutes later, Katherine started downstairs. She wandered down the hall and peeked in a few rooms where the doors were open. She felt like a snoop but she was curious. All the rooms seemed so warm, each with its own color palette. Mitch's mother had a knack for the demure and the fantastic; a woman after her own heart. Once downstairs, Katherine followed the noises into the kitchen where Mrs. Frinnel, Aly, she reminded herself, was putting food on the table. If Katherine wasn't mistaken, there was a lot of food there.

"Can I help?" Katherine asked from the doorway.

Aly smiled, "No dear, I've got this." She motioned toward the door that led out to the back yard. "Would you like to take a tour of the back yard? We've got a small orchard and even a tire swing." She nodded to the lump of fur laying in front of the door. "Champ would probably love to keep you company."

Katherine decided she would like to walk since the drive was long and she was a little stiff. Her doctor said she should do that anyway so she nodded to Aly and went toward the door. "Coming, Champ?" she asked the dog.

Champ jumped up, tail wagging, and was ready for an adventure.

"I'll call for you when dinner is ready!" Aly hollered as they went out the back door.

Katherine nodded. She turned around to see a huge yard. Aly wasn't kidding. There was a fence that went around it so Katherine figured she wouldn't get lost. She started down the back steps and crossed a stone patio, Champ close to her side. She smiled at the dog as they started to explore.

Mitch and his dad parked the truck in the driveway and got out. They grabbed the bags they filled at the store and turned to go into the house. "We have company," Mitch said to his dad and nodded toward the unfamiliar car.

Just as they reached the door, cars pulled into the driveway. Mitch smiled and continued into the house. He wouldn't be able to hug his brothers and sister with his hands full of groceries.

He walked into the kitchen, his dad right behind him and placed the bags on the island in the middle of the room. "Mom, we're back!" he yelled.

"I heard you," Aly replied, coming out of the pantry. She walked over to Matt and kissed him, "Hello there."

Matt smiled, "Hello there," he returned. "The gang is all here. They pulled in just after us."

Aly nodded and busied herself cutting up some vegetables.

Mitch put the milk in the refrigerator and turned to face his parents, "Whose car is that out front?" he asked.

Matt looked at Aly who was, thankfully, not looking at her son.

"A friend," she said lightly and continued to cut up vegetables. They were very interesting all of a sudden.

Mitch was going to ask who when two of his brothers entered the room, "Mitch!" his brother Nathan yelled. The men embraced.

Mitch's other brother, Oliver, was next, "Hey, big brother," he hugged Mitch tightly.

His sister Shelley stood at the doorway to the kitchen, "You couldn't wait until the birthday girl got here?" she asked and tried to look offended.

"Sis," Mitch said and grabbed her into his arms and spun her around the dining room.

His sister giggled with his attention, he loved spoiling her. He set her down and planted a big kiss on her. "How are you? Are you feeling older?"

Shelley gave him a bored look, "You'll have to do better than that."

He smiled slyly, "I intend to."

They were interrupted by the front door slamming, "Hey!" Craig, Mitch's other brother, yelled.

"Hey," They all yelled back in unison.

Matt Frinnel came into the dining room, "Okay, okay, settle down." He picked up his granddaughter and gave her a kiss. "Tell your uncles to settle down?" he asked her.

"Settle down, uncles!" Little Allison yelled.

The adults laughed. Mitch glanced out the dining room window when something caught his eye. He walked a few steps over and looked out. There was someone walking with Champ but they were too far away for him to see clearly. He squinted but couldn't make out who it was. He went back into the kitchen.

"Mom," he said as he made his way around his siblings. He said hi to his brother-in-law Rob and mussed the hair on his nephew, Bobby's, head. "Who's out in the back?"

Aly Frinnel looked at her son and did something she never liked to do to her children; she omitted. "A friend." Lying was a little harsh because she did consider Katherine a friend.

Mitch waited for more of an explanation, his eyebrows raised. His mother was cutting up vegetables and seemed really intense about it. "Mom, what friend?" he asked.

Matt stepped in and touched his son's shoulder, "Why don't you go out and get our friend and invite her in to dinner?"

Looking back and forth between his parents, Mitch was lost. He shook his head and gave up, "Okay." He went to the back door.

Shelley walked up to her mother as soon as her brother walked out, "What did you do?" she demanded in hushed tones.

Aly wanted to cry; she only wanted her son to be happy. Hopefully Katherine was the woman to do that.

Mitch turned and went in the direction of the orchard. He saw the woman and Champ in that area from the dining room and, after a few minutes, he finally found her. She was pretty far away from the house now so he had to pick up the pace to catch up.

"Champ," Katherine looked down at the dog beside her as they walked, "I'll bet you're just happy walking around with a crazy lady, aren't you?"

The dog wagged his tail in response. Katherine assumed that was a yes. She smiled and rubbed the top of his head. When he turned around, gave a small bark, and took off, she turned to see what got his attention. The man was tall with broad shoulders and dark hair. Short hair, she looked closer, very short hair. The man was Mitch!

Seeing Champ coming toward him, Mitch leaned down to pat the dog then straightened. He was closer now so when he stood up he got a good look at his mother's friend. "What the hell?" he said out loud. It was Katie.

Katherine stopped and saw that he did as well. She couldn't run, although she wanted to. But what would be the point? Although every fiber in her being told her she should go, she started to walk slowly toward him.

Mitch just stood there and watched Katie come to him. He was stuck to the spot, in awe of how beautiful she looked. Her hair was pulled back into a pony tail that swung when she moved. She had on a cotton sundress with bright colored flowers that reminded him of her bedroom. He tried to crush the awareness that thought brought to his mind. Damn it, what was she doing here?

Katherine stopped a few feet away from him, "Hello, Mitch." She wanted to roll her eyes since the comment sounded so dumb.

"Katie," he took a step closer, "what are you doing here?"

Looking around him at the house, she wondered why his mom hadn't told him she was here, "Your mom invited me."

Heaven help him and heaven help his mother when he got back into that house. His nostrils flared in annoyance. "She did, huh?"

Why was he questioning her, "Yes, she did. She said you weren't able to make it." Great, she just told him she was avoiding him.

Mitch didn't miss the remark. It hurt. "So you came down to my parents' house when you thought I wouldn't be here?"

She was caught! "Yes," she said with more confidence than she felt. "Your mom called me a couple of days ago and asked me to come."

"She did," he said plainly. "She asked you to come and you did." He was just verifying the facts.

He was moving closer and Katherine's heartbeat was speeding up I response. She couldn't answer, she only nodded.

What were they doing? He wondered. He moved another step closer. "Why did you want to meet my family?"

Katherine shrugged. He was only a couple of feet away now and she had to look up to see his eyes. They were dark blue and she remembered that they turned that way from desire. The thought that she made him respond like that empowered her. "I wanted to see where you grew up."

"Not going to fly," Mitch said when he stepped yet closer. If he reached out now he could touch her.

She looked up into his eyes, "Mitch, I just wanted to be near you," she started explaining. "I was wrong and acted like a crazy person in New York." She looked around, searching for the right words, "I was jealous and then I fainted, and…"

The last part of her statement brought him out of the sexual trance he was in. "Are you okay?" he asked, the concern inflecting his voice.

Katherine nodded, "I am now." She took the last step and raised her hand to touch his shirt, "Now that I'm here with you, I'm perfectly fine."

Mitch growled and pulled her to his chest. He wrapped his arms around her and held her soft body to his. He could feel her shoulders shake and set her away so he could see her eyes. "What is it?"

Tears fell down her cheeks. "I'm sorry, I don't know what's gotten into me."

What did he do? She was crying and he never saw Katie cry. "It's kind of tough to be in this situation," he said softly and pulled her to him again.

Katherine held onto him as if her life depended on it. He felt so good; so strong and safe and she was getting warm thinking about him holding her and how he held her before. Her cheeks brightened and she smiled, which helped quell her tears.

Katherine stepped back and absently ran her hands over her dress in an effort to make herself feel more in control. "I'm sorry if my being here is upsetting," she said quietly, looking up into his eyes.

"It's not," It surprised Mitch that he was being honest. Katie being here was the best thing that happened since the argument in New York. "Do you want to talk about what happened in New York?" He really didn't but his parents always told them to talk out the problems so they didn't linger. He never thought he'd use that little piece of advice.

She nodded, "Yes but it was really just me being insecure."

They started to walk past the last of the orchard trees. There was a bench closer to the house so they walked over and sat down. Mitch looked up and saw eyes looking out of every downstairs window that faced the back yard. He looked at the wanna-be eavesdroppers and gave them a nasty look. Everyone moved away from the windows quickly so he turned his attention back to Katie.

He put his hand under her chin and gently lifted it so she would look at him. "We're all insecure, Katie."

Katherine appreciated his attempt to make her feel better. "I was jealous." She closed her eyes to take a breath and then looked back into his blue ones, "I saw that woman kiss you and I wanted to scream."

Feeling a little smug, Mitch grinned. "She's an old high school friend of my sister Shelley."

Nodding, Katherine smiled, "She came up to me after I ran you off and told me. I wanted to just die."

His smile grew, "Listen, I know this is all pretty still new for both of us and, let's face it, we really haven't talked about our lives outside of the bedroom." He liked it that she blushed at the thought of their lovemaking. "But I've missed you."

"You did?" Katherine asked, hope blooming in her chest.

Mitch nodded, "Hell yes." He looked around trying to find the words. "I was so pissed at you and myself." He placed his hand over hers and held it. "I feel so different when I'm around you."

She smiled, "When I'm with you I feel safe and loved."

His heart literally jumped in his chest, "Loved, huh?"

There was the word they'd been skirting around for some time. Katherine never used the word outside of her family and it was like trying on a new jacket and wondering if it looked right. "Yes," she finally said and felt sure it was right.

"I suppose," he said slowly, "it could be a term I could get used to using."

Now he was teasing her, "Mitch, I'm trying here."

He could see this was difficult for her and felt a little bad. With his loud and demonstrative family, it was easier for him to admit his feelings. He'd seen firsthand how her family could be somewhat repressed in that department. "I know, Katie."

Katherine looked at Mitch and figured that the tables were finally turned. In the whole time she knew him, he was always open and honest with her. She, on the other hand, wasn't open about anything but sleeping with him. If she figured out anything in the last two months, it was that she was accustomed to playing by her own rules and not taking anyone else's into account.

She always wondered why everyone else was able to find someone to love and she couldn't. Now she knew. And here, sitting beside her, was the man who could change all that. She only had to have the courage to say okay.

She turned to look at him, his dark hair, his beautiful blue eyes, and knew, in the core of her being, that he would be there for her and their children for the rest of her life.

"I love you," she said softly. "I don't know when it happened, only that it has and I'm not going to love anyone else for the rest of my life." Tears snuck out of her eyes.

Perhaps there were some romantic words out there but he couldn't think of them right now. "Good," he responded, "I love you too."

Katherine smiled, the hope in her heart bloomed and covered her body like a warm blanket. "You do?" she asked weakly.

"Yes," Mitch pulled her closer, "I think I have since the first moment on that plane when you were scared."

She laughed through her tears. "Would you consider marrying me?" she asked.

He couldn't help it, he laughed. Not at her, but with her. She was anything but conventional. "I might," he answered, and kissed her.

The kiss was soft and hinted at pleasures they both looked forward to. Well, Katherine thought, might wasn't a no.

Mitch wanted to do something right so he knelt down in front of her. "I happen to have something I think you might like," he said, a twinkle in his eye. "I was talking to my dad this morning and asked him for something." He pulled a little velvet bag out of his pocket. "I asked him to stop by the bank and get something for me." Opening the little bag, he pulled out a ring, "this was my grandmother's engagement ring."

Katherine started to cry. She hated being so emotional. Looking in his eyes, she could see the beginnings of tears in his.

"I would like you to wear it, Katie." He took her left hand and put the ring on her finger, "we have a ton of stuff to work out but I love you and I want you with me forever."

Her hands were shaking so hard that she laughed as he tried to get the ring on. It was a gorgeous solitaire surrounded by little diamonds in an antique white gold setting. There was no ring in the word she thought would look more beautiful.

Mitch looked at the ring on Katie's finger and knew it was right. It fit perfectly. "You are not at all what I expected but you are so much more than I deserve. I love you. Marry me."

Katherine smiled and nodded, "On one condition," she said.

"Name it," Mitch said quickly.

She nodded behind him, "We let them know before they all come running out and tackle us."

Mitch laughed. "Deal." He stood up and pulled her to him. He held her in his arms until they were bombarded by his family surrounding them in the backyard of his parents' house. This was the best day of his life.

Everyone was around them, offering congratulations.

Aly took Katherine into her arms and hugged her tightly. "Thank you," she said through happy tears, "for making our boy so happy."

Katherine nodded and thought she would definitely love her new family.

"Just don't wait too long to tell him about the baby," Aly winked and turned to give Mitch a hug.

Yep, she thought. Quiet? No. Boring? Of course not.